I0819056

THE
BEAST
YOU LET
IN

THE BEAST YOU LET IN

DANA MELE

sourcebooks fire

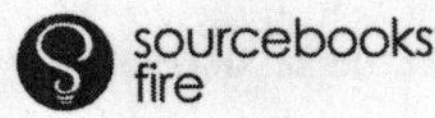

Cover art and design by Ash Jon/Sourcebooks
Internal design by Laura Boren/Sourcebooks
Internal images © Val_Iva/Getty Images

Published by Sourcebooks Fire, an imprint of Sourcebooks
1935 Brookdale Rd., Naperville, IL 60563-2773
(630) 961-3900
sourcebooks.com

Cataloging-in-Publication Data is on file with the Library of Congress.

Printed and bound in the United States of America.
LB 10 9 8 7 6 5 4 3 2 1

For all the trans kids (and adults) who may not
have visible allies right now:
You are not alone.
You are not alone.
You are not alone.
And as always, for Ben.

1

HAZEL

My sister is a liar. A good one. The kind you want to believe, and believe again, after she's broken your heart into bits and stomped it under her snowy, fur-lined boots. She has an unreadable face, heart-shaped, with eyes the cool pale gray of the sky before it opens up and rains down hell. She's utterly remorseless. She's pretty when she smiles, but there's danger in it. Her teeth are sharp and whiter than they have any right to be. She cares for her teeth obsessively, my sister, constantly brushing and flossing, rinsing and whitening. She wears her long, straw-colored hair in a single braid down her back to hide the streaks of white that started snaking through it last summer. She's good at hiding things. An expert. There is no one in the world I trust less than Beth.

That's why I should say no when she asks me to drive her to Ezra Elwood's party.

She sits on her hands on the twin bed that matches mine, an angelic expression on her rotten face. Our room still looks like the bedroom of a pair of ten-year-old twins. It's embarrassing. Symmetrical placement of beds, simple walnut dressers with identical oval mirrors hovering above. Matching plaid quilts, one in scarlet and one in forest green. A window by each pillow with a view of the pine-covered mountains. Two hand-carved wooden plaques, gifts from my father when we were born, perhaps to remind our parents which of us was which, hung over our cribs, and still hang over our beds. They say Hazel and Elizabeth, but they could easily say Plain and Changeling, or Demon, or simply Mistake.

If it seems like I'm being hard on my sister, wait. I always end up being right, and no one ever appreciates the "I told you so." I'm not perfect either, but I'm sick of being punished for telling the truth. People don't like to hear it. The problem is, it comes out whether you say it or not.

"I'm busy." I flop down on my back with the book I've been reading for school—*The Crucible*. "Puritans call."

Our loyal golden/shepherd mix looks up from his spot at Beth's feet and yawns loudly at me, as if to protest I know damn well that I'm not *that* busy. Artax is such a meddler. And he always takes Beth's side. Beth is the one who brought him home last summer, and he's clearly chosen her as his person, though we all adore him equally and spoil him to bits. How could you not with that angel puppy face and snuggle-monster personality? He *will* show his disapproval if you go against Beth, though. And right now, he has no patience for me.

Beth picks up her own copy of *The Crucible* and flips through it. "I'll write your paper for you."

Lie. She'll buy one online and I'll get caught, have to rewrite it, and be penalized an entire letter grade. I've fallen for that one before. "I don't see that ending well."

She throws herself down next to me and takes the book out of my hands. "Pretty please? I'll tell you the ending."

This isn't an offer. It's a threat. One of my biggest pet peeves is having the ending of books and movies spoiled for me. It's *The Crucible*—I know the gist—but I have a compulsive need to read every line for myself.

"No!" I leap off the bed.

She reclines on her elbow, smiling up at me. She's already dressed as a witch, at least some costume party semblance of a witch, in a black steampunk dress and striped tights with a cat charm necklace around her neck. Beth started dressing sort of goth recently, to my very traditional parents' despair. Their idea of high fashion is a new flannel every day of the week. I'm not much better, so I shouldn't talk. But the dress is much nicer than anything Beth would usually have in her closet.

"Halloween party?"

She stares at me pityingly. The loser sister who doesn't get invited to things. "You know..." She rises and walks slowly to our closet. A deep sense of dread washes over me. "You don't have to drop me off. I could take you. No one would care."

I sink back onto the bed, trying to look like that didn't really sting. "I love the 'no one caring that I exist' part. I hate the 'showing up at a party I wasn't invited to' part."

"Hazel May." She flings the closet open and starts rifling through my clothes. "You are not letting me show up to Ezra's dateless."

"So you were always planning to strong-arm me into going." Lies. I told you.

She whirls around, her face flushed bright pink. "I didn't say that." She hands me an old ballet costume from three years ago when we did a community production of *Swan Lake*. Neither of us took lessons, but we auditioned to play swans and were cast. Beth was a natural, and I was a disaster. But something about being onstage in the costume made me feel good about myself in a way that I usually don't. Stripping off the flannel and jeans and sweeping my dull brown hair into a sleek bun made my stomach swirl—in a good way. Pulling on the tights and tulle and delicate shoes was like slipping into another skin, and when the music swept me onto the stage and into the lights, something changed in me that I still can't put into words. Wings moved inside me, and I disappeared for a while.

I stare longingly at the costume. I know I will never get that feeling back, and forcing my seventeen-year-old body into that costume is not going to help. But there's a reason I still have it, and Beth *knows* how to convince me to do something. She always knows.

"There's no way that will fit me," I say, but she's already rummaging through the old costume trunk for a larger pair of white tights.

Artax, ever the opportunist, snatches a balled-up fuzzy sock that falls to the floor and darts to the corner with it, batting it back and forth like a kitten.

"Please don't make me show up to Ezra's alone."

"What about Jack?"

She and Ezra broke up last summer. They had been together for almost two years, and if Beth weren't such a good liar, I would absolutely believe the tinge of regret I hear in her voice. She broke up with him, that's clear, and she started dating Jack Sawyer, a new kid who embodies the weirdo outsider vibe. Weirdos, outsiders, and, to be honest, vibes do not do well in Ashling. We like tradition, the familiar, that which we recognize. Ezra is the Reverend's eldest son. Going from Ezra to Jack was not Beth's savviest social move. But she doesn't really need to consider things like that.

Beth is a town sweetheart. She sang in the church choir for ten years. She's friendly and outgoing. She's our parents' daughter, and maybe that matters most. Family lines mean a lot in Ashling. Social status is highly influenced by how long you've lived here, who your family is, and what they do. Our family has always lived in Ashling. My father is a landscaper and city councilman; my mother is a florist. My parents love all that is of the earth, and Beth and I were raised to do the same. I may not be the most popular kid in Ashling, a smart-mouthed bookworm somewhere that's green, but there's a place for me. Namely, in the town library where I work after school. Jack is shit out of luck. I almost think Beth chose him to spite Ezra...or to prove that she could date anyone, and no one would give her shit. It's the sort of thing she would do.

"Please." She rolls her eyes, but I'm not sure I get why. Jack is quiet and keeps to himself, but if he were to go to a party, I guess it would be a Halloween party. I attribute Beth's sudden interest in black clothes, steampunk, and goth music to Jack, because that's his aesthetic. He seems like a nice enough guy. When Mac Wendell, one of Ezra's crew, tripped me in the hallway earlier this year—because it's apparently hilarious to give a girl a bloody nose—Jack helped me up and walked me to the nurse's office while almost everyone else pretended not to see. Teachers included. And this was before he and Beth were dating.

I sigh and pull on the costume for Beth and Artax's appraisal. With the tights, it fits, albeit snugly. I hate how much I love putting it on again. Going to the party *would* be an excuse to wear it. Damn you, Elizabeth Jean Whitman.

The bright, wicked grin on her face as she grabs her stage makeup kit tells me she knows she's won. I sigh as she twists my hair up away from my face and begins to powder and paint.

"One hour." I attempt to talk without moving my mouth and messing up her work. Artax licks my hand in approval. "I still have to write this paper."

"I promise," she says, too quickly. Too easily. But I don't argue. And that gives me the uneasy feeling that I actually *want* to go.

We try to slip out of the house unnoticed, but we're not exactly dressed to blend into the wallpaper, and Operation Subtle Exit fails.

"Freeze, ladies." Mom looks up from the kitchen table where she's carefully bundling baby's breath into dozens of little mini vases for an event at the Elks Lodge. Being scolded by Mom is surreal, because she looks like me returned from the future to correct the timeline. We have the same round, birdlike face, light brown hair and eyes, and sharp nose. We even wear similar round glasses. Beth has my father's temperament and features, the high forehead and straight nose, the firm chin and golden hair. In my costume and makeup, though, you can barely tell the difference between us.

Beth pauses at the front door, her posture rigid, but she doesn't take her hand off the doorknob. "We're going to Ezra's for a minute."

"Oh?" My father says too casually from his perch in front of the TV just beyond the kitchen in the den. My dad's convinced that if she got back together with Ezra, she would magically revert to the old Beth. He was always too invested in their relationship.

Ezra's dad is one of his closest friends, though our mothers do not get along—some ancient grudge from high school. In the grand Ashling tradition, it's never spoken of, but everyone knows. I think in Dad's mind, the power of love was meant to break the curse, like their relationship would heal the bad blood between our mothers. But it never did.

"Don't lose your shit, Owen," Beth says in a flat voice. "If I come home knocked up, Ezra won't get bragging rights."

"Ignore her," my mother says. She takes my dad's side. Of course. But she shed zero tears over the Beth and Ezra breakup. Mom's grudges are built to last. She turns to me, glowing with enthusiasm. "Hazel, you look beautiful." She gestures for me to turn in a circle, and I reluctantly obey, feeling like a pawn, lavished with praise for Beth's benefit. *See how much love and attention I'd give you if you'd only be good?* "Is there a boy?"

Mom flicks a meaningful glance at my father, then back to me, and my face flushes scarlet. There's so much *hope* in her voice. I hate it.

Beth grabs my hand, dragging me toward the door. "I won't let anything happen to her."

My dad lets out a snort, and Beth glares back at him.

"What?" She stares him down coldly.

He shrugs and mutters something inaudible.

Beth flinches almost imperceptibly. "I hope you don't mean that."

It isn't only Beth who's changed over the last year. The months of screaming matches between Beth and my parents have made my mother anxious, and she's clingier with me. But they've made my father closed off and angry. It's almost like he doesn't just resent

Beth; he resents my mother for not being able to keep Beth in line. Sometimes, it feels like this extends to me, too. None of this is fair, and his temper sucks. Still, Beth is the one who transformed almost overnight from a golden child to Satan's heiress.

The mood in the room has changed. Mom gives me an extra-long hug and tries to give Beth one too, but she shrugs out of it, and I see Mom turn to yell at my dad as Beth closes the door behind us and we slip out into the cool, crisp night.

I don't want to ask, but I have to.

"What did he say?"

Beth doesn't look at me as she heads toward the truck. "Maybe something *should* happen to her."

I halt, feeling like I've been smacked in the face. Beth turns around. She smiles reassuringly. "Forget him. You deserve to have serious fun for once in your life. Trust me. You want to go to this party."

And this time, I really do.

The second we step into Ezra's house, I change my mind. Ezra's family is loaded, and his house is about three times the size of ours. We live in an old one-story cottage built around a century ago, lovingly restored by my grandfather before he died and left it to my father. Ezra's mother had their home custom-built in the style of a luxury mountain chateau on his father's family estate—acres of farmland and forest where his grandparents also live, in a more modest home. Normally, this is the sort of thing that only an outsider would do—a city person looking to spend their weekends up in "quiet country." Which translates into trashing our parks and trails, feeding wildlife and drawing them into their yards and then freaking out when the wild animals don't respond to their verbal requests to leave, and disregarding most of our local ordinances, from waste management to fire containment. We get an earful from my father on the regular. Fun times.

But honestly, the outsiders bug me too. Ashling is a nice place to live. Nothing's stopping anyone from moving here. But mostly, they buy generations of families out of their homes and then set them up as Airbnbs that sit empty nine months a year, abandoned after the final snowfall. I don't like when people are too "us vs. them" about it, but I get why the animosity exists. The outsiders are the reason many of our friends and family no longer have homes. I wish I wasn't treated like one.

That last part lingers in my thoughts as I take in Ezra's palatial house. I've never seen the inside before. Mom would call it showy. The downstairs is arranged in an open floor plan with high ceilings hung with several gigantic chandeliers carved to look like tangles of thorny branches. Black streamers and strings of purple lights crisscross above us like an intricate spiderweb, and real candles flicker in sconces on the walls.

In one corner, an expensive-looking bronze sculpture of a beehive is adorned with plastic spiders. In the center of the living room, billows of dry ice flow from a cauldron on a round table piled with plastic cups and liquor bottles, and in the corner, a bar is set with paper plates and snacks. Music is pounding, and people are already dancing as Ezra and his friends move the last of the furniture against the wall to clear out the dance floor.

Beth makes a beeline for the cauldron where some of her friends are congregated, downs a Jell-O shot, and drags a friend onto the floor. I stand uselessly in the doorway as the wrestling team pushes past me, carrying a keg.

Well, the mystery of why Beth invited me is solved. She didn't care about Ezra or having a date. She wanted a designated driver.

I seriously contemplate driving home and leaving her to find her own ride, but I feel Beth's jacket being lifted off my shoulders and turn, startled. Ezra stares down at me, a wide grin on his face.

"You came." He slips a hand around the small of my back and before I can react, his lips press down on mine.

For a second, I'm too shocked to move. I've heard people say that before and doubted them. Moving isn't hard. Sleeping people move. But my brain glitches.

First of all, I've never been kissed. It doesn't sync with what I'd expected. It barely feels like anything at all. The disappointment is stunning. Second, it's Ezra. Beth's boyfriend of two years. The guy who *laughed* when his best friend tripped me in the hall and gave me a bloody fucking nose. He's a terrible person. Third, whatever Ezra and his awesome friends think of me, I'm not a kissing doll. I'm not desperate for attention. I may not be prom queen, but I have standards, and consent to give, and there are people I would actually *like* to kiss.

I push him back, gulping the air.

"Never." I stare at him furiously and register the shock on his face.

Maybe something should *happen to her.*

Amanda Laurence, the school's reigning queen bee and Beth's former best friend who's been secretly in love with Ezra forever, whispers, "Told you it wasn't over." Then it slowly dawns on me.

He didn't kiss *me*. At least, he didn't think he did. I'm not even supposed to be here. And with my hair pulled back and obscured by a crown of feathers, face made up, and dressed elegantly, I look like Beth.

Who, naturally, has witnessed the entire thing.

She storms up to Ezra and grabs his arm. "What are you doing?"

His mouth drops open at the sight of her. Then he looks back at me. "Ew." His face reddens. "I am so sorry."

"Yeah, you are." I cross my arms over my chest. I'm the wrong sister, not a cave troll.

"I thought..." Ezra indicates from Beth to me and back to Beth again.

"So?" Beth looks at me accusingly, as if I had some part in planning this. "What were you thinking? We're not back together."

"I don't get you." He lowers his voice to a whisper. "You always say nothing's changed. But when anyone else is around, you act like a total stranger. Make up your mind."

Now I almost feel sorry for Ezra. He's a gigantic hulk of a guy, and I always think of the Jolly Green Giant when I see him. A meaner, less jolly version with wavy, sandy hair and green, green, vacant eyes that stand out vividly against his pale complexion. Those eyes look so confused, I want to pat his hand, make him a cup of tea, and sit him down to explain about Beth. It doesn't particularly surprise me that she would continue to see Ezra in secret. Why she would date the cool guy in secret and the weirdo publicly is a head-scratcher. It's also very Beth.

Beth's face has fallen. I turn to see Jack standing by the back door, the blood drained from his face. "I asked him to come," she hisses, and runs out after him. Shit.

Ezra puts a hand on my elbow. "It's cool. We'll take care of you." But there's an icy undertone to his voice I don't like at all.

I start to pull away. "I'm going to head out."

He draws me into his circle of friends. Nausea washes over me as someone passes me a beer. I try not to panic. I know all the ways this scenario goes wrong. But it's not like it's only me and a room full of guys—Ezra, Mac, their whole lizard-brain crew. There are girls here too, enough to keep the vibe from tipping from "party monster" to "creep chic." Pretty girls, even, and no one ever looks at me the way people are looking at me right now. Mom's words float back to me as Mel, a girl from my chem class who I have long had a crush on but zero nerve to speak to, waves from across the room. *Is there a boy?* Not exactly, Mom.

Maybe it's because I look like Beth. But it's very hard to walk away, though I know I should. So I take the beer and stand stiffly in the circle until one of Beth's friends, a cute soccer player named Julie, compliments my costume. At first I don't know what to say. Our fathers are close friends, and I work with her mother at the library. We used to play together as toddlers, but I've been virtually invisible to her for years. Somehow we get into a conversation about the *Crucible* paper. And I begin to let my guard down.

Mistake number two.

THE TWISTED MIND OF VERONICA GREEN

JANUARY 1

i

I arrive in hell.

2

HAZEL

0 HOURS

I don't remember handing over my keys, but I do. I don't remember asking for a Jell-O shot, but I do. And another, and another. I don't remember joining the circle and spinning the sticky beer bottle, but I do. I *do* remember kissing Ezra again, on purpose this time. For a boy, he isn't too objectionable. But I'm not interested in boys. I kissed Mel, twice, which was exciting, Julie once, which was new, and Phoebe Crane, a quiet girl in a stunning Victorian dress, which was intriguing, because Phoebe was another of Beth's summer friends. When Beth began to shed the old ones like downy feathers, it wasn't only Jack who flew into her life. There was Phoebe too, a weekend girl with deep brown skin, a quirky Victorian-era wardrobe, and hair always drawn into two trademark waist-length braids interwoven with silky ribbons. A girl with money, impeccable style, and a constant glare. No one knew much about her family except that her parents were divorced, and her father didn't spend his weekends in Ashling anymore. There were rumors her dad made Marvel movies. I bet Beth got her dress from Phoebe.

I remember Phoebe pulling the game out of the velvety bag slung by her side. Mother forbade Beth and me to play as children because it was "the devil's game." I stared at the stiff beige board stamped with letters in an old-fashioned font and crowned with a *yes* and a *no*. A sun smiled sweetly from one corner, and the moon eyed it resentfully from the other. A carved wooden heart—the game piece, the magic—was placed in the center of the board. One by one, people's fingertips drifted to its edges and their gaze fell on me.

This is the thing about me and people. I go blank. Words don't come easily to me like they do for my sister. I don't know what people want to hear.

"Ask her something," Phoebe prompted.

"Ask who?" My words ran together a little, and so did the letters on the board. I knew it was time to go home, and I wouldn't be driving tonight.

Ezra grinned. "Veronica."

No, not Ezra. Ezra had left the circle. It was one of his friends, Mac or Randy or Jason.

I shook my head, drawing a blank.

Amanda rolled her eyes. "Everyone and their knockoff sister knows some version of the Veronica story."

Mel cradled her beer between her chin and her shoulder, her sky-blue hair falling into her eyes. "No. This story makes me sad." She started to scoot away from the circle, her eyes on me, and I wondered whether this was a goodbye or an invitation to join her. But she didn't say it. So how would I know?

Julie's eyes lit up and she clapped her hands, drawing my attention back. "Let me tell it. A girl died in these woods ages ago, before we were even born."

The memory shook loose. A campfire story. A cautionary tale. It was as forbidden in our house as tarot cards and summoning games. Speak of the devil, and he will appear.

Then again, we weren't in our house. And I was tired of being good. So I said the words. "Are you here, Veronica?"

The heart jerked beneath our fingertips, like it does in the movies.

Yes.

"Do you want to tell us something?"

Yes.

"Um. Go ahead."

Whispers. Laughter. There was fog in my skull. I needed sleep, but I'd had a taste of being Beth, and I was drunk on that too.

The heart moved slowly now, uncertain of its course. A message, a puzzle, a clue spelled in fragments.

H

W

I

D

I

D

"Ho, what I did?" Mac exclaimed, erupting into giggles.

Amanda punched his arm with a smirk. "What didn't you do?"

"How I died," Phoebe corrected him sternly.

Again, the heart moved erratically, this time with no ambiguity.

B

A

N

G

B

A

N

G

I blacked out.

When I woke the next morning, unsure how I got home, the bed next to mine was empty and untouched. Artax gazed up at me from beneath it with worried eyes. Beth had never come home.

Maybe something should *happen to her.*

12 HOURS

It is disorienting to go to sleep hating your sister with every fiber of your being and wake up desperate to find her. But here we are.

I woke up knowing. There was an evil in my stomach, and I just knew. Not that Beth had disappeared; I don't claim to be psychic. But that something was terribly, terribly wrong. We share a bedroom, and I could see through the late morning light filtering through our gauzy yellow curtains that Beth wasn't there. Her comforter lay undisturbed on her bed, smooth as ice on a frigid lake.

A chill swept over me, and all my anger evaporated. Beth may be rebellious, but she always comes home.

I could hear my mother down the hall, her slow, unbothered footsteps creaking across the old hardwood floors. Going about her day like nothing was wrong. Our house is ancient, and the rooms are small, but everything is wood, and it creaks and sighs with every movement. My father would be out hunting with his crew, a small, tight-knit group that includes Ezra's dad as well as Julie's. My parents wouldn't notice Beth was gone.

Why would they? They don't watch us sleep.

One text message, from Mel Sanders.

Had fun! Talk later?

Any other day, I would have been so freaked out over a text like that. In a good way—because I don't *get* texts from crushes. I definitely don't get texts from crushes the night after kissing them at a party. But I was confused by the fact she left early and maybe didn't approve of me staying and playing that game. And right now, the only thing that mattered was that it wasn't a text from Beth that she was okay. The timing felt deliberately cruel. I shoved my phone into my pocket without responding.

My body felt stiff as I forced myself to stand and pull on a sweatshirt. I resisted the walk down the hall, where I could hear my mother in the kitchen. I checked my phone again. Nothing. And then I had to face her.

"Good morning, Hazel," she said pleasantly, pointing to a stack of pancakes with her coffee mug. An apology for last night. Comfort food is my mother's love language. "Did you dance all night?"

I stood, stuck in place, Artax planted firmly between my ankles, a soft whine wafting from his throat. "Have you heard from Beth?"

She looked up from her coffee and magazine, and the expression on her face said what was coming next would be hell.

13 HOURS

I was told to stay home, but I'm not sure I know how to do that right now. So, I find myself in the police station, sitting next to my parents and across from Chief Merritt, an old friend of my father's, who's double-tasking filling out paperwork and issuing what sound like empty reassurances. I focus my attention on my phone, googling doomsday statistics.

Crucial fact #1: 90% of missing minors are runaways.

Except Beth ran off in the middle of a party. She wasn't even wearing a jacket.

Crucial fact #2: Most abductions of minors are by relatives.

All of our relatives are in this room, minus our Uncle Paul who is currently in Hanoi on his honeymoon.

Crucial fact #3: In the very small percentage of cases when a minor is kidnapped by a violent offender, 74% of the time the minor dies within three hours.

It's been thirteen.

I sip the watery hot chocolate from the Styrofoam cup that was handed to me without being asked if I wanted any. It burns my tongue. I can feel the singed taste buds, rough and useless against the back of my teeth. The feeling is comforting, somehow. All of this is partly my fault.

"Hazel?"

I whip up my head. "Yes?"

"You say Beth was fighting with a boy before she ran out into the woods?"

My parents turn their attention to me.

"I didn't see her run into the woods," I clarify, uncomfortable with this scrutiny. If I make a mistake, remember one detail wrong, or say something too vague, it could send a search party in the wrong direction and cost precious time. "She went out the backdoor toward the woods behind the Elwoods'. And yes, she was fighting with...two boys, actually. Ezra Elwood and Jack Sawyer."

Chief Merritt furrows his brow and scribbles a note. "I'll call in the Sawyer boy."

"And the Elwood boy." I shut myself up with another sip of burning chocolate water. Golden boy Ezra and his glittering, golden family. Why would the police question him when there's an outsider like Jack Sawyer to zero in on instead?

Merritt raises his gaze to meet my father's. *This is how you raise your daughter, Owen?* he says with the arch of his eyebrows. "I'll have a chat with the Elwoods."

"So you will speak to Ezra?"

He casts me a withering glare. But I didn't ask him to chat with the Elwoods. I asked him to speak to *Ezra* Elwood. Saying he'll speak to the Elwoods leaves room for him to have a pleasant passing word with Reverend Elwood, his drinking buddy, with no intention of considering Ezra as a suspect. He's humoring me.

"Hazel," my father says sharply.

I avoid his eyes. I need to know *all* the leads are being followed. That Beth is not going to become another tragic unsolved case because the chief of police gives his buddies special treatment. I need to hear him say he *will* bring Ezra in for questioning.

"Excuse us." My mother takes my arm and pulls me out into the hallway. "Hazel. You can't talk that way. It's disrespectful."

"He's making a mistake, Mom. Do *you* think the Elwoods are above the law?"

She presses her lips together so tightly, they turn white, and a wave of guilt washes over me. I only meant to play on her feud with Mrs. Elwood, not plant thoughts of the worst-case scenario in her head. "No one said anyone is above the law. But you will get yourself in trouble if you speak out of turn like that, and that's the last thing we need."

I disagree. I think the last thing we need is a corrupt, biased cop. But I nod, because as much as having your sister disappear is a nightmare, I'm pretty sure it's nothing to losing a child.

Mom leads me back into Merritt's office and clears her throat, nodding at me meaningfully.

"Sorry," I say curtly.

"I'll speak to the Elwoods," Merritt repeats, without glancing up from his files.

I'm sure it's meant to be a magnanimous gesture to show my parents that in exchange for my apology, he can be reasonable. But all he's done is repeat his shitty ambiguous nonresponse. I *hate* when people speak ambiguously. I can never tell if it's on purpose or not, and it eats at me. No one else ever seems to see those ambiguities. My parents sure don't. It makes it hard to have a pleasant conversation in the best of circumstances, and this is arguably the worst. I need to know the truth, including whether someone is really *sure* when they say "sure" or if they're only speaking colloquially. Or trying to shut me up.

"Is there anything else you need from me?" I ask.

Chief Merritt looks over his notes, then finally makes eye contact. "Not for now."

Mom squeezes my hand. "Go home. Get some rest."

Dad nods, worry etched across his face. I wonder what he's thinking. If he's beating himself up for fighting with Beth, for the last thing he said before she walked out the door. That must be haunting him. It ought to be. It haunts me.

Maybe something should *happen to her.*

I hesitate, wondering if I should mention it to the police to give the full picture. Except this isn't a gritty true crime drama, and even though Dad has a temper, so does Beth. They're cut from the same cloth. And anyway, he said it about me, not her.

"Remember something?" Chief Merritt looks at me expectantly and I realize my mouth is hanging open.

I swallow the words. It's family stuff. Merritt doesn't need to know. "My place."

"Girl's got a mouth," he says before I close the door behind me.

Girl's pissed off. And if the police won't question Ezra, Girl will.

14 HOURS

The house *looks* like the wreckage of a party. Empty bottles, plastic cups, and crumpled paper plates are everywhere. I press my face to the window beside the front door and knock loudly, then push the doorbell repeatedly. A shadowy figure eventually makes its way down the spiral staircase, moving with the speed and precision of a sleepwalker.

Ezra opens the door wearing sweatpants and a T-shirt and

squints at me through half-open eyes. He clearly just rolled out of bed. “Party was last night, Chip.”

He certainly seems to know which twin I am now. *Chip* was my nickname in second grade after I fell off the swings attempting a 360 and chipped my front tooth.

I touch my permanent filling with my tongue. “Can I come in for a second?”

He glances at the toxic wreck behind him. “Sure you want to?”

“I am sure.” And when *I* say it, I mean it.

“Sorry about the mess. My parents are off at some wedding weekend in Miami.”

“And the maid is off,” I say sarcastically.

“Exactly.”

I can’t tell if he’s kidding. He leads me into the living room and selects a glass from the bar. It has a delicate etching of a honeybee on it, and I glance at the beehive sculpture I noticed last night.

Ezra follows my gaze. “My mom. She’s, like, obsessed.” He pours himself a glass of orange juice. “Ever had Lillabee Honey?”

“Who hasn’t?” Mrs. Elwood’s honey regularly earns honors at the county fair, and she’s built the brand into an extremely successful business. The decor still feels a bit much, though. Like living in an advertisement.

“I can’t stand it.” Ezra adds a splash of vodka to his glass and offers it to me.

I look at it with distaste. “This is how you live?”

He appears offended. “It’s a hangover cure. Look it up.”

“I’ll take your word for it. I wanted to ask about last night.”

He pushes his thick hair back from his face. “Look, I’m sorry about that. I thought you were Beth.”

"During spin the bottle as well?"

He blushes. "It's a game, man."

"I'm not a man. I know it's a game. And I'm not a weirdo. I meant I wanted to talk about Beth."

His face disappears into his glass. "No."

I gape at him. "What do you mean 'no'?"

"I mean 'none of your business.' Sorry. Beth wouldn't want me talking, either."

For a second, we stare each other down, and I wonder if she *did* run away and tell Ezra her plans.

"It's complicated," he adds, blushing again. "I don't really know what's going on with Beth. Unless you do?"

"I'm sorry, do you know where she is?"

The confusion on his face answers my question. My heart sinks into my stomach. He thinks I've been asking about *their relationship*.

"Should I?" he asks.

I take his glass and place it on the bar.

"Beth is missing."

My voice is way too calm. I'm hyperaware of how unnerving I sound, but it's the only way I can get out the words. Any words at all, really. "She was last seen leaving your party. Right after you fought."

His face drains of color.

"From what I gather, she fought with you and Jack, left, and ran into the woods. No one has seen or heard from her since. I think that makes you a suspect."

"Suspect?" he echoes, looking nauseous.

"I was there when the police report was filed." He doesn't need to know what the police actually *said*.

"What about Jack? Why isn't he a suspect?"

"Who says you both aren't?"

Ezra jumps up, grabs a bubblegum-pink puffy jacket someone left draped on a lampshade and throws it on, then strides to the foyer, snatching his keys from a basket beside the door. "Come on."

I imagine the way he sees himself: a badass, a take-no-prisoners detective, a rebel beholden to no one. The jacket falls about an inch above his wrist and waist, and staring at me with bedhead and bloodshot eyes, he looks like a party boy freshly out of coke.

"Where are we going?"

"To find Jack fucking Sawyer."

THE TWISTED MIND OF VERONICA GREEN

MARCH 3

ii

I meet the cast:

CERBERUS

canine, vigilant, loyal.
fond of flesh, especially royal.

DEMETER

beautiful, equine, earless.
a black hole of reason
approaching darkness.

DEADEYES

ravenous, bloody, hungry.

eyes with arms and arms with purpose.

CHORUS

empty bodies and air,

bodies and air,

bodies and air.

LILLABEE

quiet, on the inside.

until—

—wait for it

there.

3

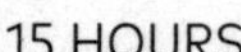

HAZEL

15 HOURS

Jack Sawyer lives in a trailer off Lonely Mountain Road, about three quarters of a mile from our house. No one lives particularly far from anyone else in Ashling, but he's very literally around the corner. I'd never realized that.

When we pull into his gravel driveway, the windows all light up, and my heart flutters in my chest. Part of me was hoping that he wasn't home. That maybe the police had already called him in for questioning and are getting answers right now.

Ezra cuts the engine and meets my eyes before swinging open his door. Another thought suddenly occurs to me. I have a bad habit of focusing hard on the worst-case scenario, sometimes to the exclusion of all possible positive outcomes. I blew right past that first statistic because there's a caveat to the fact that most missing teens are runaways. It's that this includes kids who get lost, or miscommunicate plans, or don't tell anyone where they're going.

The point is—this subset, they're not actually missing. They're just *missed.*

I jump out of the car, hope soaring through me as my feet hit the ground that when the front door swings open, there will be two figures looming in the doorframe. Jack and Beth, their fight resolved after talking through the night and eventually passing out, too emotionally exhausted to think of calling home.

It isn't like Beth. But maybe.

I reach the door breathless as Ezra bangs a fist against it for the second time and I resist the urge to call out for my sister.

"Beth!" Ezra shouts. As if he can hear my thoughts and instinctively knows to do the opposite.

"It won't make the door open faster," I say through gritted teeth.

But the door does open. And Jack is the only one standing there in a black long-sleeved t-shirt and skinny jeans. His ginger hair is meticulously styled to look messy, and he's wearing his usual black eyeliner and frosted pink glasses with the lenses popped out. Jack sticks out in this town, but he wears a glorious air of *I don't give a fuck.* His chin is covered in light stubble, and he clamps his teeth on a vape pen before addressing us with studied disinterest. As if last night never happened. As if he could not care less about Ezra Elwood or that Beth cheated on him. It's an act, and it feels like a gigantic, frantically waving red flag.

He takes in Ezra. "Slept well, did we?"

Ezra places a firm hand on the door, preventing it from closing. "Where's Beth?"

Jack nearly matches him in height, but he doesn't have Ezra's muscle mass, and he moves slowly, deliberately. Ezra is the type to bound into a room fists first.

He backs away from Ezra, maintaining his air of total disinterest. "I'm not doing this."

"Jack." I take a hesitant step toward him. For me, it's a bold move. "What happened last night after you left the party?"

He looks back and forth between me and Ezra. "Why?"

"Come on, Jack," Ezra says softly. His expression is threatening, but there's an undercurrent of fear in his voice. "You know."

Ordinarily, I'd tell him to fuck off.

Except he's right. Jack does know. He's smart enough to recognize something is very wrong with this picture. Ezra Elwood and Hazel Whitman are not friends. And yet, we showed up on his doorstep together. The only thing we have in common is Beth. And the last time we were all together, she left an entire party full of witnesses and followed him out into the darkness.

"Beth is missing," Jack says. I can't tell whether it's a statement or a question. I can't read his face. That makes me very, very nervous.

Ezra turns to me. "I told you." He looks back at Jack. "What do you know?"

Jack throws up his hands. "Back up. I didn't say I knew anything. I left the party early, remember?"

"She ran after you," I remind him.

"I didn't want to be found." He tucks the vape pen into his pocket and invites us inside. It's a cozy space, brightly lit and filled with living things: plants and herbs and a collection of small-animal habitats—tropical fish in a rainbow of colors, a snake as green as new spring leaves, a delicately spotted leopard gecko. It doesn't fit with his sleek, muted aesthetic.

I wonder about his family. Families don't define you, but I

think you are who you are because of what you're surrounded by or actively resist. My parents and I might as well have been conjured from the pages of *Mountain Living* magazine, cut from flannel, denim, and wool with unfussy hair and practical footwear. Lately, Beth looks more like Jack and Phoebe with their dark eyeliner and fine Victorian boots.

It's the boots that bother me.

Footwear reveals a lot about a person. If you don't know these mountains, you won't know the worst flooding comes from snow melting, not from storms. Ice can fall in blocks or spears, or it can solidify into a parasitic shell, pry under shingles, and bite through roofs and siding, invading slowly, insidiously. You won't know how the water got in, what softened the walls and bred the rot. The thaw is always worse than the freeze.

Beth knows these mountains. Beth dressing like an outsider is a *choice,* like dumping Ezra for Jack was a *choice.* What I don't get is why, and why last summer?

Jack sits on a battered armchair and motions for us to sit on a loveseat. "I heard Beth follow me out," he admits. "But I wasn't in the mood to talk. I took off through the woods, ran straight home, and I've been here ever since."

Ezra raises a skeptical eyebrow. "You *ran* home."

"Ran, walked, skipped, what do you want from me? Some of us don't have rich parents who throw cars at us instead of love."

Ezra stares at him, more perplexed than pissed. His parents do spoil him, but they're not assholes. To hear my dad talk, Ezra's father was the most popular guy in school in his day—prom king, football captain, the whole nine yards—and nothing has really changed. The Elwoods are Ashling royalty—town spiritual leader and PTA president with a house bursting full of wholesome, rosy-cheeked children. Maybe I don't love the Elwoods. But they're not bad people.

Jack is flailing, trying to hit a nerve. From the many fishing and hunting trips my father took Beth and me on from the time we could lift a rod or trudge through the woods in an orange vest, I've learned that animals don't flail when they're in control. And that includes people.

They flail when they're cornered.

I focus. "Jack. I just came from the police station, and they only want to talk to you."

His face goes pale.

I continue, "They're jumping the gun. But you, me, Ezra—we were there. We all want the same thing. We can work together if we can be honest with each other."

Jack's gaze strays to Ezra with contempt and distrust.

"We can," I insist. "So how about it? We can find her before the twenty-four-hour mark if we work together. After that..." My throat goes dry and my voice cuts out.

"What?" Ezra asks.

"Outlook not so good," Jack finishes darkly. "Okay, I'm in." He steeples his fingers and stares at the floor, then looks up at me. "How much did you and Beth talk the past few months?"

"We're not close." The admission floods me with shame, as if being sisters confers a moral obligation that we be friends.

I can *feel* the judgment.

"Whose fault is that?" Ezra says under his breath.

"Did she ever mention Veronica Green?" Jack asks.

The name sounds vaguely familiar, but I can't place it.

Ezra rises with an annoyed huff. "We don't have time for this."

"Who's Veronica Green?" I ask.

"An urban legend." Ezra glares at Jack.

"Only some of it," Jack tells me. "She was a girl around our age who died in Ashling."

Last night flashes back to me. The Ouija game. "I know the story, just not the name. The ghost girl of Ashling."

"She wasn't from here," Ezra says dismissively. "It's not exactly the town legacy." He eyes me. "You have to make an effort *not* to talk to anyone to not know about Veronica Green."

I blush. I have friends. A couple. We talk about shared interests. True crime isn't one of them. And it's embarrassing to explain that growing up, we were never *allowed* to talk about the murdered girl because Mom thought devil worship was involved. "Murder doesn't do it for me."

Jack arches an eyebrow. "Well, Beth...is a special kind of person."

"What does that mean?"

He shrugs evasively. "Beth was very interested in Veronica and what happened to her. I don't really know what else to say."

Ezra looks at him distrustfully.

I try to process. My choir-girl sister was secretly obsessing over a decades-old murder we were forbidden to speak of. And then she vanished. "What does that have to do with her disappearance? Was she trying to investigate the murder? How did no one know about this?"

Jack smiles apologetically. "I knew. Phoebe knew."

"Phoebe brought the game," I remember. "At the party. She brought a Ouija board, and someone wanted to contact Veronica. I mean, 'contact.'" I use air quotes. "So I did."

Both of them stare at me oddly.

"Fun fact," Jack says slowly. "Last night was the anniversary of Veronica's murder. Halloween Eve."

My mouth feels sour. "Oh." The blur of gleeful faces around the game board takes on a different tone. Only Phoebe was serious, concentrating intently, almost studiously.

"Where were you?" I ask Ezra suddenly. He looks at me blankly. "You didn't know about the Ouija board. Or that your friends casually had me summon the soul of a dead girl."

Ezra shifts his weight uneasily. "We're getting off track. That shit is just a game. It's kindergarten."

"You know what's not a game? My sister disappearing."

"*And* on the murderversary of the girl whose death she was investigating." Jack rises and pulls on a black wool coat. "I have an idea. But no questions until we get there."

Ezra follows him out the door, frowning. "Why can't you tell us where we're going?"

Jack glances over his shoulder as he heads out to Ezra's gleaming SUV. "You think I trust you? That's cute. Nice jacket, by the way." He hops into the driver's seat as Ezra gapes at him. "It brings out your softer side. If it does in fact exist." He gives him a thumbs-up and pushes the ignition button.

Ezra turns to me indignantly, like I'm the referee. "This is my car."

Jack nods dismissively. "And I already explained that I do not trust you, so I'll be driving. You'll be in the backseat with a blindfold over your beady eyes."

"Ezra," I say curtly. He turns to me, mouth open, like a child protesting an unfair punishment. "We have no time."

He stalks over, climbs into the backseat, and slumps down. “Dent it and you’re dead.”

“Blindfold,” Jack reminds him, unfazed.

Ezra shoots him a murderous look, then digs a crumpled sports jersey from the floor and tosses it over his head. “Happy?” he asks, his voice muffled.

“Thrilled,” Jack replies.

“So…where are we headed?” I snap my seat belt into place as Jack backs out of the driveway.

“Blindfold, Hazel,” he says softly.

Stunned, I pull my hood down over my eyes. So much for the trust circle.

THE TWISTED MIND OF VERONICA GREEN

APRIL 4

iii
I meet the King.

EVERYONE KNOWS THE STORY, OR AT LEAST THE BONES—

—it was against her will.
But the body, buried and risen
buried and risen
and buried
and risen
has not been put back together quite the same.
She was taken
But not for love.
Her mother, with promises of endless summer,

fairy gardens and golden hives, pushed her
down to the dark place.
It was against her will.
And in the dark place, there he was.

SOMETIMES, A KING ASKS PERMISSION.
Even a King with all the fires of hell at his fingertips.
To dance in the light of those fires is to taste power.
It tastes like forever.
So maybe she says yes—
not to the body,
but to the fruit.
Because why should one yes
mean an eternity of false memories?

Everyone knows the bones.

4
HAZEL

16 HOURS

We make a lot of twists and turns as we drive, and there's a steady incline the whole time. At some point it occurs to me that we've made the classic murder victim mistake—we confronted the killer, got into a car with him and *went to a second location.* And once it's in my head, I can't get it out. It prompts me to start asking a string of inane questions, but Ezra is more direct.

"You'd better not be taking us into the woods to murder us."

Part of me admires his straightforwardness. It's soothing. But it isn't very strategic.

"I'm taking off my blindfold," Ezra warns.

"Do what you must," Jack says.

I slip my hood down as well. We're deep in the woods, though not in the middle of nowhere. The mountain has become so developed with vacation homes and tourists desiring to live secluded from society that seclusion has become impossible. Every few miles, there's a house. Even government-protected lands are bordered by homes.

Still, the narrow dirt road, winding ever upward, isn't reassuring.

"Where are you taking us?" Ezra asks. He's nothing if not persistent.

"A friend's." Jack slows and makes a sharp right down an even narrower, unmarked road. An enormous house comes into view, one that makes Ezra's look like a quaint little cottage. It's perched at the edge of a cliff, a creation of unstained wood and glass that looks like it could be straight out of *Architectural Digest*. Through one of the enormous glass panels in the front of the house, I see a fireplace that takes up an entire wall, and a collection—*a collection*—of deer heads.

"Holy shit," Ezra says.

"Yeah." Jack parks, and we climb out of the car. "If I were going to run away, this might do."

Ezra turns to me as we reach the door. "That's a lot of heads."

"Scared they might need one more?" Jack rings the doorbell.

Ezra rolls his eyes at him. "I run fast."

The door swings open as he speaks. Phoebe Crane stands there wearing black silk pajamas. Her face is made up, as always, with dark, dramatic makeup. Half of her nails are done in glossy black, and she holds a bottle of nail polish in one hand as she carefully fans the other.

She takes in all three of us with a dubious expression. "What is this, and why? And be brief. I have a headache because of you." She points a long, glossy nail at Ezra, then curls it to beckon the three of us to follow her inside. She leads us into an enormous living room filled with plush, fur-covered furniture and settles down on a giant, pouf.

Jack sits on an armchair that resembles a bear. "Have you heard from Beth?"

Phoebe resumes painting her nails with long, careful strokes, scraping the edges and examining each one for imperfections. "I have not."

Ezra paces. "Thanks. Can we go? I say we take Jack to the police."

I sink back into the sofa helplessly. "What are they going to do?"

He shrugs. "Lie detector? You said so yourself, the first twenty-four hours are crucial. We're running out of time."

Jack ignores both of us and speaks directly to Phoebe. "Beth went radio silent last night."

Phoebe places the nail brush back in the jar, screws on the lid, and fans her hands back and forth slowly, regarding him carefully. "What time?"

"No one knows."

I look at her impatiently. "Do you have any idea where she might have gone?"

"I might." She picks up her phone with her dry hand and balances it on her knee, typing carefully. "Last night was the anniversary."

"Veronica Green's death," I say.

She looks up at me. "Beth talked to you about Veronica?"

"Everyone knows the story."

Ezra raises an eyebrow at me. I glare back.

It *is* true. Everyone else knew. Now I do too. Hence, everyone knows.

"Maybe. But I'd guess she never discussed her take on

Veronica." Phoebe opens a text conversation and shows it to me. It's a long string of eager, almost obsessive check-ins, notes, and questions from Beth with short answers from Phoebe. It doesn't sound like the Beth I know.

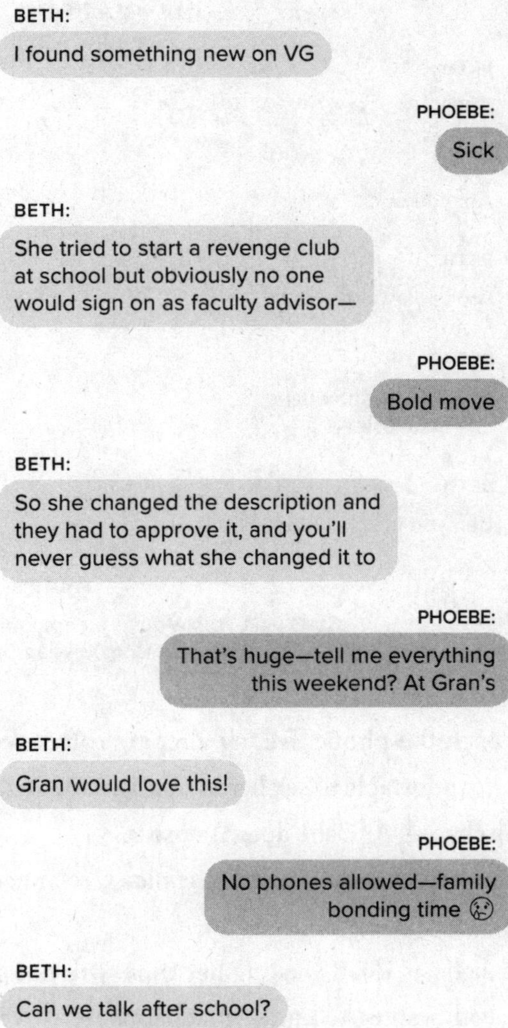

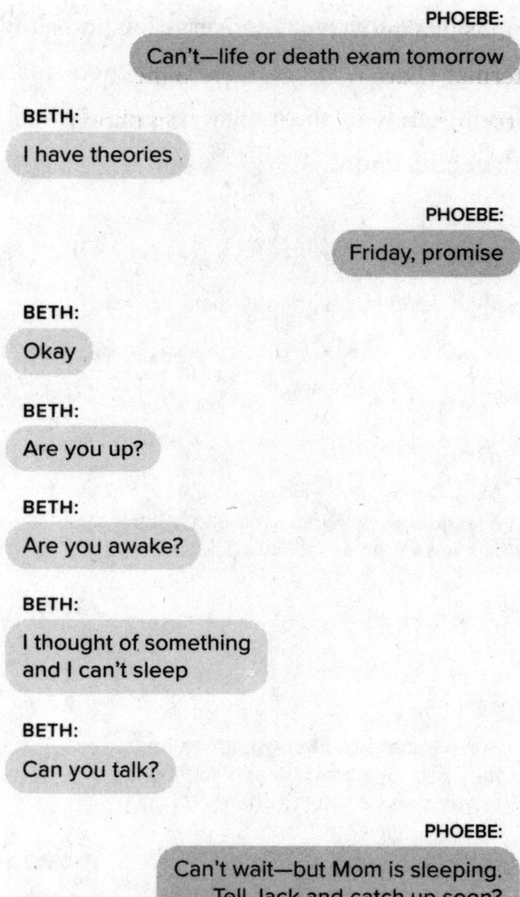

I hand back the phone, feeling almost protective of Beth. It makes me uncomfortable to see her in this light. Beth doesn't chase people. She's chased. And she doesn't obsess.

"Okay, so Beth texts a lot and Veronica Green had a grudge. Where's the clue?"

Phoebe sighs as if I'm wasting her time. "It's not a clue. It's a pattern. We *both* wanted to know what happened to Veronica. But Beth couldn't wait. She had to dictate all the terms."

That sounds like my sister.

"What terms?" Ezra crouches next to me.

Phoebe reclines in her chair, slipping her phone into her pocket. "We were supposed to call to Veronica during the party—at the time she supposedly died. Beth wanted to go about it differently, which I was strongly against. But we agreed on the Ouija board, and when you make a plan, you stick to it. So when she bolted, that's what I did. I followed the plan." She nods to me. "Well. With a twin stand-in."

I rub my temples with my fingers, a headache forming. "Why would it matter if it were either of us?"

"Veronica responded, didn't she?" Phoebe snaps. She recovers her calm, centered composure. "The point is, it worked."

Jack scrunches his nose. "Did it, though? Because we're missing one."

Phoebe sighs and stares down at her nails. "I'm sure she stayed over at a friend's house."

"We're it, and you know it," Jack says flatly. The four of us stare at each other. "What was Beth's plan?"

Phoebe averts her eyes. "She wanted to do a more advanced summoning ceremony."

Ezra looks unimpressed. "Any chance Beth planned to do this summoning on a bus out of town?"

Phoebe glares. "She planned to do it in the woods behind your house. You know, where Veronica was found dead."

I turn to Ezra, stunned. He looks a little pale but not surprised. Clearly, he knew this little factoid. So. Maybe there *is* a reason the Veronica murder is both known and hushed around town. It's an Elwood family scandal.

Jack flicks his hair out of his eyes nervously. "If you *want* to see that as a lead, I guess it has all the markings."

"Beth planned to go to the place a girl was found murdered on the anniversary of her death, and now she's gone." I feel sick to my stomach, my head reeling with all the worst-case scenarios. "We have to retrace her steps."

17 HOURS

No one speaks on the drive back to Ezra's house. Ezra takes the wheel this time, with Jack and Phoebe silent in the back seat. They look like paper dolls tucked into the wrong book. Jack, ripped from the pages of a music magazine; Phoebe, an illustration from a Victorian novel, prim in a velvet waistcoat and veiled hat. The jeep smells like the sawdust, sweaty jerseys, and empty pizza boxes that litter the floor. Even I feel like an outsider, and I was conditioned to embrace all of this. Boy smell, big car, a permanent place in the passenger seat.

Mom texts me in a panic because they just got home, and I'm not there.

I lie and tell her I'm at a friend's house. *I have friends. I do,* I tell myself. None close enough to tell that my sister is missing. That she may be hurt or dead. That's the sort of thing you tell someone who doesn't mind the burden of caring. Because girls our age aren't supposed to go missing. Not in the age of smartphones. Not in the mountains, in the cold. Not on the anniversary of the night another girl died.

Ezra is speeding, taking the snaking curves like he's playing a video game, and my body slumps from side to side, slamming into the car door, the console, and back again. I want to tell him to slow down, but the silence feels like an unspoken agreement between the four of us. Suspicion hangs thickly in the air. Ezra wasn't at the party when Beth disappeared. She followed Jack into the night after he witnessed Ezra admitting they were still seeing each other. Phoebe and Beth apparently had friction between them about how to solve Veronica's murder. And it might have involved the occult.

It occurs to me that I don't know for a fact that Veronica's killer was never caught, and hope flutters in my chest. I turn around to look at Phoebe. "Did they catch him?"

She raises a meticulously shaped eyebrow. "Who?"

"Veronica's killer."

Suddenly, the jeep swerves sharply, and the world spins. I'm filled with a dizzying sense of weightlessness as gravity abandons me, then the wheels find the pavement again with a jolt, and the jeep screeches to a halt. The seatbelt digs into my chest, and for a moment, I can't breathe. I lift my hands to my head, as if to steady it, then turn, in slow motion, to look at Ezra. His hands are gripping the wheel, white as bone, his shoulders drawn up to his chin, his expression rigid. I twist my head around, and in the back seat, Phoebe straightens her hat and punches the back of Ezra's seat, but she's shaking.

Jack's hands are plastered over his eyes. "Are we in a river?" Panic ripples through his voice. "I have a recurring nightmare about crashing into a river."

"No," Phoebe says softly. She stares out the window, one hand on the car door.

I follow her gaze, my head still spinning, and my heart leaps into my throat.

Beth is standing in the middle of the street, still in her costume from last night, her long, white-streaked hair loose around her shoulders. Her skin is pale, pink and raw in places, her lips purple. Her expression is blank, sickly.

She's alive.

My sister is alive.

Beth is alive, and I don't feel relieved. I feel shame. I *didn't care* that she left the party, and I didn't care that she didn't come back. I didn't wait for her, and I didn't call. And oh god, it could have been so much worse than this.

I tug on the handle and throw my shaking body against the door, trying and failing to run, each step unsteady after the almost-crash.

"Beth," I gasp. And by Beth, I mean *I am sorry, and I am wrong, and things will be different*. Because this changes everything. It's inevitable. It's the third act moment, the near-tragedy that makes everyone realize what's really important, and forces you to set aside all the pettiness and jealousy and shitty behavior and dark thoughts that ruin all the good things we could be if we weren't so awfully human.

I unzip my jacket and give it to her, but she holds it awkwardly and looks at me with suspicion. Which I deserve. I fully own that. "Beth," I plead. "You're freezing."

"I'm freezing," she repeats slowly. "But I'm not Beth."

"Holy shit," Phoebe whispers from behind me.

"What do you mean, *not Beth*?" Ezra says.

She tilts her head up at him. "My name is Veronica Green." She looks me dead in the eyes. "Could you call 911 for me, please? I've been shot."

THE TWISTED MIND OF VERONICA GREEN

JUNE 17

iv

I summon a beast.

SOMETIMES A KING ASKS FIRST.
Sometimes, no.
Sometimes he forgets
A girl is more than bones.
A girl may be beast when you peel back the skin,
may summon a beast within.
When words fail,
white teeth may prove
that love's no fairy tale.

KINGS HAVE BONES, TOO

blood they may miss
white teeth prove all of this.

ONE HEAD FOR KISSING THE QUEEN'S NOBLE HAND

One head for guarding her royal land
One to eviscerate very bad men.
A hound is a girl's best friend.

5

HAZEL

Beth was not shot. But she is not okay. The paramedics were the first to arrive, then the police, then my parents, and finally the ambulances. There are two ambulances on the mountaintop, and with the winding roads and steep cliffsides, and many hazards of simply being alive, it can sometimes take a while to claim one when it's needed. Sometimes too long.

But Beth has no bodily injuries. The paramedics assured us of this quickly. She was disoriented and confused—but unharmed. Still, my mother cried inconsolably and my father paced by her side, the blood drained from his face, as she stared up at them vacantly from her cocoon of blankets. "Where is my mother?" she repeated over and over. "Where is Olivia Green?"

"Veronica's mother moved away from Ashling shortly after Veronica's death," Phoebe whispered to me as the two of us stood huddled on the sidelines. Ezra was filling out a police report for the car crash, and Jack was answering questions about the night before. I wanted to be closer to Beth, but just when I thought I had my chance to put our past behind us, this new perplexing development appeared.

Veronica.

Now we're home and quiet has settled. I sit in the kitchen with my father over a warm Campbell's cream of chicken soup casserole. The neighbors filled our fridge in the less than twenty-four hours Beth was missing. The rules apparently hold. My father eats mechanically, smiling at me occasionally and nodding to my grease-stained paper plate, as if to reassure me that everything is okay and eating is how we prove it. Eat, Hazel, or something weird might happen.

"She's okay, though?" I ask for maybe the twentieth time.

"The doctors said she wasn't hurt."

I want to ask some of the obvious questions I don't have the nerve to ask and maybe aren't my business. How are they *sure* she wasn't hurt? Did they do a rape kit? A psych eval? Do they mean her outsides aren't hurt? How much does that count for? Ninety-nine percent not hurt doesn't count for shit. But I'm not a doctor.

My father is staring at me with a furrowed brow. "She's fine."

I take a delicate bite of slimy green bean. I know exactly who brought this dish—who brought every dish. Every baptism, graduation, town picnic, funeral brings the same offering from the same family. It's not perfunctory; there is love in the gesture but also obligation: the favor is expected to be returned.

The apple pie is from Ezra's aunt and is sweetened with his mother's famous raw honey. The chicken soup, right from the coop, is from Julie's mother, the head librarian and my boss. Spaetzle from Principal Laurence and family, probably made by Amanda,

Beth's former best friend. I wonder if she feels guilty too. And the dish no one ever wants but always gets: an enormous jar of pickled beets from Ed Wendell, editor-in-chief of the local newspaper, who has tried too hard to be involved in the community since his wife died, though not hard enough at home that his son didn't turn out to be a little shit. Mac is the one who broke my nose.

A short, sharp shriek and a loud splash pierce the thin walls, followed by a low, protective bark. It startles me out of my wandering thoughts, and I look to my father.

"She's fine," he repeats.

"Beth or Veronica?" The question hangs in the air between us.

"She's tired and confused," he says shortly, then rises with his plate of food and retreats to the den.

I trail after him, resentment building at his repeated dismissals. "She's not fine."

He looks startled, hurt even. He's used to Beth talking back and me being *reasonable*.

"Why don't you help your mother?" he suggests.

I waver. I want to talk now while the resentment is giving me courage. I want to tell him I'm not fine either, ask what he meant when he said maybe something should happen to me. There are so many ways to interpret that statement.

"Please, Hazel."

It is a plea, but it's not a request.

I walk down the narrow hallway toward the bathroom. Through the closed door, I can hear my mother struggling with my sister like she's a toddler. There's rapid-fire whispering from Beth, soothing sounds from my mother, more splashing, another shriek. Then a growl, the kind dogs give to strangers as a warning—but it's not coming from Artax. It's coming from Beth. A helpless whimper from Artax follows, then finally, silence.

The door opens, and my mother emerges, her hair frizzing out of her low ponytail, her shoulders sagging.

"Can you watch your sister for a minute?" she says.

"Why?"

"I don't want her to drown." She sloshes down the hallway, her clothes drenched.

Dread overwhelms me as I push open the bathroom door.

Beth is sitting in the bathtub, looking straight ahead with the unblinking stare of a mannequin. The water is filled too high, almost to overflowing. It's cloudy and opaque with soap. The entire room is soaked—the carpet, the mirror, the curtains.

"Aren't you going to tell me this is your bathroom and I can pee in the woods like a bear?" Normally, if I so much as knocked while Beth was brushing her teeth, this is exactly what she'd say.

Instead, she looks directly at me, and without a word, she slowly begins to slide down into the water. Inch by inch, past the old, toothpaste-blue tiles, she sinks into the cloudy white haze.

I freeze, unnerved.

Her expression doesn't shift. She doesn't break her stare as her shoulders disappear under the cloud-colored water.

I open my mouth, but nothing comes out. She mirrors me, mocking me. The water rises, creeping up her neck toward her chin.

"Mom." It comes out too faint. Not even I can hear myself shouting for help.

Beth's lips form the word "Mom" soundlessly, her eyes locked with mine. The water begins to pour into her mouth. It spills between her lips, pools between her cheeks, rushes toward her throat.

The soapy, filmy water swallows her in little waves. Her mouth, her nose, her tongue, her lying voice, the baby with the bathwater, and oh, god. She's going to drown.

I am letting her drown.

I unfreeze and leap forward, hooking my arms under her armpits as her head rolls back on her neck and dips under. I shriek out loud this time, and Mom and Dad both come running as Beth coughs and shivers in my arms. She shakes harder and harder until I can't hold her any longer.

Dad catches her in a towel and pulls her from the water while Mom unplugs the drain. I back out of the bathroom.

Artax is barking wildly, pacing up and down the hallway. I try to loop my arms around his neck and hold him against me, but he pulls away. He won't calm down. He saw what I did. He saw me hesitate. Beth is his person, not me. I let go of him and he scampers away from me and refuses to meet my gaze. I don't blame him. I let them both down.

My phone buzzes in my pocket. It's a message from Julie Merritt asking if I'm okay. My head pounds, and I shove my phone into my pocket impatiently. Mom's got a dry towel around Beth, and Dad scoops her up and carries her to our room. Mom hurries after them and the door slams shut, leaving Artax and me anxious and agitated on the other side.

I go outside instead and climb into the driver's seat of Dad's truck. It's quiet and cold, and I can slowly feel my body relax. After a while, Mom emerges from the house with a warmed slice of apple pie and a travel mug of chamomile tea. I roll down the window.

There are dark circles under her eyes. "Come on back inside when you're done?"

"I don't want to," I say, but I take the tea and the Elwoods' pie. I think of how long I've disliked Ezra, and suddenly I feel unsure. "Can I ask you something?"

"Of course." She leans against the car.

"Why don't you and Mrs. Elwood get along?"

"We were friends once," she finally says. "When we were young. We had a fight, and we never made up."

I try to imagine Beth and me at Mom's age, never speaking, avoiding each other. The thought fills me with such heavy sadness, I don't know how to handle it. "Did you ever try to fix it?"

"I didn't want to," she says simply.

"Do you ever miss her?"

She pauses. "Yes." Her eyes go misty, and again, I feel guilty for making her emotional. Except then she adds, "But not enough." She squeezes my shoulder. "Don't stay out too late. You'll freeze." She kisses my forehead, then goes inside.

I'm not ready to go back into that house.

I stare at the wheel for a while, but there's nowhere to go. I take out my phone and scroll through my contacts, but there isn't anyone to call, either. I will text Mel back eventually. But not until all of this is over. And Julie is out of the question. Our first phone call can't be about my increasingly disturbing family, possessed sister, and brush with negligent homicide.

I wonder what happened to Jack after we drove off to the hospital. If the police believed him. I don't know if I believe him. Because something *did* happen to Beth. I don't know who or what to believe.

I turn the key in the ignition and back out of the driveway. I doubt my parents will even notice I'm gone. I slowly drive past Jack's house, but the lights are out, and there's a cop car in his driveway, headlights on. Not a great sign for Jack. I start to continue but pause when I see Phoebe outside arguing with one of the cops. I brake, park, and jog over.

"What's going on?"

Phoebe looks over at me, startled. "They won't let Jack go."

The officer, a rookie from down mountain, looks at me wearily. "No one can enter the premises until they've been searched." Then he recognizes me. "I'm sorry about your sister."

"She's not dead," I say sharply.

"Of course not." He awkwardly puts his cell phone to his ear, as if it rang, which it hasn't, and backs away.

Phoebe and I both watch him, speechlessly.

"That just happened," she says in a monotone.

"All of this is surreal. Beth tried to drown herself in the bathtub. Like right in front of me. I can't be in that house anymore."

Phoebe's eyes widen. "You know that's one of the signs, right?"

"Of the apocalypse descending on Ashling, centered squarely on my house? That tracks."

"No." She tries Jack's front door again, then whirls around, her jacket flaring like a vampire's cape. "It's a sign of a possession. Old-school, biblical demonic possession."

"Sure." I follow her up the driveway back to the street. "I went to Sunday school. I know my fallen angels. You got Lucifer, Beelzebub, and lest we forget, Veronica Green."

Phoebe gives me a dead-eyed stare. "Laugh."

"Does it look like I'm laughing?"

We reach Phoebe's car, a sleek antique straight out of an old James Dean movie, and she leans against it. "I could use a drink."

"I shouldn't." I can never tell if that sort of statement is an invitation or just a fact. But I don't want a drink. My head is already spinning. "Beth isn't herself. Do you have any idea what happened to her?"

She shrugs. "I told you what she planned. But honestly—and I'm the first person who would be open to the idea it worked—she couldn't have single-handedly summoned a spirit with that kind of ritual. It wasn't necromancy 101."

"What was it?"

"Nothing I want anything to do with. Beth had a book. It might be somewhere in your house. Or somewhere in the woods." Phoebe opens her car door. "I think she was out all night in the cold and is in shock, clinging to what she was thinking about before she...maybe fell and hit her head, or something happened."

"Then you agree something happened."

Phoebe averts her eyes. "Let's not assume the worst, okay? I have to head back to the city tomorrow. Tell Beth to call me when she's feeling better. And that I'm sorry." She opens the car door wide to climb in without crumpling her outfit and something sparkly on the floor of the passenger side catches my eye.

"Wait. Sorry for wha—"

She slams the door and the car roars to life, and a moment later, she's gone.

But not before it dawns on me that the sparkly object is Beth's personalized phone case peeking out from under the passenger seat.

THE TWISTED MIND OF VERONICA GREEN

JULY 22

V

Elegy for winged things.

SPRING BABIES, IN WINTER'S LAND, DIE
pale, studious daughters
in the valley of the shadow.
The girls were promised springtime
in exchange for sweetness.
That home was not a battlefield.
You could be safe in Lillabee, at least, asleep.
In the end, maybe none of them suffered.
But who knew?
Spring babies, in their coffins, do not speak.
Wings lie still
and if you cry, you cry alone.

6

HAZEL

When I get home, Beth is asleep in her bed with Artax positioned protectively at her feet, and my mother has passed out in her clothes on my bed. My father is sitting in the hallway, beside the door, keeping vigil. No one noticed I was gone. I pull my sleeping bag down out of the attic, unroll it on the couch, and go to sleep, clutching my phone to my heart like a teddy bear. Questions swirl in my head as I drift off. Why did Phoebe have Beth's phone? Did Beth have it when she ran out into the darkness after Jack? She didn't have it on her when we found her. Was it in her coat she left at the party? If she did leave it behind—why would Phoebe take it?

When I wake the next morning, everything is quiet. It's an unsettling quiet, a low vibration, like a toothache. Dull. I tiptoe from the couch into our room to find it empty. So is my parents' room, the bathroom, the whole house. Artax is parked by the front door, staring watchfully out the window. He glances at me as I pass, then, as if to say "oh, it's only you," turns right back to the window again.

I fire a quick text to my mother and get a terse "we're fine." She doesn't tell me where they all went. But we should be getting ready for church now, and I don't know what else to do with myself. I have mixed feelings about church, but it's part of our routine. It's what we do, like attending school, work, hunting season, or fall festival. In Ashling, church is as much a social obligation as a matter of faith. It's something we do on autopilot. But not without thought. I think about everything. And something that bugs me about church is the whole premise is man cannot be trusted, right from scene one in the Garden of Eden. We are liars, every one of us. I'm a believer, but I'm a believer with questions. And not the *why do bad things happen* brand. That's easy. We are people. We make bad things happen. We are fragile. Our bodies break. We live in a fragile world, and we make it sick and unstable. We could take better care of it, ourselves, our communities, but we don't. Bad things happen because we are who we are.

So I don't question why bad things happen.

I question why, of every creature that walks the earth, God would choose to speak through humanity. Because in His name, man does monstrous things. You can't say that about any other living thing. God made man in His own image, but then, technically, it was a man who said that. And if God could speak through man thousands of years ago, why fall silent and leave ambiguities about His will that inspire men more toward harm than healing?

I have questions.

I shower and dress, the silence like a film on my skin, and I make it as far as the driveway when the truck rumbles up, crunching the gravel, clouding up dust. It brakes abruptly, and my mother tumbles out of the cab, landing hard on her side. I rush forward to help her up, but Beth jumps out after her, wild-eyed and frightened, looking almost feral, and drags me down the driveway by my elbow.

"Run," she pants.

My mother calls after us, her voice pitched like a siren, and I hear my father's pounding footsteps closing in.

Panic surges through me. "What are you doing?"

"They'll never let us go," Beth whispers. Her eyes dart erratically and with her short, staccato breaths and nervous energy, she reminds me of a cornered rabbit. "We can make it to the road," she continues. "She's slow, and he can only get one of us. The other will get to a neighbor, call the police, and send help."

I'm at a complete loss. If I take her words at face value—*if*—that would mean she believes we're both being held hostage. By our parents.

My father grabs Beth, and she cries out.

"Run!" she screams.

The desperation on her face is so real, I freeze. This is Beth. My sister, the liar. My sister, the victim. My sister, the total stranger.

I glance at my father, a desperate man, then my mother, slowly disintegrating. For an instant, I squeeze my eyes shut, unable to act. Then I make up my mind. I will do whatever it takes to find out what happened to Beth that night—and what the fuck is going on right now. And the only way to do that is to play by Beth's rules.

I turn and run.

An hour later, I open the bedroom door and fling myself in, kicking the door closed behind me and glancing over my shoulder with a practiced frightened expression. Unlike Beth, I am not a smooth liar. Massaging the truth to get my way does not come naturally to me, and even little white lies to give bad news a gentler landing make me uncomfortable. Like I'm being judged on both my performance and my morals, because I know with regard to both, I could and should do better. But it's crucial that Beth believes my performance—that I followed her instructions, ran for help, and was captured. Because she'll only trust me if she believes I trust her.

I rub my wrists, wincing, as I glance up at Beth. "I tried."

She sits on her bed stiffly, staring straight ahead. "They're smarter than they look. Hard to crack."

"I guess they are." I sit across from her gingerly.

She doesn't shift her gaze. "They're liars. They put one face on for the world and another for their *friends*." She says the word 'friends' like it has jagged pieces of metal embedded in it.

"Beth—"

She nods, eyes half closed, as if processing the information. "That's what they call me."

"Right." Slip-up. Lazy. "Their friends...?"

"Don't be naive. They're all tangled up in this too. The chief of police? I tried to tell him the truth. He already knew."

There's a plate sitting on the nightstand next to Beth with a sandwich on it. I gesture at it. "Maybe we should eat. We have a better chance of escaping if we keep up our strength."

She sighs wearily and glances down at it. "I can't eat that."

"When's the last time you ate anything?" I don't like the way she looks. She has dark circles under her eyes, and she's pale and unsteady. An occasional shudder jolts her body, like an electric current. Her voice is dry and raspy. I feel guilty about what happened in the bathtub. Very guilty. Like I'm now responsible for her survival.

A faraway look passes over her face. "I don't remember. Before I was shot. I feel sick all the time."

I offer her half of the sandwich. "I'll take a bite if you take a bite?"

She glares at me, then tears into the sandwich viciously, like a wild animal, swallowing it in a giant gulp. Then she stares at me with hard eyes, breathing heavily, her shoulders rising and falling under her bulky Ashling High sweatshirt. Suddenly, she throws her head back, whips it forward, and vomits repeatedly until she's choking up nothing. She lifts her head and meets my eyes. "I feel much stronger now."

"Sorry," I whisper. The urge to gag rises up my throat. The smell is sharp and my stomach churns. I haven't eaten, but I feel my throat contract. I want to bolt for the door, but I've committed to this. I turn and open the window instead.

She eyes me suspiciously. "What was your name again?"

"Hazel. Hazel Whitman."

"Veronica Green." Her gaze is even, unblinking, conscience clear.

"I remember." I press my temple against the cool glass and feel the old resentment stirring in me. This could be another one of Beth's games. Revenge for me abandoning her at the party. Shame sets in again. How quickly did I start to break because it got unpleasant? No one would go this far for spite. I need more information. "Where did they take you this morning?"

"Some doctor." She wipes her mouth with a tissue. "Therapist. I heard him talk to them after. He told them what they needed to hear. *'Beth' suffered some kind of trauma. 'Beth' is in a dissociative state. 'Beth' should not be left alone.* I hope a truck hits him, and he's decapitated."

Jesus. Whoever Veronica was, she wasn't very nice.

Nope, nope, nope.

Veronica is dead. This is Beth.

I tiptoe to the door and open it carefully. "I think I can get to the kitchen and back. They've been keeping me here a while. If you play along with their delusion, they give you a lot of freedom."

She stares at me distrustfully.

"I could get cleaning supplies," I offer, gesturing toward the vomit on the floor.

She hesitates. "Fine."

"Is there anything you would eat?"

She shakes her head. "I *want* to. I just can't."

Beth is asleep when I get back to the room. She should be completely exhausted, which means I can finally sneak away.

Mom is whispering into the phone when I emerge, but she hangs up and jumps when she sees me.

"It's okay. Beth is fine. She threw up."

Mom pales. "She won't eat."

"I know. I tried... It was a mistake. She's sleeping now."

Mom sinks into a chair, looking slightly relieved. "She has to eat sooner or later."

"She will when she's hungry enough," I lie. I hesitate, then go on. "You know how they always say you shouldn't challenge a person's delusions? That it can bring on some kind of crisis or something?"

She looks at me sharply.

"Maybe we should try playing along. When I did, she talked to me."

Her expression hardens. "You want me to role-play kidnapping my child?"

It does sound bad phrased like that. "I guess not."

"She'll snap out of it."

"But...have the doctors figured out what's wrong? Why Veronica?"

"You know I don't like you girls talking about that," she says softly.

"Don't we have to? This isn't an urban legend anymore. It's Beth." I sigh, frustrated. "You don't really believe Veronica was killed by the devil, do you?"

Mom's eyes flash. "Hazel May, I do not like you girls repeating that story. Have I made myself clear?"

I flinch, and she looks guilty.

"I apologize." She hesitates. "It was never an urban legend. What happened to that poor girl was scary and hard to understand, and for a long time, no one felt safe in this town. People tell those stories to make themselves feel better. But stories can't save you, Hazel. And they're not respectful. Now, I do not believe your sister is in her right mind at the moment. But you are. Enough about the Green girl, and that's the last I want to hear about the devil."

"Fine." I grab the keys, storm out the door, hop into the truck, and head directly for the library. It's time to find out who Veronica Green was. When I get to the library, I find my boss, Julie's mother and the wife of Police Chief Merritt, sitting behind the desk working on a crossword puzzle.

"Hey, Mrs. Merritt."

She looks up, and her customary warm smile melts into concern. "How are you?"

"Holding up." I very much do *not* want to be dragged into a discussion about Beth and the fallout of the past two nights. "I had a question. How far back do the newspaper archives go?"

She frowns. "Thirty years. We were supposed to digitize them, but the budget is..." She indicates around the run-down room. The Ashling library is a little bit behind the times.

"Thirty years is perfect."

She raises an eyebrow but turns back to her crossword.

You'd think in a tiny town where nothing ever happens and a spelling bee is major news, Veronica's murder would have been front-page material for a while. But after the initial story and a couple of follow-ups with scant updates, there's almost nothing.

I do a Google search before combing through the papers and learn this much to distinguish fact from myth: Veronica died twenty-six years ago at age seventeen—that would put her at Ashling High roughly at the same time as my parents. Which suddenly makes me a *lot* more interested in what my mother said, both about the occult and how the stories developed out of fear of the reality. *It was never an urban legend.* From the papers I learn a bit more: it's true Veronica died in the woods behind the Elwood house, but it wasn't technically on their property—it was public land. No info on how close to the house she was found. But Beth must have known, because she headed there that night. And Phoebe knew, because she was in on Beth's plan. So there has to be some way to find out the specific location.

I take a break from sifting through the stacks of newspapers to text Phoebe, asking if she knows where exactly Veronica died, but she doesn't answer right away. I make a mental note to follow up later.

I learn from a newspaper article that what I've heard of Veronica's story so far is mostly, but not totally, true. Local legends have a way of evolving the truth over time.

According to the *Daily Journal,* Veronica Green was sixteen when she moved to Ashling from Prospect Heights. She died of a gunshot wound sometime in the middle of the night, but it's not certain when she was shot, and the coroner estimated her time of death to be between the hours of midnight and 4:00 a.m. on October 31, in the early hours of Halloween. But no one ever reported hearing shots fired, so the timeline is murky. It was suggested she was killed by someone moving through town, but no suspect was ever identified, and the local media coverage petered out before a theory of the case evolved. There isn't much else there, and there are no mentions of devil worship.

I put the papers back carefully and say goodbye to Mrs. Merritt, feeling disappointed.

My next stop is the *Ashling Daily Journal.* Ed Wendell, editor-in-chief and father of Mac Wendell—Ezra's shithead buddy who broke my nose—is hunched over an ancient-looking desktop computer when I tap on the glass door. It's such a sad image. The guy probably spends ninety percent of his waking hours in front of that twenty-year-old aqua neon iMac. Treat yourself, Ed.

He jerks back from his desk, startled, then hurries to unlock the door for me. He's a nervous guy, the kind of nervousness that possesses your entire body. It makes me anxious to be around him, like the buzz from three cups of coffee. He gestures to a seat across from him at his desk and offers me a little paper cone of water from the cooler, which I decline.

"Can I ask you a few questions about the paper?"

He looks faintly surprised. “Fire away.”

“The previous editor-in-chief was Paul E. Wendell. A relative?”

He nods. “My father. My family has worked on the paper in some capacity for generations. I was a paperboy as a kid. That’s how they rope you in.” He grins, but there’s a wisp of regret in it. The *Journal* is a nonprofit owned by the town, but the Wendells have run it as far back as I can tell. I’m not sure Ed is thrilled about it.

“And now you run the whole operation.”

He looks around the small room. There are a couple of other desks, but they’re empty. Are they always that way or only on Sunday? I wonder where Mac the wonderdouche is.

“Not single-handedly. And most of my writers are freelance. This is the mother ship.” He furrows his brow. “We usually don’t take interns during the school year.”

I shake my head impatiently. “Oh, I have a job. I wanted to ask about a series of stories from a while back. I saw your name on a couple of bylines, and I had a few questions. Do you remember Veronica Green?”

He pales. “I was sorry to hear about your sister.” Of course he knows.

“She isn’t dead,” I say, déjà vu making me feel nauseous. I wish people wouldn’t use that language. I think part of what I hate about the phrasing is that it’s more consistent with if my sister *were* Veronica. I shake it off. “You wrote about what happened as a young reporter.”

He nods. “One of my first assignments.”

“But it was a huge story.” *Or it should have been.*

He looks embarrassed. “Perhaps there was a little nepotism at work.”

"So what happened? Story of the century, yet it disappeared after three articles?"

He shrugs. "We report news. There wasn't anything *new* to tell. The murder happened, a potential suspect was identified, and the mother threatened and then dropped a lawsuit against the police department."

"She left town," I clarify, and he nods in agreement. "But your articles said a suspect wasn't identified."

"A profile was identified," he clarifies.

"'A stranger passing through town' is a profile?" My criminal expertise is limited to watching a few episodes of *Law & Order*, but even I know that isn't right.

"It's enough," he says.

"Can I ask you a question off the record?"

He looks at me over the top of his glasses. "This has been on the record? For what?"

I return his gaze blankly. "No. It's not. That was embarrassing. I'm just trying to understand what's happening to my sister. I wish you would help me."

He sighs and gestures for me to continue.

"There have been rumors of devil worship—"

He stands, switches off his monitor, and gestures toward the door. "Can I walk you out?"

I eye the overflowing filing cabinets stubbornly. I can see how Beth could get hooked on this case. Honestly, to me, the mystery of what happened to the investigation is more fascinating than what happened to Veronica. People are murdered all the time. What *doesn't* happen all the time is a small town with one murder per century giving the investigation as much attention as the death of a deer on a midseason hunt. I wonder if that's what caught Beth's notice.

If so, we may finally have something in common.

"You must have known Veronica," I press. "You were around the same age, right?"

He hovers by the door and works his jaw. "I saw her around the school when she bothered to show up. She was an odd duck. Sad what happened to her, but I'm not sure anyone was shocked, exactly."

"No one was shocked a teenaged girl was murdered?"

He shakes his head and waves a hand back and forth as if to erase the words from the air. "Of course they were. Death is always shocking. It does seem to seek out the troubled girls, though." He freezes. "I'm sorry. I didn't mean it like that."

"Why are you sorry?" We stare at each other awkwardly. "Because I'm also a troubled girl?" I'm losing control of the conversation. My heart is pounding so hard in my chest, I can hear it. That is what he meant. And sometimes, in a town like Ashling, when older people say things like *troubled*, that's code for *queer*.

"I didn't say anything like that. I only meant Veronica was—" He trips on his own words, flustered. "A lone wolf," he finally says. He opens the door roughly and nods toward the street, perspiration gleaming on his forehead.

"Lots of people have no friends and manage not to be murdered over it," I say.

"And others don't know when to quit."

His response hits me like a slap in the face. Did Ed Wendell just threaten me? Or does he know more about what happened to Veronica than he's letting on?

"But—"

My phone buzzes, interrupting me, and my heart drops into my stomach as I read the text from my mother.

Beth is gone again. Where are you, Hazel?

THE TWISTED MIND OF VERONICA GREEN

AUGUST 6

vi

Wraiths.

DEMONS ARE NO SMALL THREAT.
The cut of them, blunt force, and rotten will
the stench of their trail
is hard to kill.
Once you face one,
let alone five,
they are yours forever
even unalive.
They follow you like a curse,
shadows sewn into your skin,
lost boys. Still—

Wraiths are worse.
Invisible at first,
In puppet mouths and unseeing eyes
and the cruelest part,
they look like you,
flower girls in frosted fields,
They were supposed to be like you.
They were supposed to be sisters.

7

HAZEL

My heart pounds as I drive, and a million worries flood my mind. But I don't have time to entertain them. Because half a mile down the road, a crowd is forming on the front lawn of the school. I jerk the wheel to pull over and jump out, fixated on the scene unfolding.

The double glass doors to Ashling High are smashed. *Smashed.* Police haven't arrived yet, but a few volunteer firemen have blocked the entrance and keep back those who have congregated from the shops and nearby homes on Main.

An eerie feeling creeps over me. Beth is inside. I *know* Beth is inside. I'm not the only one who thinks so, either. The crowd parts as I approach the school. I feel dozens of eyes on me, but Mrs. Merritt catches my gaze. She looks dismayed, like it's terrible what Beth is going through, but did she *really* have to destroy public property? Allison Laurence, the older sister of Beth's former best friend Amanda, is also here. She rushes to my side.

"Hazel. Are you okay?" Allison is quieter than Amanda, every bit as popular but less snarky, a community college student and preschool teacher.

"Fine. I'm fine. Where's Beth?"

She points to the school.

I try to ignore the whispers as I make my way through the parted crowd. *Troubled*—that word again. *Out of control*—no shit. *Veronica.* I whip my head toward that last comment, but everyone shuts up.

A hand closes around my forearm, and I flinch. When I turn around, it's Mel. She looks at me with concern. "Hazel, wait."

"For what?" I slide my arm out of her grasp. I don't want to see her right now. It's too stressful. I don't want to see anyone whose opinion I care about.

Behind me, there's a loud snort and Mac loud-whispers, "Enter crazy's sister, crazier."

Mel gapes at him, then turns back to me. "Beth isn't herself."

"Veronica," Mac fake coughs.

"What's your problem?" Mel snaps. She continues, "It's a bad idea to take that on alone. I'll wait with you until help gets here. If you want, I mean."

"She's not alone." Ezra's voice breaks through the crowd. He looks to me as if for permission. "Are you?"

I resent the idea that I need a guy by my side. But the gathering waits expectantly for my answer, and Ezra is a trusted person in this town. Part of me wishes Mel would volunteer, but I can't *ask her.* "He's with me. Let's go."

He scowls at Mac. "You're a dick."

"And you're wasting your time with *that* Whitman. She's defective." Mac shoots me a contemptuous look.

"Ignore him," Ezra mutters. But it's hard to ignore the muffled laughter rippling through the crowd. I turn away abruptly. I don't want to see if Mel is laughing along with the others.

"What's that supposed to mean?" Glass crunches beneath my shoes as I step into the school, careful to avoid the jagged remnants of the glass in the metal doorframe.

"It means Mac Wendell is full of shit. *He's* defective. Watch yourself," Ezra cautions, sticking close behind me.

"Then why are you friends with him?" I duck, my face burning with humiliation.

"He used to be decent. When his mom died, it brought out the worst of him."

"No excuse."

"I didn't say it was."

"But you do think he's funny. Like when he broke my nose."

He stares at me. "Are you kidding?"

"You laughed."

"You never laughed from shock before?"

I have. But knowing his reasoning doesn't change how it made me feel. And I'm not ready to relate to Ezra Elwood. "What are you even doing here?"

"My Dad had to fly home early when I busted the car. He only gets two Sundays off per year, so I'm grounded for the rest of my existence. But I'm not going home until I know Beth is okay. Are we in this together or not?"

I size him up. I may not be ready to relate to Ezra, but we're on the same side. "Clearly."

The locker-lined hallways look menacing in the dark, like something out of a slasher movie, and I turn on my phone's flashlight. At any moment, someone or something is going to jump out at us from the shadows, a monster with razor teeth or a killer with a useful but deadly instrument—a hatchet, a chainsaw, an ice pick. It's scarier if it's a mundane object. People who make the movies know this shit. Our imaginations are working against us at every moment, convincing us that even in our own homes and workplaces, schools and parks, we are not safe.

Because you know, we aren't.

"Word is, Beth showed up a little while ago with a baseball bat," he says grimly. "Smashy smashy."

"You have such a charming way with words."

"I'm sorry. Elizabeth doth the glass door smashethed."

"I get the point. We need to find her."

"Try the roof," a voice says.

Ezra screams and grabs my arm as my heart leaps into my throat.

Jack emerges from the darkness, his own phone illuminating his face.

"The fuck are you doing here?" Ezra grasps me by the shoulders, holding me in front of him like a human shield.

"I live here now," Jack says. "My parents kicked me out after Beth went missing. I sleep on gym mats and subsist on vending machine food."

"That's not funny." Ezra releases me, and I rub my shoulders. Dude has an iron grip. For once, though, I agree with Ezra. Being rejected by your parents and having nowhere to go is about as funny as roadkill. "You're not serious. About the roof?"

"I *was*," Jack says. "I got her inside and bolted the door. But she was mad, so she cracked me in the face and gave me the slip." He rubs his jaw. "Now I don't know where she is."

"Thanks. Helpful," I say, but I'm flooded with relief. Inside is definitely safer.

Ezra doesn't let him off that easily, though. "How did you trick Beth into coming inside?"

"I pretended to be a super hot guy," Jack says. "Hard to resist that."

"Who?" Ezra narrows his eyes.

"Your dad," Jack retorts. "But I'm still looking for Beth, so if the inquisition is over...?"

"It is for now," I say decisively. We continue down the hallway. "Do you know why she came here?"

"Far as I know, she was looking for Ezra's dad," Jack says.

"Shut *up*."

Jack shrugs. "I hear Chet Elwood was a handsome fella in his day."

Ezra rolls his eyes. "I'm not taking the bait." It's hard to backtrack on taking the bait, though. After a moment, he adds, "And no one's called my father Chet since high school."

There is something needling about that. Jack's whole disinterested vibe doesn't match the things he says. He knows a lot for an outsider. Maybe too much. There's information about the town he would have absorbed from spending time with Beth, but he drops little details here and there that no one would mention in everyday conversation. Like the Rev's high school nickname. Things Ezra might be sensitive about, or only I would care about. Sometimes it feels like Jack has lived here a long time.

"Jack, have you heard from Phoebe? I can't get in touch with her."

"Probably at her grandmother's," he says. "Gran Crane says cell phones obstruct communication."

That reminds me of Beth's phone in Phoebe's car, but before I can say anything, an earsplitting sound cracks the air and we cover our ears. Music blares over the speakers, a familiar clanging acoustic guitar riff. It's so loud it takes me a second to recognize it as the classic rock song "Good Riddance" by Green Day. My mom drops everything whenever that song comes on the radio and tries to get my dad to dance with her, but he hates it. It was their junior prom song, and Mom is a sentimentalist. Not Dad. He's country all the way, and all the way back too.

The song sparks hope in me, and I whip my head in the direction of the AV room. The school has a PA system in the front office—but it's not hooked up to musical equipment. The AV room is where the radio and broadcast journalism classes take place, and they're also hooked up to the speaker system. That has to be where the sound is coming from.

If Beth is the one playing the song—she must be—she chose it because it's a connection to our family. That means she isn't completely gone. *Or she* has *been faking it this whole time.*

I run toward the AV room, but Ezra has a head start. Behind us, deep voices shout Beth's name over the blare of the music, then a warning to any trespassers. The police have arrived.

The shit has officially hit the fan.

The AV room is at the back of the school, down three corridors, past the gym, and before we make it down the first corridor, the song cuts off and Beth's voice comes on in a dull monotone.

"That was 'Good Riddance' by Green Day. I think I speak for all of us when I say it's a song very close to our hearts. I'd like to dedicate it to the deadeyes. Get off me—"

She's cut off and I hear the sound of struggling down the

hallway. Ezra grabs my arm with one hand and Jack's with the other, and we halt, flattening against the wall.

"Okay, Beth. You can relax. We're just going to give you a ride back home."

It's Chief Merritt.

"They must have come in the back," Ezra whispers.

"Aces, Sherlock," Jack replies.

I shush them.

"Where's Chet?" Beth demands, before their voices fade and the door slams shut.

Jack turns triumphantly to Ezra.

Ezra's mouth drops open. "You were serious?"

"I'm always serious. It's a me thing." He starts cautiously toward the front entrance.

I shake my head. "We're stuck here until the cops leave. Unless you want to get arrested for trespassing."

"No, thank you." He slides to the floor.

"But... What does Beth want with my father?" Ezra sinks down next to Jack.

I join them. "She played that song because it was important to my mom—so I don't think she's one hundred percent gone. But she's obviously going through something. Phoebe told me the ritual Beth was planning the night she disappeared was no joke. She used the word *necromancy*."

Ezra's eyebrows shoot up. "As in, to raise the dead?"

"Not like zombies. But maybe like a medium?"

Jack hesitates. "Beth was fascinated with the foxes."

Ezra looks dubious. "We have tons of foxes on my property alone. I could have trapped us one."

Jack gives him a sharp look. "Aren't you a hero?"

My stomach twists. Dad trained Beth and me to hunt from the time we could bear the weight of a gun. Never my mother—she said it was a father's job to teach his daughters how to hold and shoot a weapon. She had a huge hang-up about the fact that her father never taught *her*. But whenever my father offered, she would glare at him so coldly, it ended the conversation. I don't have qualms about killing animals. To me, if you eat burgers and chicken wings, but you have an issue killing the food you put on the table, you're not being completely honest with yourself.

Gun safety is another discussion. There's a world of difference between saying people should be allowed to hunt for food and that instruments of death should be treated like toys. But we're talking animal ethics. And trapping has never sat right with me. It seems cruel. There's an element of deception to luring and baiting. I know enough about traps to question their humaneness. And I've read stories about dogs being killed by traps that haunt me.

Maybe I'm a hypocrite. Some would argue that no form of killing is humane, even if you eat all you kill. But I don't believe in all-or-nothing thinking. I can think something is acceptable up to a point, but no further. That's another difference between Beth and me. With her, everything is all-or-nothing. Like the night she stormed into the house after midnight, smashed the glass door of the antique gun case, dragged all the guns into the backyard, and started *digging*. It was never enough for Beth to quit a thing; she needed a ritual of severance.

Ezra waves a hand in front of my face. "Still with us?"

I blink. "Just thinking about Beth."

His expression softens. “Right. So what do you think? About the foxes?”

Jack looks at me expectantly.

“I…didn’t know Beth had taken an interest.” My sister—always full of surprises.

“Well, she did. And considering the ritual, it might be worth looking into.”

“Veronica and the foxes,” I say.

“Exactly.”

The sound of footsteps ends our conversation.

“I think we’ve officially worn out our welcome,” Jack whispers. “Let’s split, see what we can dig up, and touch base when we have anything. Ezra, you’re on dad duty. Hazel, you’re your sibling’s keeper. I’ll try to stay on the right side of the law. In the meantime, look for the foxes.”

“Who made you project manager?” Ezra whispers.

“Nepotism. I inherited the position. Didn’t ask for it, didn’t want it. But here we are.” Jack shakes Ezra’s shoulders roughly, then silently leaps to his feet, and we all make a run for it.

THE TWISTED MIND OF VERONICA GREEN

SEPTEMBER 7

vii

Vengeance song.

STRENGTH IS A BURDEN.

When they hear of it, they'll come.
They'll bring armies.
They will fight you,
not because you are the enemy,
but because they've heard of you
have heard that you are strong
and strength is a threat
to those who know what it looks like
but not how it feels.
Here's the thing:

Strength isn't in numbers,
it's in biding time.
Vengeance is a song,
a relentless rhythm in your chest
good riddance
good riddance
good riddance.

8

HAZEL

I immediately break my promise to Ezra and Jack. Home is the last place I want to be right now. I have a finite amount of energy I can devote to my family, and they're going to have me for a night that's going to feel like a century. Before that, I have about a million questions I want answered, and I have an idea where to look next. I don't know exactly what to make of Beth smashing up the school. I know either Beth or Veronica has a clear interest in Chet Elwood, though.

So he's my next stop. Even though it's Ezra's job to keep tabs on his dad, I hedge my bets and head straight to the Rev's office, banking on the fact Ezra will likely avoid his grounding sentence as long as he can, and his father will most likely avoid the house until Ezra cleans up his own mess. And yes, everyone calls Reverend Elwood "The Rev." He insists on it. Which could feel cheesy and forced, but we've known him since we were babies. He *was* the cool preacher who played in a Christian rock band at youth group socials and school dances. He told homilies that didn't feel totally condescending, that acknowledged, yeah, he made mistakes too, and we were definitely going to do the wrong thing, probably repeatedly, and God didn't hate us for being flawed creatures, because he intentionally made us flawed.

The Rev won you over because he made you feel like religion wasn't a sword hanging over your neck, or a battle between the saved and the damned. It was simpler than that. We were all cast out already, some sin committed by an ancestor, and we could redeem ourselves because God was good. I can sit with that version of faith. I don't have to accept it wholesale, but I can sit with it. By his logic, it wasn't even Eve's fault. She was designed to do the wrong thing sooner or later, because all of us are. Only immortal beings are capable of always doing the right thing. We're bound to fuck up, face some kind of reckoning, and be altered, hopefully enlightened.

The Rev doesn't answer the first time I knock, but I can see the car is in the church driveway, so I'm persistent. Eventually he answers the door, wearing his usual smile, but looking a little tense and distracted. There are shadows under his clear blue eyes and his shirt, usually ironed to a crisp, is rumpled and dotted with crumbs. He follows my stare and hurriedly sweeps it clean.

"Hazel. How can I be of service?"

"Can I come in?"

He glances over his shoulder reluctantly, then holds the door open for me. I've only been in the Rev's office a couple of times, but from those experiences, he keeps it spotless. Today, there are papers scattered everywhere, takeout cartons, coffee cups, soda cans, candy wrappers. He picks up a few self-consciously and tosses them in the trash before taking a seat behind his desk and pointing to an armchair. “Have a seat.”

I hover over it, too jumpy to sit. “I’m worried about my sister.”

He nods and steeples his fingers. “I am too. But she’s in good hands. Your parents are strong, and their love will give Beth strength.”

I hesitate. “Right. I just had a couple questions.”

His brow furrows. I try to read his expression, but I can’t.

“Beth is saying weird things. She thinks she’s someone else. A girl who died long ago.”

“She’s confused. Traumatized,” the Rev says gently. A little condescendingly.

Of course a girl who disappears and turns up twenty-four hours later completely disoriented and deeply upset has probably undergone something traumatic. *Read between the lines, Hazel.*

“I think there’s more to it than that,” I press. I hate arguing with authority figures. But what alternative is there? Nod and get nowhere? “Trauma doesn’t fill your head with facts. She knows things she’s not supposed to know.”

“Kids today are fascinated by unsolved crimes, no?” the Rev points out.

“So you know about the Veronica thing.”

He doesn’t answer. Does he look guilty? I can’t tell.

“I mean, that Beth is claiming to be Veronica Green.”

“Ezra mentioned it.”

“She asked for you. As Veronica. Did you know her? When she lived here?”

The Rev sighs and pushes his seat back.

"Hazel, you're obsessing. Playing along with Beth's delusion is not going to help her. It's going to push her farther from reality. The best thing you can do is give her space."

"But for my own peace of mind, so I can understand where Beth is coming from. Did you know Veronica?"

He stands wearily. "It's Ashling. There's no way *not* to know anyone a little. But the truth is, she was as much a stranger as anyone could be. She'd barely moved here, and then she was gone. It was very sad."

"But she knew you," I say.

His eyes catch mine, as if trying to read me. "I doubt it."

I hesitate, not wanting to repeat Ed's words. "I heard people weren't shocked by what happened to her."

He looks genuinely surprised by that, and I have to admit, I'm relieved. "Where did you hear something like that?"

"Just a rumor."

"I don't like rumors, as a rule. They distort the truth, and they can take a nasty turn."

"There's another rumor. About devil worship?"

He tilts his head. "This isn't really about Veronica Green, is it?"

I want to say that it is, because I do want to know about her, but in my heart, I know it's not. Veronica is a stranger who lived and stopped living before I breathed my first breath. "I need to understand why this is happening."

"Because you need to fix it?" he asks gently.

And that's why the Rev is so good at what he does. He hears the unsaid part. Every time.

"Would you have called Veronica odd or troubled?" I have to ask. It means too much to me.

"I wouldn't have called her anything," he says. "She was a face in a sea of faces."

I hesitate, unsure how to ask what I want to ask. "Did she have a boyfriend?"

He considers for a moment, then slowly nods. "I think she did."

"Oh." I can't explain why, but I'm disappointed. I had started to feel like I knew her. Like we had certain things in common. Like I might have understood her. I'm falling into the true crime trap. She's just a random girl who lived a long time ago. She has nothing to do with me. And it would be best to remember that. Or I could end up like Beth. Dangerously obsessed.

"One more thing. The church *does* recognize possessions, right?"

He shakes his head firmly. "Not by dead girls. Only demons. You need to watch fewer movies, Hazel." He gives me a sympathetic smile, then rises and holds open the door for me to leave.

Thanks, Chet. The words are on the tip of my tongue. But I chicken out, of course.

I mull over what he said on the drive home.

If only demons are capable of possession, and Beth is not Beth, then there's a demon out there with a very strong interest in Veronica Green. Not that I'm actually entertaining the possibility of possession. It's a trauma-based delusion.

An incredibly detailed trauma-based delusion.

When I get home, I find another surprise waiting for me—Julie Merritt is sitting in the driveway on the hood of her pickup, casually scrolling on her phone, like it's no big deal for her to be there. She looks up at the sound of the tires crunching on the gravel, and her eyes brighten. Julie Merritt has these round, velvety blue eyes with pale brown lashes and thin, high-arched eyebrows, so she always looks a little more interested in what you're saying than she probably is.

As I park and climb out of the car, I stumble on an uneven bit of gravel and nearly fall on my face. Because of course I do. I wave awkwardly, and Julie smiles, not a mocking smile, a real one. She's so honeycomb sweet, I always wondered where she fit into Beth's clique, a gossipy knot of pure pettiness that Amanda Laurence reigns over. I *know* why Beth went over to the dark side. Beth is drawn to drama, spectacle, glamour, and villains are always more glamorous. There was never any contest between me and Amanda where Beth was concerned.

Julie was harder to figure out. Although, the truth is I don't know her very well. In every brief exchange we've had, she's given the impression of being exactly who I *want* her to be: funny, warm, and kind. She smells like horses, which is a good thing, and her smile is like New Year's Eve: hope, excitement, and giddiness. But smiles are mirrors. And kindness can give you hope that isn't earned. The Julie who exists in my mind is one I've pieced together from a hundred little interactions, but none that really count. Until Ezra's party, where *I* wasn't acting like myself. It's impossible not to notice Julie, because she's one of the most popular girls in school. I figured I was completely invisible to her.

Contrast that to Mel, who I have actively planned to borrow a number two pencil from for three months. It feels somehow traitorous to abandon the number two pencil plan and the lined sheet of paper plan that was to follow because one of Beth's friends suddenly decided I existed. But then today happened. Mac said that awful thing. And Mel was there. And she didn't disagree with him. She probably laughed with everyone else.

Now isn't the time to figure it out, though. Julie hops off the truck and hurries toward me, shoving her phone into the pocket of her fleece jacket. "Hey." She knits her brows in concern. "Are you okay?"

I get stuck on a response. I'm not *really* okay, but I don't think that's the right answer.

"You didn't reply to my text," she prompts.

"Beth," I say, nodding my head toward the door. I hate my brain. Why can't I speak like a human?

She bows her head. "Sorry. I should have given you space. I only wanted to see how Beth was doing. And you." She glances up briefly then darts her eyes away.

"I honestly don't know how Beth is doing." I gaze past her toward the house. There's a flash of movement in our bedroom window, but it's so quick, I might have imagined it.

"I'm sorry," she says softly. "She and I started to drift apart this year, but I still really care."

I nod awkwardly. "She knows." I mean, I have no idea what she knows. But it seems like the right thing to say.

She clears her throat. "Is she allowed visitors? Her phone is going straight to voicemail, but I'd love to tell her in person."

"I don't think that's a good idea. She's really not herself." I imagine it: Julie standing nervously in the hallway as Beth growls at her from the bedroom, the stench of vomit seeping out from under the door.

"That's what I heard," Julie says softly. She stares at the ground, her expression troubled.

"She'll be okay," I say, sounding a lot more convinced than I am. My phone buzzes, and I feel my face warm as I read the text from Mel. *Sorry about before,* it says. *Can we talk?* I guess that answers that question. Yes, she laughed, and no, we can't.

Julie interrupts my thoughts. "You're friends with Melody Sanders?"

I shove my phone into my pocket. "No."

"Sorry. I saw the screen by accident. I'm glad you're not friends, though."

"Why?"

"I've just heard bad things. I don't like to gossip. Bad karma. Hazel?" When she says my name, a wave of excitement ripples through me, and I forget about Mel and how awful it feels that the person I thought so highly of thinks so little of me.

"What?"

"I had fun the other night. Before...you know."

"Oh. I did too. Before."

"We should do it again. After."

She smiles, and hope floods through me. There's going to be an after. I *will* remember that the next time Beth wanders onto a roof or disappears underwater like the urban legend she's rapidly morphing into. There's always an after.

"We could see a movie in Everton or something," she suggests, and my hope dies a little. Everton is forty-five minutes away. There is a tiny local cinema in Ashling, and two more between here and the Everton Multiplex. It could be my trademark pessimism, but my gut says you don't plan a date with someone in Everton unless you don't want to be seen with them.

"Sounds great," I lie.

"Well..." Julie gazes back at her truck and takes a few slow steps toward it. "Don't keep me in the dark?"

"I'll try. Honestly, though, we're all pretty much in the dark right now. Black Hole Sun." I cringe at my reference to the ancient music video Beth used to watch obsessively of this creepy town where everything is *off*, stuck in slow motion, poisoned by some dark unknown wrong. It feels like Ashling since Beth returned. Everyone is trying to act like nothing is wrong, but something *is* wrong. Every "I'm sorry about your sister" hits exactly like the stretched, cadaverous smiles on the Black Hole Sun citizens' faces. Every attempt at normalcy slashes like a rotten chord. Because that town was cursed by some awful secret, and I'm starting to believe we are too.

"I get it." She tilts her head sympathetically. "You can call me, though. If you need to talk. I know how close you and Beth are. She adored you."

"Sure, maybe." I step toward the house. I'm starting to like Julie. Maybe. I like being near her. It's a buzz. But a buzz isn't always a good thing. And if I'm being honest, I'm not sure Julie is to blame for wanting to meet in Everton. I feel one way about kissing Julie Merritt at Ezra's party when I'm alone, and another way standing in my driveway in full view of my parents. That's partly Beth's fault too. Or maybe it's mine.

Focus, Hazel.

This is the problem. Julie is a distraction. Spending too much time *not* thinking about Beth and the Veronica puzzle makes me jumpy, like pins and needles under my skin. And anything that makes me angry at Beth makes me feel like a terrible person. And that's the opposite of what I need right now.

I wait for Julie's truck to pull out of the driveway and then let myself into the house quietly. Artax peeks around the corner cautiously, then slinks away when he sees it's only me.

The rest of the house is eerily still. I tiptoe past the kitchen, where Mom has fallen asleep at the table, a mug of cold coffee next to her head. Dad is in his easy chair in the den, his sturdy frame motionless, facing away from me and toward the television, which is off. It's creepy as all hell—like walking through a frozen frame in a horror movie. But I don't feel like talking to my parents right now. Neither of them has cornered me for a sit-down yet, and I'd like to avoid that as long as I can.

After Beth had that epic meltdown last summer, they were on me immediately. Was I all right? Did I understand what was going on? Everything was going to be okay—I had to trust everything was going to be okay. But that was different. That was Beth being dramatic and selfish and a liar. This is...something else.

When I get to our bedroom, I see Beth is asleep in bed, the covers pulled all the way over her head, adding to the eerie "everybody's gone to the rapture" vibe.

But her laptop is open on her desk. I sit, careful not to scrape the chair against the floor. Although the computer itself is open, I'm facing a lockscreen, which makes it useless to me unless I can somehow guess her password. I glance at Beth's bed again, but for once, all is peaceful. Her body is still and serene under the quilt, wisps of her blonde hair trailing out onto the pillow. I exhale shakily and turn back to the screen, pulling out my phone.

Any idea Beth's password? I text Phoebe and wait.

No answer. Figures.

I fire off the same question to Ezra and Jack, and get a smartass answer from Ezra, and an ever-helpful reminder from Jack to look out for foxes. I pause and text Julie as well.

JULIE:

Try Bethanhazel?

A lump forms in my throat.

Beth and I weren't always sibling strangers. As kids, you couldn't pry us apart. I was her shadow. I haunted her classes, her friendships, dance class. It wasn't my fault; it was family policy. We weren't allowed to have playdates or go to parties if the other wasn't invited. Mom tried *so* hard to fight the inevitable: Beth was cool and I was the weirdo. It was obvious from infancy. Beth was the star baby in playgroup; I collected spiders in sippy cups and tried to make friends with worms. It always went that way. Beth led the gymnastics team to victory in third grade while I got lost in the sports complex. Beth spent the fifth grade dance actually dancing while I hid in the bathroom. By middle school it had become ridiculous. Beth would make sleepover plans with her friends and our parents would drop us off together, then Beth would smile apologetically and ask if I wanted to take a walk or something. I'd close out the library, then spend the rest of the night in the Gingerbread House—an old abandoned cabin we used to play in in the forest behind our house.

That's where *Bethanhazel* came from—the sound of our names blended together, back when we weren't allowed to be separate people. It sounded like a witch from a dark, dangerous forest, and it became our game. One of us would be the evil witch, the other the ravenous wolf. We've never had much in common, but we've always shared an obsession with fairy tales, and not the frothy, sugary kind. When we were little, our grandmother read us grisly German fairy tales where children met all sorts of bloody ends. They terrified Mom, but Beth and I were entranced. We were as thrilled by poison apples and deadly spindles as by glass slippers and true love's kiss. And we firmly agreed on one thing: a fairy tale wasn't good unless it ended in proper revenge. The witch burned to a crisp in her own pastry oven, the wolf filled with stones and shoved into the river, the wicked queen dancing to her death. *Bethanhazel* was a sacred game.

Here's what I have a problem with. I know Beth's friends don't like me. We spent a year lying to Mom and Dad based on that knowledge. I thought we had an understanding—our parents were unreasonable, but we were in this elaborate lie together, because telling Mom and Dad the truth wouldn't get through to them. I understand why Beth is so practiced at lying when it comes to my parents. The truth doesn't yield change. But I don't understand why she felt she had to lie to me. That's how *Bethanhazel* ended—with the first lie Beth ever told right to my face: that she was afraid of the woods. She had a *feeling*. Something bad happened out there. She couldn't go back. *Bethanhazel* had to end. She was so convincing, too. Dead pale, feverish fear, contagious fear—I inhaled it and became infected instantly. It's so easy with Beth. She's so convincing. But with fear, maybe it always is. Danger is always more credible than safety.

I'm not sure why she thought I couldn't handle the last bit of truth—that it wasn't good enough to have Mom drop me off in front of Amanda's house. And then a block away. And then at the library. She needed a clean break, separate friends, separate lives. It would have been totally reasonable. It was the *only* reasonable thing to do. But instead of telling me to my face, I headed out to the Gingerbread House one night to find Beth, Amanda, Julie, and Rosalyn huddled together around a shared can of beer, the cabin newly decorated with strings of pink lights and posters of boy bands. Part of me wanted to storm in and confront her, tell her I knew she lied to me, that I was angry and hurt, and her new clubhouse was stupid. But I sat down in the dead leaves and waited. For almost three hours, limbs numb, fingers white, jeans stiff with frost, my body slowly petrifying in the heartless cold. When they finally left, I still didn't get up. I sat in the darkness while Beth and her friends walked right by me. I didn't have the guts to say a word. I thought about breaking into the cabin and trashing it, tearing down the pretty fairy lights and the cool posters and everything that made it a clubhouse and not a witch's home. It would have felt better, a little. Isn't a fairy tale supposed to end with revenge?

But I didn't do that either.

Instead, I fastened the door, because Beth had left it loose like she always did, and all those pretty lights and glossy posters would be ruined by the wind and rain that would descend before dawn. I fixed the broken door to her broken fairy tale cottage, and I left the spoiled ruins of *Bethanhazel* sturdier than I found it. Only then did I let myself cry. Because the beautiful fairy princesses had stolen my wicked witch, and in real life, revenge is not sweeter.

I type *Bethanhazel,* and some deep, aching part of me really wants the password to work. I know it won't. But I'm willing to try.

The screen lights up, and I'm staring at Beth's desktop. A wave of hope, guilt, and uncertainty hits me hard. Maybe I don't know Beth as well as I think. Maybe our friendship isn't as dead to her as it is to me. My head spins. She has let me down so many times, so painfully, and the one time I truly needed her, she ghosted me.

I turn toward her bed, wanting this to be my sign to wake her, to say the words I've never had the guts to say. *I loved you, and you let me down. I'm afraid I don't love you anymore, and that scares the shit out of me.*

But she lies there, motionless as a corpse, a mound of blankets and tangle of hair, a shell of Beth. Maybe that's all that's left.

No. It's not fair to give up now. Not before I have a chance to speak to her one last time. Not if *Bethanhazel* still meant something to her.

I turn my full attention to the desktop. There's a password-protected file titled VKG1031. My heart skips in my chest. *V* and G for Veronica and Green? And 1031—the month and day she died.

One more code to crack. I pull out my phone again and type "Veronica Green Foxes" into a search tab. Nothing useful. Then I try "Veronica Green Deadeyes"—from Beth's song dedication at the high school. Again, nothing. Then—"Ashling High Foxes Deadeyes."

Jackpot.

THE TWISTED MIND OF VERONICA GREEN

SEPTEMBER 13

viii
Deadeyes.

IN WINTER'S LAND, THE LIVING—FOR A TIME—
walk among the demons and the dead.
Indistinguishable, unless you know the signs.
The dead speak only when spoken to
and never out of ire.
Their bones are soft in the neck,
and they fold when demons walk,
their teeth gum into gel
while their tongues, thick slugs, swell.
Demons have just one tell.
It's in the eyes.

You can see your own death
if you have the guts to look inside.
A demon knows how things will end,
if he has his way—and an alibi.

9

HAZEL

I stare at the top hit, a Facebook page for the Ashling High yearbook, and Beth's texts with Phoebe rush back to me. Veronica had started some kind of "revenge" club at school, but she was forced to change the description to mask the purpose. According to the page, Veronica Green was the *sole* member of a club called the Echo Foxes. I google *echo foxes* and an e-sports organization named "Echo Fox" comes up—but it was formed after Veronica's death. Dead end.

I tap my fingers on the keyboard impatiently, then try "echo foxes" in quotation marks. Still nothing. Back to the yearbook page. Veronica's photo stares back at me from the screen. It's the first time I've seen Veronica Green in color. The newspaper articles offered only a blurry black-and-white photo of a ponytailed girl hugging a dog. It was hard to see much detail. This image is crisp and clear: a dark-haired, bright-eyed girl with a sharp, defiant gaze. She's dressed in the same yearbook outfit as everyone else—an emerald green cap and gown—but on her it's eerie, because even though I know all of the photos were taken at the beginning of the year, long before graduation, Veronica was dead before finals. The graduation photo is like a ghostly glimpse into a future that never was.

It occurs to me—with a shiver that snakes its way through my entire body—that Beth *does* bear a slight resemblance to Veronica. It's hard to pinpoint exactly what it is. Maybe it's the defiance, the stubborn set of her chin, the fire in her eyes that seems to burn through the laptop's screen. It's like one of those trick paintings where someone's eyes follow you. It feels in motion, alive. Maybe that's Veronica's allure. The mystery is so vast, the investigation cut so unsatisfyingly short, it feels like she can't truly be gone. What do we really know for sure?

There's a quote under the club title and Veronica's name, and I take a moment to jot it down in my notes app. "*Splitfoot/Deadeyes/Mariana.*" Apparently, I've started a Veronica Green case file. Deadeyes again. At least I know where Beth found it.

I try "splitfoot" and "mariana" as the locked file passwords, but neither works. Then I search "foxes, deadeyes, splitfoot, mariana," and my heart catches in my throat.

The search page is filled with articles about the supernatural.

The top one is a historical society website about three sisters, who I vaguely remember reading about at some point in a magazine—Margaretta, Leah, and Catherine Fox. *The Foxes.* They lived in upstate New York in the mid-1800s and captured the attention of the world when they claimed they could communicate with the dead, beginning with the spirit of a man who they said was murdered and buried in the basement of their home. Eventually they convinced their community, then thousands of believers in the spiritualism movement, that they had the power to reach beyond the veil. The Foxes became celebrity mediums, until a serious falling-out led to an estrangement between the sisters, and Margaretta and Kate disavowed both Leah and spiritualism, publicly swearing they'd faked the whole thing. But Margaretta later walked back her confession, claiming spirits prompted her to do it. Leah died before they could reconcile, but spiritualism outlived them all in the form of the National Spiritualist Association of Churches.

I skim the article but stop at the name the sisters used to refer to the first spirit that supposedly spoke to them in that old farmhouse. There, they spun a lie about a dead man, a nameless stranger passing through town, someone easily invented because no one knew or cared if he even existed in the first place.

They called him Splitfoot.

Another name for the devil.

I send a text to Jack:

HAZEL:

I found the Foxes.

JACK:

Took you long enough. And?

HAZEL:

I think they're the key to getting into a file Beth has about Veronica on her computer. Do the words deadeyes or mariana mean anything to you?

JACK:

Beth dedicated that song to Deadeyes. Good Riddance.

Another text pops up from Ezra.

EZRA:
Where are your parents?

The question takes me aback. I pause, then reply:

HAZEL:
Right here, why?

EZRA:
Tell them to come get Beth okay?

EZRA:
My house

EZRA:
Before someone gets hurt

I turn to the bed where Beth is sleeping peacefully. To the long strands of blond hair trailing from beneath her quilt. My whole body feels metallic, heavy, rusted in place. I place my palms on the solid wood of the desk, force myself to my feet, and walk to her bedside.

Dread is the worst of all the bad feelings. It feels like drowning inside your own body. I know what I'm going to see before I look, but there's no way out of it, and that's the scariest part of dread. The inevitability of facing the horror you know is certain. Not possible, not probable, but certain.

I reach out and grasp the corner of Beth's quilt because I have to. I lift it, and peel it back over the Halloween Central wig I should have been able to distinguish from Beth's hair but didn't, because I saw what I expected to see. Like a fool. A side character. No princess or witch. And when I throw back the rest of the quilt, there it is: a carefully arranged row of pillows. It's the oldest trick in the book, the prank we pulled as kids to go play in the woods after dark.

What comes next is a slow dance, a horror movie sequence that can only be done in slow motion and set to gorgeous orchestration, because in real time, it's too much. No—there is no real-time version. None of this is real.

I float down the hallway to the kitchen, like I have in a hundred nightmares, the walls constricting with my throat. I don't touch the floor because gravity is part of the world where there is order and reason, and this is not that world. I don't get to choose what happens next. Since Beth disappeared, I am stuck in a bad dream, and there is no control over anything anymore. It is not real.

It's not *acceptable* as real. It's not acceptable that Mom's head is still resting on the table, motionless, next to her mug of barely touched coffee. A cold terror begins to creep over me.

She's not sleeping. She didn't fall asleep. No one falls asleep like that, skull-first, cheek-to-wood, slouched spaghetti-spine. Not unless something made them. Something in their drink.

The terror is tangible, a moving, living thing. It's unbearable, like bugs crawling over my skin and under my clothes, everywhere and unstoppable. I start to scratch subconsciously, but it does nothing, offers no relief. It's under my skin, but I won't allow it to go any deeper. When terror gets inside your bones, there is no way to get it out.

I look over at Dad, propped up in his chair, unconscious, posed like a taxidermy animal. I scratch harder, breathe faster, but the terror burrows deeper, and I feel it start to ice out goodness, rationality, forgiveness.

Beth.

What did you do?

Or maybe, *what did Veronica do to you?*

I know what I'm supposed to do. I'm supposed to run to them, shake them, spiral into hysterics, make something *happen.*

But I stand there, rigid, useless as stone, a vessel for terror. There's a humming sound in my head like a discordant violin. Pins and needles sting my fingertips, and I clench and unclench my fists to get rid of the feeling. My throat is so dry I can't breathe. I should call 911. I should do the shaking thing. Feel for a pulse.

But I. Don't. Want. To.

I just want everything to stop.

Then my mother lifts her head and looks directly into my eyes.

I scream.

THE TWISTED MIND OF VERONICA GREEN

OCTOBER 1

ix

Splitfoot.

THOSE FUCKS.

Those *fucking* fucks.

This is not the end.

This is NOT the end.

You come for my dog, you fucking die.

10

HAZEL

I want to call 911, but neither of them will let me. All of a sudden, they *don't* want to involve the police. I've never seen my parents like this. Both of them are panicking. There is true terror in my father's eyes, and my mother won't stop crying. Artax has holed himself up in his safe place, the space between the washer and dryer. Numbed and in shock, I go to the kettle to make a pot of tea and discover one of my mother's mason jars of dried herbs with the orange *do not consume* stickers sitting next to the coffeemaker. Next to it is a mortar and pestle with flecks of powdered herbs still in the bottom with an oily residue.

I stare in disbelief. It shouldn't even be in this room—any inedible herbs should be with the cleaning products or in the gardening shed. Mom makes her own organic cleaning sprays, disinfectant wipes, laundry detergents, and pesticides with the plants she grows in the garden. But Beth and I have known since we were toddlers to stay away from some of the plants. *Just because they're from the earth doesn't mean they're safe*. I shakily take a photo with my phone. The jar doesn't have a label, but I carefully reseal it, shove it in a garbage bag, and hide it under the sink. I don't know what to do about it right now, but I'm pretty sure it's evidence. And my parents are in no state to talk about it or Beth. The sight of my parents unraveling, the fact that my sister *poisoned* them, may have tried to kill them, supersedes everything else.

My mother is huddled in the living room under a blanket, crying. She doesn't seem sick—only upset. I don't know what to do. Since the night Beth went missing, Mom has been preoccupied, and it feels like I went from secondary to invisible to irrelevant. It brings up that dread again, but a sharper, deeper kind.

I sit on the floor at her feet, legs crossed, feeling like a little kid again. Crying makes me uncomfortable. I've never been a crier, even as a baby. My parents thought there was something wrong with me. When we were two, Beth threw a rock at my head at a town picnic. Mom insists it was an accident, but how do you accidentally throw a rock at another child's head? Apparently there was an impressive stream of blood, and plenty of screaming, fainting, and general panic among the parents and the other children. Not me. Mom was pretty sure I'd suffered a head injury. Luckily, I hadn't. Scalp lacerations just bleed a lot. But I never cried.

Whether it was a rock to the head, scraped knee, or the general unfairness of life, I'm generally stoic. Being abandoned by Beth twice—is one of the few exceptions. There haven't been many others. And I don't know how to deal with people when they cry. Especially my parents, who you expect to have the answers and the innate ability to make a nightmare go away. The problem is, this time, they're part of the nightmare.

I reach out a hand tentatively. "Mom?"

She looks down at me with crimson-veined eyes, and I'm startled by the *depth* of it all. Mom is lost to me. She's drowning, miles deep in her own terror and sadness and helplessness. She has the look of someone in mourning, funeral eyes, glazed and bottomless and dangerously contagious, swamps-of-sadness eyes. But there's the shadow of something even darker, a fear that reaches straight through my chest to my heart and squeezes until I gasp. I never want to look my mother in the eyes again.

I stumble to my feet, my heart pounding, and make my way to the kitchen, where my father is pacing the floor. He grabs my elbow and pulls me into a chair.

"What did she say to you?" His eyes are wild, his face red and agitated.

Suddenly, all I want is to get out of this house. "Nothing."

"Beth, I mean." He mops the sweat from his brow with a paper napkin. "Did she tell you *anything*?"

"She thinks she's Veronica and that she's being held hostage. She thinks you're the enemy."

"*I* am the enemy?" He raises his voice, and I shrink back instinctively. My father has a habit of yelling at the person in front of him when the person he's angry at isn't there, and I want to tell him *you're not being fair*, tell him *don't shoot the messenger*, but I am angry right back.

"You didn't even notice she was gone!" The words whip out sharply, and he stares at me, speechless. My father looks at me like I'm a stranger. A dangerous stranger. "The last words you said that night were *maybe something* should *happen to her*."

He stares at me in disbelief. "I never said that."

"You did. You said it about me."

A spark of recognition ignites in his eyes, then fades. "For God's sake, Hazel, I wanted you to meet a boy."

Because you can't stand the idea of a lesbian daughter? I can feel the words fizzing on my tongue. I can't say them, though. I'm too afraid of the answer.

Across the room, a soft sob issues from my mother.

"What are you doing to fix this?" I demand.

"We are handling it, Hazel," my father says. But he doesn't sound sure of himself.

I shake my head. "No. You're losing her."

Something in his expression breaks. Once again, I'm ashamed and guilty because the only thing I should feel is relief that they're alive, but instead I'm angry. It's Beth all over again. I can't stand it anymore. The way my parents look past us. The way they don't listen. The way they've divided our lives into two versions: the real one and the one they can *handle*. They're wrong. They're not handling it. They are losing Beth. They are losing both of us. And they have been for a long time.

"How are you handling it when you can't even say her name?" I plead.

"You have no idea what you're getting into," my father says, his voice unsteady. "Leave it alone."

"Did you know the real Veronica Green?" I ask, tired of needing to know a stranger to know my sister. "If what happened to her wasn't just an urban legend, then tell me the truth. Why is everyone so afraid of her?"

My mother breaks into frantic sobs. "She's taking Hazel too."

I flinch.

My father's gaze flickers to my mother, and there's fear in his eyes. My head swims. Taking Hazel? Up until this point, neither of them showed any sign of believing Beth was possessed. Fear starts to grip me, and then my father speaks again.

"Veronica Green is a scary story. You and Beth are real." His voice trembles. I don't believe him. I don't think he believes himself. Veronica Green is more than a scary story. My mother admitted as much. Veronica Green is real.

I feel the heaviness that sets in when I think other people might start crying. It feels like all systems powering down. I can't do this anymore. I can't save the day. I can't help my parents, and I can't help Beth. She didn't tell me anything, because she didn't trust me. And she didn't trust me because I didn't trust her. The sad fact is, she let me down when I needed her. And even though I want to make things right between us, it doesn't change the past. Beth was a bad sister. And if she wasn't, maybe I could help her.

I smile, because sometimes I smile when I'm supposed to cry. It makes my insides feel thick and heavy with rot, and my father stares at me like I'm a monster. I'm not a monster. My feelings just aren't for his consumption. Or anyone's. I don't cry for anyone else's satisfaction. I don't owe anyone that. I don't owe anyone shit. Suddenly, the only thing I feel is anger. But it's bigger than anger. It's consuming, combustible, dangerous. Fury throbs in my brain and in my chest with a life of its own, feeding off my exhaustion and sadness. I'm tired of fighting it off. I'm tired of fighting anger at not being allowed. I don't want to feel like a failure anymore. I'm not a failure. I'm not a fuckup. I'm not a design flaw. I'm not second best, either. I am exactly me. And I don't want to be in this house anymore.

I push myself abruptly back from the table and grab the keys, not caring that I don't have permission.

"Hazel," my father calls after me.

"Don't let her go," my mother begs.

My poisoned parents. Unsuspecting victims of the witch of the woods.

Well.

Make way for the wolf.

When I arrive at Ezra's, it's eerily silent. All the lights are on, but there are no cars in the driveway. I knock on the door and adjust the backpack where I've stashed Beth's laptop, then glance over my shoulder. I can't shake the creepy, horror-movie feeling someone or something is following me, will jump out and grab me if I don't continually check for its presence. But as I scan the expansive, well-manicured lawn, nothing materializes. After a moment, Ezra answers. His clothes are rumpled, his face is red and sweaty, and he looks like he *may* have been crying.

"You look like shit," I blurt out.

He raises a weary hand and points up the stairs. "My room."

I follow him up cautiously. He walks hesitantly, as if afraid some heavy object will come hurtling down at us. There's a loud crash, the sound of breaking glass, and an earsplitting shriek. He turns to look at me.

"I had to restrain Beth. Veronica didn't like it."

"I'm sorry, *restrain*?"

"You'll see." He leads me down the hallway, past the room with the thumping and shrieking and nudges a door open with his knee.

My mouth drops open. It appears to be his parents' bedroom, and it looks like a crime scene. Every door, every drawer, every cabinet of the honeybee-themed room is flung wide open, and the closets, bureaus, and dressers are empty, gaping hollows. I stare into the shadowy depths of a hope chest nestled at the end of a bed that's been stripped down to the mattress, and a sense of doom settles over me. It's roughly human-sized, coffin-like. There's something final and hopeless about it. The way the lid yawns up and seems to wait, to beckon. A warning, or a heads-up. *Dark times ahead.*

My eyes skim over the heaps of clothing littering the floor. Trails of glittering jewelry and fragile perfume bottles scattered like seashells on the shore, among shoes and pill bottles and tiny artifacts of an intimate, behind-closed-doors life we're *not* supposed to see and I don't want to know about. There's an object I *think* is a sex toy lying smack in the middle of the room along with a retainer—do adults wear those for real?—acne medication I recognize because I used it religiously between the ages of thirteen and fifteen, a shiny packet of condoms, a locked safe box, and shredded bits of paper.

I look to Ezra questioningly.

"My parents would flip out if they saw any of this." He looks too shocked to panic. But not far off.

"At least they can't ground you twice."

"They're not going to see it. My dad already took another flight to Miami to join my mom for the afterparty and post-wedding brunch. I convinced him I wouldn't get into any more trouble." He pushes his hair out of his eyes nervously.

"What are the papers? Did Beth do that or did your parents?"

"Like I would know?" He picks up a scarf gingerly and lets

it fall over the suspected sex toy and condoms. "The less I know about my parents' private lives, the better."

"Amen," I murmur, crossing myself like a jerk. But my eyes are fixed on the safe. "What's in the lockbox?"

"Papers? Jewels? The Holy Grail? Knowing my parents, it's probably something boring like life insurance docs."

I sidestep a mountain of shredded paper and nearly crush a fragile silver earring. "What was she looking for?"

"There's nothing *to* look for. My parents are the least interesting people on the planet."

"Well, that's not true. Everyone loves your parents." Except one person. I look at him. "Ezra, do you have any idea why your mother and my mother don't get along?"

He shakes his head with a touch of bitterness. "Anyone who doesn't worship Lori Elwood doesn't exist to her."

"They used to be friends."

He nods. "Supposedly. Cheerleader co-captains and whatnot. Dad said they used to do the fair circuit together for the school garden, but Mom quit gardening and moved to beekeeping so there would be a clean break."

"Really." I wonder if Mrs. Elwood's bee obsession is partly an ongoing competition to show up Mom. If so, enough already.

Ezra jerks his head up. "Hey, do you hear that?"

I listen. "No."

"Exactly." He turns to the door with a look of dread.

When did Beth go silent?

He leads me down the hallway, careful not to make noise, then pushes open the door to his bedroom.

Beth is standing as still as a statue in the center of the room, one wrist raised to the railing of Ezra's bunk bed where it's fastened with a shoelace. Her other arm hangs at her side. She stands stiffly, her spine straight, staring dead ahead, transfixed, as if looking at something visible only to her. I turn my head to follow her gaze to a blank wall over a desk covered in books and computer accessories. Nothing to stare *at*. She's breathing hard, as if she's running instead of standing still. And the expression on her face is frightening.

"Beth," I say softly.

She doesn't answer. Doesn't register that she's heard me at all.

"Mom and Dad are okay. They want to know you're all right."

Ezra laughs nervously. "What do you mean *okay*? Why wouldn't they be?"

I ignore him and take a step closer to her. "Beth, I know you can hear me." But I don't know that. Not for sure. Not anymore. I don't believe Beth would try to hurt our parents. Period. And I'm not sure what that means. Either Beth has had some kind of breakdown and lost herself to an alter ego... Or the other possibility. The impossible possibility: we're no longer dealing with Beth, and Veronica, or some other sinister entity, has taken over my sister's body.

"Beth, please. Let me—"

She spins on me before I can finish the sentence. Her hand slips easily out of Ezra's shoestring "restraint." And she hits me hard, palm flat against my cheek, the surprise stinging more than the contact. Still, it's enough to knock me breathless.

Ezra's mouth drops open, and Beth and I stare at one another. For a moment, the shock immobilizes all life, stilling and silencing the house. Her eyes are unfamiliar, fevered and frenzied. She's nothing like the Beth I know.

Then she says, "Deadeyes." And before I have time to react, she shoves me into Ezra, knocking us both backward into the desk, and darts past us into the hallway and down the stairs.

"Beth!" I run after her, but the front door slams before I'm halfway down the stairs. By the time I fling it open, she's in the truck and starting the engine.

"Did you leave the keys in the ignition?" Ezra says incredulously.

"I didn't think..." I trail off.

We watch helplessly as the truck jerks out of the driveway and speeds away.

I whirl around to face him accusingly. "Where's your car?"

"I crashed it trying to track down your possessed sibling." He scowls at me. "Or sort-of sibling, whatever. Still trying to figure that one out."

I take out my phone and begin to text.

Alarm flashes in Ezra's eyes. "Please don't involve more people. This is getting out of hand."

"Do we have a choice?"

"Yes! Call your parents."

I hedge. "I don't want to bother them any more than they already are."

He eyes me suspiciously. "Why?"

"They're not well."

I send the text to Julie. Luckily, she responds right away—happy to help.

"Are they okay?"

"Beth poisoned them. I found an open jar of toxic leaves near their coffee."

His eyes grow wide. "Jesus."

"I'm going to text Jack." I send him a quick one, telling him we're coming.

"Why?"

"Because he's part of this too. He might know where to find Beth. And the truth is, I think he knows more than he's telling us." I bite my lip. "Remember how he kept talking cryptically about foxes?"

Ezra nods impatiently. "Beth was into foxes. Whatever. They *are* kind of adorable. Like mutant squirrels."

I close my eyes, praying for patience. "Jack was playing with us. He was leading us toward the Fox sisters. Remember in Cutter's class when we read that article about the spiritualism movement? The three girls who claimed they could speak to the dead?"

He stares blankly. "You're asking about an article we read in eighth grade during last period, when I'm more likely to be in the woods behind the school than in it?"

I roll my eyes. "Okay. Well, we learned about them. And that's what Jack meant. Beth was interested in the Fox sisters because Veronica was interested in the Fox sisters. We have to figure out why."

Two headlights appear in the driveway, and we head outside. Ezra raises his eyebrows in a *well, well, well* as I climb into the front seat, and I shoot him a warning look. But he behaves, climbing into the back with a quick thank you to Julie.

"Where to?" she asks, her forehead creased in concern.

"Jack Sawyer's house." I give her the address as Ezra sighs his eye roll out loud.

"So tell me more about the Foxes. Why should we care?" he asks impatiently.

"Foxes?" Julie glances my way.

I hesitate. Jack is part of this, but Julie isn't.

As if Ezra can sense my thought process, he barrels in like Mr. Kool-Aid. "TL;DR, Beth is either a very good liar or possessed by the ghost of Veronica Green."

I glare into the back seat. "Why would you say it like that?"

"That's the situation, is it not?"

"Because it sounds crazy." I press my forehead into the cold car window, mortified. Mortification is another word for necrosis, the literal death of living tissue. That is exactly how I feel in this instant now that the absurd thing we've all avoided saying out loud is tattled to the girl I have been spiraling further and further into a massive crush on.

"Okay," she says slowly. "Catch me up."

Ezra explains, more or less, while I shrivel and die inside. But at the end, she doesn't come out with a dubious *okaaaay* or dismissive *anyway*. She reaches over and rests a hand on top of mine for a split second. No words. Just an almost-handhold.

Then we pull onto Jack's street and that's over with.

"So wait. Hazel. If you're right, then Jack is lying about how much he knows. Why are we picking him up?"

"Because liar or not, he's helping us. He led me to the Foxes, and the Foxes led me to Veronica's yearbook page. It looks like she left some kind of code or clue there, which might be the key to a secret file on Beth's laptop. And the file almost definitely has information about the night Veronica died. I know how Beth thinks. She loves puzzles and riddles. She would absolutely lock the file with the answer to the clue. We just need to crack it."

"Shit." Ezra raises his eyebrows. "What's the code?"

I sigh in frustration. "Splitfoot/Deadeyes/Mariana." I pass back my phone to show him the yearbook page, and he studies it with a deep frown.

"The devil," Julie says.

"Right." I nod, a little taken aback that she made the association so quickly. How is she so much better at this than me? Oh. Right. Because she actually knew my sister.

"Splitfoot is a name for the devil," she tosses over her shoulder.

"Sure, everyone knows that," Ezra says distractedly. "And Mariana is another name for the..." His voice tilts up at the end, curling into a question mark.

"Trench?" Julie guesses. "Islands?"

We pull up in front of Jack's house and wait for him to emerge, but the windows are dark.

"Why does that sound familiar?" Ezra passes back my phone.

"The Mariana trench," Julie recites. "It's the deepest part of the ocean."

"The devil and the deep blue sea," Ezra recites blandly.

Julie and I turn to him.

"Say that again," I blurt.

"Splitfoot. Mariana. Between the devil and the deep blue sea," he says again. "It's an old-timey expression. Like a rock and a hard place, but with the devil. All the best expressions have the devil in them. *Before the devil knows you're dead, idle hands, speak of the devil—*"

"You called?" A voice comes out of the darkness, and a shadowy figure emerges.

THE TWISTED MIND OF VERONICA GREEN

OCTOBER 13

x

Echo fox.

A MYTH IS ONLY A MYTH
when there is no one left to remember
how it really happened.
A lie is only a lie
when there is no one
willing to believe the truth.
A miracle is made
when faith meets the impossible:
where light comes from darkness,
where life comes from nothing,
where death is undone.

In the true winter's land, the barren land of bones and oblivion,
mysteries lie thick and deep, waiting to be excavated.
Three clever foxes told a story and made it true.
And why not?
A universe from nothing, life from the grave,
the miracle is always in the believing.
The sisters knew, and I do too.
If you believe the story, isn't it true?

11
HAZEL

Ezra screams. Julie grabs my arm with a gasp, and my heart attempts to escape my body through my ribcage.

Jack.

Of course it's Jack.

Ezra collapses on the seat, clutching his heart dramatically. "You will die for this," he gasps.

Jack slips into the seat beside him. "Not today, Satan." He looks between the three of us. "And then there were four?"

I gesture at Julie. "This is Julie Merritt."

It could be my imagination, but I think I see a waver in Jack's customary confidence. He *has* to know who Julie is, who her father is. You can't live in Ashling without a basic knowledge of who is who; the town is basically a giant *Guess Who* board.

Our family is no exception. Mom's brother Paul runs the wastewater station. He just married Jennifer Cutter, middle sister of the teacher I'm relatively certain showed us the article on the Fox sisters. The youngest Cutter daughter, Abby, is engaged to Amanda Laurence's older brother Ty, and when *they* get married, I'll officially be related to the largest family in town. The Laurences own enough of Ashling, they could probably buy the rest of us out if they really wanted to, rename it Laurencetown, and brand it "the land where high school never ends." They even own the Slashwheel, the mountaintop's iconic carnival/arcade mash-up. The Laurences live forever as if it is the spring of senior year. The moms all dress like cheerleaders and the dads go out drinking every night, not to the pub, but to the abandoned summer camp at the edge of town, same as they did when they were seventeen. Not Principal Laurence, of course—he has a reputation to uphold. He's careful about his curfew.

It's odd living in a place where everyone can see virtually everything you do. You have to be dead sure of your every move. It all goes down on your permanent record. Hence my childhood nickname Chip making an appearance over a decade later. Yet the Laurences, all but Amanda and her parents, don't seem to worry about what goes down in the history books.

"Hazel. Hazel. Hey, hey." Ezra waves a hand in front of my face, and I blink.

"Where to?" Julie asks.

I look to Jack for a sign, but he gives nothing away. Instead, he gazes back at me with *how can I help* eyes. He could help by telling me what he knows instead of dropping cryptic little clues. Ezra seems to sense my frustration and opens his mouth, but I cut him off before he can make an accusation. "Head for the school again."

Julie backs out of the driveway and makes her way down the narrow road toward town.

"Did you find Deadeyes?" Jack asks.

"Between the devil and the deep blue sea," Ezra can't help saying smugly.

Jack turns to him, total poker face. "What does that mean?"

"It's code," Ezra says confidently, and then falls quiet, because he's just given away everything we know and our leverage to get more intel out of Jack. I should have left him to clean up the mess at his house, or as I'm beginning to think of it, the pit of despair.

"It's from Veronica's yearbook page," I explain, shooting Ezra a warning look, like *play along*. "Beth mentioned Deadeyes, so I think there's a good chance there's a connection. And the first part of the clue was Splitfoot, which is another word for the devil—and it comes from the Fox sisters—which you tipped us off about. I'm not sure why you did it so cryptically."

"Don't shoot the messenger," Jack says defensively. "I only repeated the information I was given. Beth started mentioning Veronica and foxes. She didn't specify what *kind* of foxes."

Ezra *uh huhs* and I narrow my eyes, watching the village lights in the distance slowly grow more distinct and take shape. Even when you know someone very well, or think you do, it's hard to tell when a person is lying. My sister taught me that. Her early lies were the most tolerable kind, if you can tolerate any lies at all. They were well-meaning, therapeutic—meant to keep unkind gossip out of my ears and shield me from rejection. Beth played social defense for me like her life was on the line. For longer than it made sense to, really. I mean, it never made sense to at all. She didn't owe me anything. It's not anyone's fault when one sibling is accepted and one is rejected. It's a fact of life in the animal world. The runt is frozen out. I'm fine.

I do notice the little things.

The way Chief Merritt talked about me to Mom and Dad right in front of my face, like I could disappear and it wouldn't make a difference. The way grown adults, dozens of them, laughed when Mac called me defective. Ed's comment about troubled girls, and how he never actually said he didn't mean me. How Mrs. Merritt, who acts so *nice*, didn't come to my defense when I needed her. The way my own parents look right through me. And the way, when Mac broke my nose and I stood bleeding in the hallway, surrounded by a half-dozen teachers, none of them did a thing.

It's like they've identified the sheep who wandered into their pack of wolves. Like I can never really know who I can trust, and I might not be safe with anyone.

And sometimes it feels like violence is inevitable in my life, and it's just a matter of time.

I don't say shit, because all of this is terrifying. And I don't want to think about it. But I fucking notice.

I sound overdramatic, but I'm fine. I'm not the one with a dead girl potentially piloting my body.

I am. I'm fine.

Julie's phone rings, and she punches the touchscreen on the dash to answer over Bluetooth. "Mom?"

"Honey, are you okay?" Mrs. Merritt sounds strange, and the air stills in the car. She's breathless, voice quavering. It's the kind of tone that makes you impatient to hear what happened, who died.

Julie sounds puzzled. "I'm fine, Mom."

A deep sigh comes through the speakers. "Go to Amanda's." Then, abruptly—"No. Not the Laurences. Go to Aunt Mindy's."

"What? Why?" Fear floods her voice. "What happened? Is Dad okay?"

"Dad is fine. He's at the station."

It's clear that everything is not okay, and Julie jerks the steering wheel to the left and makes a U-turn as her voice rises in pitch and volume. "Where are you? What's going on?"

"I'm fine. Everything is fine," her mother says, in the least-convincing performance since the school production of *A Chorus Line*. I hoped they wouldn't get it. "Julie, go to Mindy's," her mother says more firmly, a touch of panic in her voice.

"Fine," Julie relents, ending the call and jerking the wheel again, gunning the engine and slamming the rest of us into the passenger side of the car.

"We're not going to Aunt Mindy's, are we?" Jack asks in a flat voice.

"No, we're not." She slams on the brakes, and we're thrown forward. Ezra grabs my seat from behind me, bracing himself against the sudden stop, and then we're thrown into motion again.

"It's Beth, isn't it?" My heart drops into my stomach and adrenaline surges. Every single bad thing that's happened since the night of the party has involved Beth.

"Why would Beth be at Julie's?" Ezra says.

"Why would she go to your place?" Jack lobs back. "She's giving us breadcrumbs. The school, deadeyes, the yearbook, Chet, now Julie's house."

"Can you not call him Chet please?" Ezra grumbles.

"What does my dad have to do with any of that?" Julie says through clenched teeth.

Silence fills the air for a moment. None of us says anything, but I'm pretty sure even Ezra picks up on the fact that no one ever mentioned Julie's father. Jack specifically said Julie's *house*. A wave of paranoia washes over me. It feels like a tell. It shouldn't be—Julie isn't connected to any of this. But then again—she *was* there the night Beth disappeared. She never gave me the time of day until that night, and suddenly she's texting me and wanting to hang out, always with questions about Beth. And her father's the head law enforcement official in Ashling. My blood turns ice cold in my veins.

You're paranoid, Hazel. You wreck things *because you're not willing to believe anyone could possibly be good.*

And like that, I'm trapped back in one of my biggest fights with Beth. It *is* true that Amanda never liked me. I never fit into their scene of boys and gossip and roller skating and slumber parties. But way back before Mom had to start dropping me off a block away from sleepovers, the *reason* she had to do that was because of Amanda's fifth-grade birthday party at Slashwheel.

Slashwheel is what everyone fondly calls the creatively named Shoot/Tag/Wheel, a popular local hangout, which features—as you might have guessed—paintball, laser tag, and a roller rink, along with an arcade and single carnival ride, an ancient wooden Ferris wheel straight out of Bradbury. It's the premier mountaintop destination for doing anything other than sitting around a bonfire drinking beer. People still hang out there, but in fifth grade it was *the* place to have your birthday party, and according to Mom's policy, I had to be invited in order for Beth to go. So I found myself lacing on roller skates along with Amanda, Beth, and the rest of the cool kids who had already sorted themselves into separate lunch tables and elite playground factions.

It was awkward. No kid *wants* to turn down an invitation to Slashwheel. It's the greatest place on earth, unless you've ever been on a plane or visited a major city, I guess. Even then, it's a close call. The roller rink makes a good argument for itself. Roller skating on the cracked pavement at Dewitt Memorial Park is fun, but Slashwheel elevates it with rainbow light shows, a glittering disco ball, and a giant movie screen covering one wall that rotates between retro music videos from my parents' day, mesmerizing color patterns, and projections of the skaters. (That can be embarrassing or fun depending on your skill level. I'm pretty good.)

The laser tag arena is small but decent. It's dark, except for the black lights, and constructed like a maze. They pipe in music from adventure and horror movies to keep your adrenaline pumping too. Laser tag was always my favorite part. Beth hated it. She was a hider, burrowing under a foam boulder or cramming into a crevice with her eyes squeezed shut, hoping to go unnoticed. I was a hunter, betting heavily on the element of surprise. It didn't always pay off, but at least I got to play.

The arcade is the most pointless part, because it costs extra. Even though they always give you a free card worth a couple of games at parties, a couple of games is never enough, and you have to bring money from home to make it truly worth it. So it's basically a scam.

But the thing that either makes or breaks the Slashwheel experience, the reason some people (wrongly) call it an amusement park and the reason I will *never* go back there is the Ferris wheel.

I should *never* have listened to Beth. For the record, I trusted my sister at that point. I don't think this incident is part of her liar origin story, although maybe every moment plays a role. But Beth was the one who convinced me to do the thing I was afraid of. I don't just dislike heights. I get true Hitchcockian vertigo, a swirling sense that the world is dipping and tilting below me, that my depth perception has become relative and unstable. There's an irrationality as well, a sudden stream of fears, like there might be an unaddressed problem with the ride, and it will break apart under me, like in *Final Destination 3*. Or maybe it was built on a sinkhole, and I will be swallowed up. Or an earthquake will strike, and we all fall down.

There's more to it than that, though. I fear *myself* when I stray too far from the ground. I fear that I'll betray my own body and hurl myself down, powerless to stop myself. That's what I fear most, because I don't understand it. I don't want to die—I *really* don't want to die. And I definitely don't want to die like that. But I'm afraid I'll do it just the same, and the fear is strong enough to fill my mouth with bile, make my teeth ache, hollow out my chest. The effect is physical. The scariest thing imaginable is the idea of losing yourself, of drifting back and watching helplessly as the person you knew as *you* does this horrific violent act. And you can't stop it. And then you're gone. You're history.

Which is why I didn't want to ride the Ferris wheel.

But my sister is persuasive. And the argument I can never turn down is that she's afraid to go it alone. This isn't entirely her fault—our mother conditioned us to believe that we couldn't and *shouldn't* do anything without the other. I think she was afraid of what can happen to a girl who is alone in the world.

So when Beth begged me to ride the Slashwheel with her, I relented. Of course, we were next in line when Amanda came running breathlessly out of the roller rink, music pounding behind her, rainbow lights flashing, all glitter gloss and silver ribbons. She wanted to ride, and you don't say no to the birthday girl. Beth looked to me for permission, desperate to be Amanda Laurence's chosen one on her special day. It was my out. I was about to sigh the relieved sigh of someone who doesn't have to face their biggest fear, when Amanda's pink, rhinestone-studded phone buzzed. She grabbed Beth's arm and said, "One sec."

One sec was all it took for the overworked and underpaid operator of the Ferris wheel to glare at Amanda, then seize me by the wrist and hurl me into the open car, slamming the door shut and locking it before I even fully registered what had happened. Then, with a sickening, stomach-twisting jolt, I was airborne. I sat there, helpless, as I was swept up into the night sky and the darkness swallowed me. The obnoxious sounds of Britpop burst through the speakers, Republica's "Drop Dead Gorgeous." Because you don't forget the song that's playing the moment you're sure you're about to die.

And then it all stopped.

Amanda had finally boarded the ride with Beth—and immediately gotten motion sickness and vomited over the side. And for some reason I will never understand related to liability, they had to take her off the ride, then shut it down with everyone else still on it, and restart only after cleaning the area. It was late spring, but every breeze seemed to carry a dying gasp of winter. The ancient hinges on the cars wailed as they swayed. All I could see were the tiny lights on the other cars, flickering like falling stars. I was stranded at the very top, the closest I will ever get to the moon, for nearly an hour, alone with my paralyzing fear of heights. And you know what? The folk wisdom that facing your fears helps to mitigate them? Not true.

Beth apologized, of course. I don't blame her for what happened. She couldn't have foreseen how it would go wrong. The person I blamed was Amanda. Even if it was her birthday, she broke every rule by cutting. It was her fault we were there in the first place. And the worst sin of all, worse than barfing on the Slashwheel, is that she took Beth away from me. When I clearly had no one else to hang out with. She didn't even acknowledge my existence. Just ran up, grabbed Beth by the hands, and claimed her. Ignore the ghost girl. She'll take the hint eventually.

So I may have overreacted. Because when the Slashwheel finally spit me back out of its rusty jaws, I went straight up to Amanda, who was still bent queasily over the grass, a paper cup of crushed ice in her hand, and screamed at her.

"What is wrong with you?" My voice surged out of me like I had no control over it, so loud it scratched my throat.

She looked up at me, startled. "Sorry?"

"You should be." I stood there, shaking, without a good answer. What was I supposed to say? That Beth was mine, and Amanda wasn't allowed to play with her? I knew that wasn't right. And I knew my mother was fighting a losing battle. I was losing Beth, and that only made me angrier. Why was I always the one left behind? What was wrong with me? Why was I not Beth? Or literally anyone else?

Beth grabbed my arm and yanked me away from the gaping crowd and into the deserted paintball arena.

"What are you doing, Hazel?" she hissed.

I pointed to the ride defensively. "You saw what she did."

She stared at me incredulously. "Amanda didn't get sick on purpose."

"If she hadn't forced me to ride it alone, it wouldn't have mattered when or where she puked."

"*She* didn't force you. I asked you." She shot me a challenging look. "Was it my fault?"

I avoided her eyes. "Did I say it was? She could *see* we were going on together."

"Are you seriously jealous of Amanda Laurence?"

There's something so awful about the word *jealous*. It's so shameful, no one ever wants to admit to it. It's like admitting to not being a pet person. There are worse things, but the way people act, it feels like wanting something you can't have is the worst thing you could do. Yes, I wanted what Amanda had. I didn't want Beth to consider hanging out with me a chore. I wanted to be the kind of person no one would ever think of as a chore. I was jealous. And I hated that I felt the feeling you were never supposed to feel. That meant I was weak. It made me so mad at myself. But I took it out on Beth.

"*You're* the one who's obsessed with her."

She drew in a sharp breath, like I'd punched her in the stomach. "Obsessed?"

I shrugged uncomfortably. "Am I wrong?"

Beth narrowed her eyes, but they were bright, too bright, tear-bright. "She went out of her way to include you."

"By pushing me onto the Slashwheel—"

"She didn't push you. She invited you to her party."

I rolled my eyes. "She had to. That's Mom's doing."

Beth clenched her jaw. "She invited you because *I asked* her to. She was giving you a chance. To be her friend. She wanted to get to know you, she was interested. You're just...so paranoid no one likes you that you act like a jerk and then no one does. You wreck things because you're not willing to believe anyone could possibly be good."

Suddenly, my eyes were stinging. Badly. "Thanks for the information."

Her face fell. "Sorry. I only meant—" She glanced back at the party. "You can't always assume the worst of everybody and still expect the best from them."

"I don't."

"I know you don't think you do." She glanced over her shoulder again. "I wish you could see it. It's called a self-fulfilling prophecy."

"I know what it's called." I didn't, actually. But I do now. And as I waved her off to rejoin Amanda, I told myself none of it was true, that Amanda never would have been interested in befriending the weird sister. That it wasn't *actually* my fault for yelling at her on her birthday.

Later, I decided I had to be right. Amanda was a stereotype, a classic mean girl. Beth was lying. Amanda Laurences aren't friends with Hazel Whitmans, and that's an unbreakable law of nature. And doubting myself later wouldn't change the result: Amanda hated me, and there was a side of me Beth didn't like. And neither of them was completely in the wrong.

I can't even look at that wheel anymore.

It's a reminder of my biggest flaw: I wreck things because I'm not willing to believe people could possibly be good.

I glance into the backseat at Jack, who could be telling the truth that his words sound cryptic because Beth spoke to him cryptically. Then Ezra, who I always thought of as a giant bro jerk. He hangs out with some real assholes, including Mac Wendell, Optimus Prime of shits. But since Beth was in trouble, Ezra has been a constant presence. Maybe under his surface is fear, loyalty, and determination. And then there's Julie. I have no *real* reason to believe she's anyone but a genuinely nice and helpful person. She's here, I have to remind myself, because I *asked* her to be.

You're paranoid.

No wonder I wreck everything.

THE TWISTED MIND OF VERONICA GREEN

OCTOBER 30

xi

Point of no return.

TONIGHT'S THE NIGHT.

If it goes wrong…

Sorry, Mama.

Sorry, Mom.

12

HAZEL

As we approach the house, an ominous glow begins to emerge from the darkness. Julie slows the car, and I lean forward, craning my neck to see.

"What the..." Jack mutters under his breath.

Julie pulls to a stunned stop—the driveway has been blocked with traffic cones. The entire house has been strung with Christmas lights. A dozen or more strands of colored lights are arranged roughly in a circle that spans two floors. And two large *X*'s cross the upstairs windows. Like a cartoon dead face.

"Dead eyes," Ezra says. "Is that dead eyes?" He smacks the seat excitedly. "Guys, I'm totally getting the hang of this."

"Brilliant, Encyclopedia Brown," Jack says. "Now explain where the devil and the deep blue sea fit into this?"

Julie kicks open her car door, and we follow her out.

"So...if the house is Deadeyes, then the sea should be to the right..." Ezra points at the trailer parked next to the house. "And the devil is in there?"

Jack claps a hand on his shoulder. "I think you may have lost the trail."

"Shut up, guys." Julie walks toward the house, but hesitates, raising her phone to her ear. "Mom?" She pauses. "Yeah, I'm at Aunt Mindy's." She wanders away, talking quietly into the phone.

Jack steps between the cones and slowly approaches the house, staring up at the bright, grotesquely cheerful display.

"It's like a threat. Or a warning." I trace the lights with my eyes, thinking aloud. "If Deadeyes represents a person, it's putting him on notice. You're between the devil and the deep blue sea. No moves left. Right? Checkmate."

"Or it's a map," Ezra argues. "How could Deadeyes be one person when the symbol keeps appearing all over town? It's almost like...a scavenger hunt. Starting at the school with the song, then..." He hesitates. "Now Julie's. This marks one more piece of the puzzle."

"The other obvious point is that Beth didn't do this," I say.

Jack eyes me quizzically.

"How would she have time? She was just at Ezra's destroying his house. No one person could have done this in a half hour."

Ezra tilts his head, considering. "Veronica could."

Julie ends her call abruptly and rejoins us. "Are you serious?"

"Vengeance spirit rising from the grave on the anniversary of her death? Uh, yeah. If you knew *anything* about demons, you'd know they have superhuman strength and speed. They're basically Marvel heroes gone wrong."

"Villains?" Jack suggests.

"The *original* villains," Ezra corrects.

Julie holds her phone under her chin thoughtfully. "I'm going to assume for a sec that you have some kind of expertise on this, Ez, your dad being an actual authority on spiritual matters. A demon is a fallen angel, right?"

"Right."

"But Veronica wasn't an angel. She was a girl." Julie looks to the rest of us for backup.

"Yeah, but..." Ezra shakes his head. "Beth couldn't physically have done this."

"But Beth didn't wander out of the woods and say *I am Asmodeus*, she said *I am Veronica Green*," I protest.

"Demons lie," Jack points out.

Ezra looks at me curiously. "How do you know Asmodeus?"

I sigh impatiently. "I don't remember. And not to challenge your expertise, but I talked to your dad, and he said only demons are capable of possession. Not dead girls."

"You talked to my father?" Ezra looks taken aback and a little offended, and I wonder whether it's because I didn't tell him about the conversation, or because his dad didn't mention it. But he quickly shakes it off.

"Yeah," I say impatiently. "I talked to the one person Beth mentioned by name in her Veronica trance, who also happens to have some spiritual knowledge of possessions. And he shot the idea down, like my parents and Julie's dad. But I think they're in denial. So the question is, are we all now committed to the idea that this is for real?"

Ezra stares hard at the house. "Either that, or it's a very elaborate prank."

Jack shrugs. "I'm willing to believe anything once."

Julie looks to me. "You're the one living with her. What do you believe?"

"Beth would never have hurt my parents."

In the glow from the Christmas lights, Julie pales. "What did she do?"

"Poisoned them," Ezra says grimly.

Jack shakes his head adamantly. "No. Beth wouldn't do that."

"We just said we're not dealing with Beth," I point out. "In her mind, they're strangers who kidnapped her and are holding her hostage."

"Something doesn't add up." Ezra chews on his sleeve nervously. "If Beth is really Veronica, then your parents aren't strangers. They all went to school together. Look again at that yearbook page."

I pull it up on my phone and gasp at what flew right by me before.

Julie leans over my shoulder. "What is it?"

"Lillabee," I murmur.

Under the "splitfoot/deadeyes/mariana" quote are three more names that I had skimmed right by, assuming they were literary references: Persephone, Cerberus, and Lillabee. But while Persephone and Cerberus both fall into the same mythology, as far as I know, Lillabee isn't a reference to anything. It's the name of Mrs. Elwood's honey brand. "Did Lillabee Honey exist in Veronica's era? You said your mom started beekeeping after the falling-out with my mom."

His face falls slightly. "No. She founded the company in college. And brags about it constantly. She must have been beekeeping for a couple years at least. But still, that's a link. Everyone knew Veronica. Even if they won't admit it."

"Because of guilt? Or fear? My mom seems genuinely terrified of Veronica. She's convinced her death had something to do with the devil," I say.

We all exchange a look.

"Or maybe a demon?" Ezra suggests.

"Whatever it is, we're not dealing with Beth anymore," I say. "And our parents know more than they're letting on. We all agree?"

Jack nods slowly. "Beth has left the chat."

"Only an *actual* demon could have done this." Ezra points his chin at Julie's house.

"Clark Griswold could have done that," Julie says.

"In thirty minutes?" Jack raises his phone and takes a photo. "Nah. No *one* person did that. And Beth wouldn't hurt anyone. So either there's an entire Veronica conspiracy, or Ezra the demon-slayer is onto something."

"Love that for me," Ezra says. "But we're getting sidetracked. Beth obviously isn't here. So why are we still standing around like downstaters?"

Jack ignores the dig. "Right for the second time. You're on a roll, Buffy."

"Enough." Julie swings the door open and jumps into the truck. She glances at me as I slide into the passenger seat. "Do they always act like this?"

"Like bickering children? Yes. Always," I say.

She shakes her head in disbelief. "You think when bad things happen, people change."

"I don't." Beth would have scolded me for my unbridled negativity. I miss that.

Julie smiles unexpectedly, and that makes me sort of smile as well. It gives me hope.

"So, are we still headed to the school?" she asks.

Without any better ideas, that's what we do. I'm anxious about the fact that Beth has gone quiet. It could mean she's in trouble. We drive in uneasy silence and arrive to find plywood covering the damaged doors—now decorated in bloodred spray paint. Deadeyes.

Julie starts to park, but I place a hand on her arm. "Don't. We missed her. She's moving quickly." My eyes are already on a commotion farther down Main Street. "What happened over there?"

A police vehicle with its lights on is parked in front of the *Daily Journal* office. As we drive by, we see the windows have been smashed, and the now sickeningly familiar deadeyes symbol has been spray-painted on the sidewalk.

Julie steps on the gas and continues driving when she sees the officer inspecting the damage is her father. "Tell me where to drive. Anywhere but here."

"Aunt Mindy's?" Jack suggests.

Julie ignores him. "Amanda's it is." She makes a hard right. My stomach tightens. I don't see why we have to involve Amanda Laurence. But if that's where Julie feels safe since her house has been targeted, I don't want to tell her no.

"There's something I haven't told you yet," Ezra says uncomfortably. He pulls his phone out of his pocket. "Remember I said it seems like the deadeyes are forming some kind of map?"

"Yeah?" I say cautiously.

"I should have shown you this sooner." He leans forward to show us a photo of his house with the deadeyes symbol painstakingly laid out in luminaries on his massive front lawn, like a fiery connect-the-dots. "I panicked and took it down before you came over."

I grab the phone from him, my heart in my throat. "Why would you hide this?"

"I told you. I panicked!" He snatches the phone back. "I called you right away, didn't I? I...didn't know what to do about the dead-eyes. It feels like being marked. Doesn't it?"

Julie looks uneasy. "Marked for what?"

Jack darts a look at me. I'm pretty sure we're thinking the same thing. Veronica started a revenge club dedicated to the Deadeyes. But he doesn't say it and neither do I.

"Marked as a place that was significant to Veronica." The sinister symbol that's becoming so familiar still remains so cryptic. "She went to the school first, the same school Veronica attended, and gave us the clues Deadeyes and Chet. Then she went to Ezra's house. We know she knew Ezra's parents because of Chet and Lillabee. Next, Julie's—there's an obvious link there, because Julie's family did the murder investigation. Then back to the school, then to the *Journal*, which published the articles about what happened to her and formed the basis of the legend. Which makes four marked sites, maybe targets."

"Make that five," Julie says in an odd voice. She slams on the brakes, and we jerk to a stop.

I stare through the windshield at the Slashwheel. It's eerie at night with all the lights shut off. It's usually lit up like a carnival, the wheel blinking like dying stars in the night sky, spotlights flung over the grounds, strobes spilling out of the windows. But the only lights on the property are a set of black lights trained on the giant billboard advertising the wheel, where deadeyes covers the face of the vintage clown that serves as the Slashwheel's mascot.

"And now I have a new recurring nightmare," Jack says, hopping out of the truck to snap another photo.

I follow his lead and approach the billboard, a shiver traveling down my spine. "What else has she given us? Besides Deadeyes?"

"The Fox sisters," Jack reminds me.

"Right." I reread the notes I'd saved on my phone. "Anyone know anything about the spiritualism movement?"

"Nada." Jack lifts a shoulder and drops it, still staring open-mouthed up at the defaced billboard through his empty glasses frames.

"The talking dead," Ezra says, appearing at my side. "Or like, talking *to* the dead."

"But that was debunked a million years ago." Julie makes her way over, shivering as a breeze kicks up a swirl of frozen leaves in her path. "We read about it in Cutter's class. Remember we always had to read those 'current events' articles that were neither current nor centered on relevant events?"

I shoot a *told you so* look at Ezra, who shrugs back a *what do you want from me.*

"The popular belief that these mediums were speaking to the dead was debunked, yeah," I say, skimming my notes again. "But spiritualism still exists today in a modern form. And mediums are still around too." I pause. "Phoebe hasn't been answering my texts. Jack, you're close, right? Would she pick up for you?"

"Probably not. Phoebe isn't allowed to use her phone much during the week. She's always visiting her grandmother, who doesn't allow phones, and her stepmom is super strict."

Right—the texts between Phoebe and Beth mentioned her grandmother not liking cell phones. But knowing Phoebe isn't allowed to use her phone much casts her responses to Beth, and lack of responses to me, in a different light. What you assume people think about you can feel so obvious based on what you think you know. Phoebe is rich. She lives in the city. She's alone a lot on the weekends and stays out late to party. But that says nothing about her life the majority of the time. Not answering texts doesn't mean you *don't want* to answer them. I feel bad now. I know a lot less about Phoebe and Beth's friendship than I thought I did. Maybe they were closer than I thought, and the abruptness of Phoebe's answers was because she was sneaking her phone at the risk of being caught. Even more reason to be impatient for Phoebe's return. She may be the key to understanding Beth.

"Well, that's unfortunate, because Phoebe is the only one who can tell us if Beth interacted with a medium. And if she did, we need to talk to them."

"You think Beth *spoke* to Veronica?" Julie asks.

"Phoebe said they planned a ritual to reach out to Veronica but didn't do it, because Beth wanted to do one that was much more dangerous. Either they found the ritual online, which feels sloppy for Beth, in a book—and I doubt they have a copy of *Summoning the Dead for Dummies* in the Ashling library—or they consulted an expert. Hence the Fox sisters, hence Veronica's own obsession, hence Deadeyes...maybe."

"Veronica was obsessed with raising the dead?" Julie arches an eyebrow.

"She was the single member of a yearbook club centered around the Foxes. A *revenge* club."

"Wait." Jack looks at me intently. "What do these things have to do with each other? Veronica, some random demon, the Fox sisters, and revenge?"

"I know, it doesn't fit together yet. Revenge is the missing piece. It came directly from Beth. It's the *only* thing that's come directly from—" I stop mid-sentence, spin on my heel, and run back to the truck, my heart pounding. I grab the laptop from my backpack and flip it open. With shaking hands, I type in *REVENGE* as the password for the Veronica file.

It opens.

And it reveals a diary.

The contents are handwritten, but they've been digitized. The diary is filled with poetry and musings, and thoughts ranging from the deep to the mundane.

From the Twisted Mind of Veronica Green.

And there's a map.

A map of the town of Ashling with *six* spots marked with deadeyes and a seventh with a little red heart. I know the heart. It's drawn right over the spot where the Gingerbread House is located. *Bethanhazel.* Our cabin in the woods. And then I notice the location of the fifth deadeye, and my stomach drops.

"Hazel?"

I slam the laptop shut and whirl around. The others stare at me expectantly.

"We found something kind of huge." Julie holds out her phone to me, and I take it from her numbly. On the screen is a directory of mediums affiliated with the National Spiritualist Association of Churches. Among them is someone named Penelope Fox Crane. And along with a familiar jawline and delicately arched brows, she has the same piercing violet eyes as Phoebe. The link next to Penelope's name leads to a separate website that claims Penelope Fox Crane is a working medium who is a direct descendant of Leah Fox.

But that's not all.

At the bottom of the screen is a long string of testimonials in plain text. It's clear the website was made decades ago by someone who didn't care or was too stubborn to hire a professional to make it for her—boomer coding. But one name still leaps out as if formatted in bold, bright-red lettering amid the others.

Veronica Green.

Furious at myself for getting so close and missing *this*, the only detail that actually matters, I dial Penelope's listed number on pure adrenaline. This is why I am not built to be a hero. Neither Beth nor I would exactly make the cut. But I'm not even villain material. I was never the witch. I'm all feeling and no thought. Snapping jaws without the nerves to back them up.

"You shouldn't call old people in the middle of the night," Julie says, frowning.

No one answers.

"We don't exactly have a lot of options," I say defensively.

But Jack is already ten steps ahead of me with his phone to his ear. "Phoebe?" He shoots me a disappointed look, as if this were the obvious move.

"She never answers for me," I protest.

He holds up a hand to shush me. "Yeah, everyone's onto you, so… Are you going to tell us the truth, or do I have to send your stepmom incriminating Jell-O shot photos?" He shakes his head. "No, I'm *not* that asshole, but we have a missing Beth, informed descendants, and apparently, a medium who hasn't told us the whole truth." He pauses again. "Right." He hangs up.

Ezra looks at him expectantly. "What did she say?"

"Phoebe gave her the summoning spell."

"Spell?" Julie stares incredulously.

"Those were her words." Jack paces a few steps. "She's coming up to meet us. I think she's been avoiding all of this, because, like...if it's real, it's real bad. You know?" He scratches the back of his head nervously. "And Phoebe's the one who kind of opened the gates."

"But Beth is the one who did the ritual—right?" I grip my phone tightly. My hands feel shaky.

Jack nods emphatically. "Yes. I guess...except Phoebe got a bunch of old, mystical shit from her grandmother, who got it from her grandmother, and...I don't know. Without context, even a fairy tale can be dangerous."

"Deep." Ezra rolls his eyes. But he looks like he just stepped off a roller coaster.

"So what do we do now?" Julie asks me, as if I have a plan.

Before I can answer, my phone buzzes. Like a sign, a gift from the fates, I get what I've been waiting for almost since the moment Beth disappeared: a text from Phoebe.

It's a single word, but it's everything.

PHOEBE:

Sorry.

Because under that single word is a photo of a very old, yellowed page from what appears to be a deteriorating book. On it, in faint, scrawling ink, is a series of symbols, diagrams, and instructions under the simple heading, "Recalling the Spirit."

I look up at the others. "Let's split up."

THE TWISTED MIND OF VERONICA GREEN

(no further diary entries)

13

HAZEL

It's a Hail Mary.

But the truth is, I will never truly, fully believe with my heart and soul that Beth has been possessed by Veronica Green or any other entity until I see the ghost with my own eyes. I need more tangible proof than "Beth wouldn't do that." Because we've grown so far apart over the years, I don't know what Beth would do. I don't know if she would assume another identity for days, or why. I don't know if she would try to kill our family. I don't know if she loves me.

I don't know if I love Beth anymore either.

And I'm scared of what it means if I don't.

I'm scared of what that says about me.

Beth is a liar. She is a bad sister. She has betrayed and abandoned me many times over the course of our lifetimes. She has always chosen herself over me when given the choice. But all of that is forgivable. All of it. What I can't forgive is last summer.

To be unequivocally clear, I am a difficult and flawed person.

I'm judgmental, unforgiving, and guarded as fuck. People are like puzzles to me, and I don't like puzzles. But one thing about me that's faultless, that's perfect actually, is that I'm not straight. I'm pretty sure most people at school know this, even though at seventeen I've never been on an actual date, let alone had a girlfriend. You can't exist in the fishbowl that is Ashling High without people knowing your business, even some things that go unsaid. And again—it doesn't go unsaid because I don't love it. It suits me.

But it doesn't suit Ashling.

I think the cliché is true—our generation is more enlightened than the ones that came before it, and the future will be a better and brighter place. But I can't say for sure that being queer has nothing to do with why I've always been on the outside. You know. Waving through a window. Why Mac shoved me that day and not someone else. Why he called me "defective" in front of the school, and why people laughed. Or why his father thinks I'm troubled. Why Julie would feel the need to pick a spot for a date where she wouldn't risk running into anyone she knows. And why my mother still asks me, every time I go out, with hope in her eyes that crushes my soul, whether I'm going to meet a *boy*. Emphasis on *boy*.

I don't have Beth's charming, outgoing qualities. Still, I'm not a complete waste of DNA, personality-wise. I hope the reason I'm an outsider isn't because I'm not into guys. But I don't know. There aren't a ton of kids at school who are out as gay or lesbian or trans. It's easier to go without labels and live life. Because in a town like Ashling, labels can have consequences. I know it's not like that everywhere. I also know Ashling is far from the only place like this.

Book bans have reached epidemic status. Pandemic, even.

No one put up a fight when it happened here, one wave of challenges after the next. Parents, teachers, the board of ed—it was unanimous. Every last queer story—along with many others that weren't Christian enough, white enough, Ashling enough—gone. Even the most wholesome books about girls going to prom together or boys who had never been kissed. Gone. Without a whisper of dissent.

There's no Pride month in Ashling. Instead of rainbow flags, some people put out an *additional* American flag in June, just to make a point. I only know of one lesbian couple, and the things I hear people say when they walk down the street together make my blood boil.

The things they say also make me afraid.

We live in God-fearing, gun-worshipping country. It's not uncommon for a town meeting to have *someone* erupt in anger over how the town should be run and to remind anyone who disagrees with him how long he's lived here, his God-given rights, how many guns he owns, and that he *knows where you live*, and maybe you should shut up or get the hell out of town.

Ashling is a place where you can be yourself, as long as you do so silently and invisibly. Where you have to avert your eyes when you walk past certain folks or drive past houses with Confederate flags, ignore certain bumper stickers, and block out hateful remarks, to get by. There used to be more queer people in Ashling. Even a couple of teachers. The last of them left after the book ban. Quit mid-school year in protest.

Silent protest.

It's hard to live a silent life. And end of junior year, last summer, I'd had enough. It's not like I was ready to take on all of Ashling. But

I was ready to take on my family. So the night after classes ended, when I was feeling fairly invincible after annihilating the last of my exams, while we were lying awake in our twin beds, I talked to my sister as if she were still a friend.

"How gay do you think I am?" That's how I phrased it.

"Ninety-eight percent." She answered without hesitation, as if she'd considered and weighed the percentage in advance.

"Why ninety-eight?"

"I know there are *one* or two guys you like."

I thought about it. There were. I wasn't sure of the rules. If you were allowed to be gay and still like a guy here and there. It didn't feel like a sufficient number to count as bisexual, because the ratio was so overwhelming. Maybe *queer* was a better label. Maybe labeling was premature. But gay *felt* right. Ninety-eight percent gay felt pretty accurate. Although I resented that Beth arrived at it before me. "Give or take."

"How gay do you think *I* am?"

"Oh my God, Beth. Not everything is about you."

She rolled over on one elbow. "Okay, well, you seem to have life figured out. What do you want to talk about?"

I mirrored her pose. "I don't like feeling like it's this big secret."

"Trust me, it's not."

"Maybe not at school. But I don't want the word out officially until I talk to Mom and Dad. And I thought...you're better with words."

She tilted her head, her hair falling into one eye. "You want me to talk to them for you?"

"No, I just want you to be there. As backup. They like you better."

"They so do *not* like me better. When were you planning on the big reveal?"

"Tomorrow? I want to get it over with." I gave her my *pretty please* look.

She paused. "Can we do it after the dance? It's literally my busiest day of the year."

I rolled my eyes. Only Beth would consider getting ready for a school dance being busy. "Fine."

She reached a hand across the space between our beds, and I took it hesitantly. "You know I've got your back."

I'm mostly mad at myself for thinking I could trust her when our entire history argued against it. I didn't go to the dance because I don't do dances, but I knew when it ended. I watched the social media posts morph from *#gettingready*s to *#arrival*s to *#bestnightever*s to *#afterparty*s. Then gradually, they stopped. Mom and Dad went to bed. I sat like an asshole on the front porch, checking my phone obsessively, half in disbelief and half furious at myself for believing in the first place. I allowed myself to send only a single text asking if she was on her way home. Multiple texts would just compound what a pathetic loser I was.

But I didn't leave that spot all night. I wasn't going to let her off easy. I was going to stare her down when she finally came home, a partied-out, selfish traitor, an unforgivable liar.

And she did, eventually.

She pulled up in an unfamiliar car, looking exhausted and so thoroughly destroyed, she was barely recognizable. Her eyes were bloodshot, nose red, cheeks flushed, hair wild. No apology. No eye contact. Just a *not tonight*.

The words almost didn't compute. After waiting outside in the chilled mountain air, my T-shirt damp with fog, after trusting her when she didn't deserve it, choosing her and only her to confide in, all I got was *not tonight*.

I blocked the door. "Yes, tonight." Fury pulsed through me, a little dose of poison with every heartbeat.

She stared through me. "Mom and Dad are asleep."

"You and me tonight. I am sick of you."

A tiny flinch. "We can talk about it tomorrow, okay?"

I shoved her. I shouldn't have, but I did. She stumbled down the steps and fell into the long, uncut grass.

She looked up at me, and her eyes focused and hardened. "Okay. We won't talk about it tomorrow. You will never talk to Mom and Dad. Because if you tell them the truth, they will reject you. They'd never physically hurt you or technically love you any less. But they'll chalk you up as a loss. You know this, deep down. That's why you haven't talked to them yet. And nothing I can say will change that, Hazel. I am not the witch in the woods. I'm nothing."

"I hate you," I whispered.

"You won't talk to them," she said, her cold eyes boring into mine. "Promise me."

It only hurt so much because I already believed it. You have to bury some things in order to survive. Like the time I overheard Dad giving condolences to a friend whose daughter came out in college. As if she were dead. Mom gossiping with the ladies about a friend in a pantsuit, *she looks like an Ellen*.

They wouldn't stop loving me. I know that. But that's not enough. They're my parents. Loving me is the most basic expectation. I shouldn't even have to think about my father mourning me, as if I were gone. And why? Because he'd have to admit that his idea of me was a person who never existed? It has never been a secret. I have always been me.

If they really love me, why don't they want to know me?

I felt sick. And then angry at Beth for making me confront everything I'd forced myself to suppress. Because that gave me the uncomfortable feeling that, maybe, I was part of the problem. And that didn't seem fair.

"You're dead to me," I told her. "You are a dead girl."

"Don't call me that." Her eyes filled, as if it suddenly mattered what I did or said or thought about her.

"Dead girl."

Then I went to bed, and Beth began the process of destroying her life. I didn't care. How could I after what she said to me?

I didn't talk to my parents. What was one more year of living silently? At least, that's what I told myself. One more year in Ashling, and then the whole world was out there waiting. And it was filled with places where you don't have to live a silent life.

Now, though—now I have to act.

I arrive at the clearing and pull the items I've gathered from my backpack. I've made up my mind. I can't save Beth, save us, if I don't forgive her first. And the only way to forgive her is to take the first step myself, because she isn't capable of that. That means a leap of faith.

When Beth did the summoning ritual, she apparently believed it would work. After having read parts of Veronica's diary, I understand how Beth convinced herself that was true. What happened to Veronica was tragic on an ancient Greek scale. She never wanted to move to Ashling; in fact, she considered it to be the worst thing to ever happen to her. Her mother forced the move after a betrayal that tore apart their family, and what followed was a series of violent encounters between Veronica and her classmates written in hyperbolic, bloody, mythological language that's hard to interpret. If you took it literally, yes, you could believe the ritual could work.

Bad things happened in Ashling. It goes beyond the basic facts as reported, an unsolved killing of a sixteen-year-old girl. If I'm reading the diary correctly, there was an attempted assault, months of brutal bullying, and the cold-blooded killing of a pet. And as far as I can tell, no accountability.

I understand how someone could want to believe in the ritual after reading that.

I don't know if I can stretch my belief that far. I do believe in the symbolism of ritual, though—the power of symbolic gesture. I study the instructions for the ritual and set up the ceremony. I found all the necessary items exactly where I thought they would be—in the cabin.

First, I draw a circle of salt. I set out a series of pillar candles, black, white, and bloodred. I take the incense that looks like fragrant little fragments of amber and place it on a smoldering charcoal brick in an iron pot. There are a series of unmarked herbs, and I throw them over the fire. I study the words of the spell, written in a language I don't recognize, made more inscrutable by the fact that they're written out phonetically. There are three words I recognize—*Veronica Green* and *Cerberus*—which, according to the diary, was the name of her dog.

The temperature has dropped sharply, and I shiver inside my inadequate jacket. If there's a chance—a *chance*—that all of this is real, then what I'm about to do is incredibly stupid. Beth did this ritual and potentially ended up with a vengeful spirit trapped inside her body. If it *is* true—I'm about to risk the same thing. But what if that's the only way to free Beth?

To be on the safe side, I tilt back my head and pour a stream of salt into my mouth, choking it down. Salt is protective, according to movies anyway. I really hope that holds true in real life. I shake some down the front and back of my shirt and rub it into my hair as well for good measure. Yes, it's ridiculous, but not one thing that's happened since Beth first disappeared hasn't been ridiculous. And it's all scary as hell.

My phone buzzes and I silence it and open the spell Phoebe sent me. I take one last moment to study the unfamiliar words and illustrations, take a deep breath, and begin the ritual.

But after a half hour of chants and verses and symbols traced on earth, carefully, so carefully, nothing has changed.

SIX MONTHS AGO

"Fuck." Beth yanked their hand up as a thin trail of blood began to snake down their forearm. Beneath it, the offending shard of glass, a remnant of a discarded beer bottle, glinted in the moonlight.

"Ew." Amanda reared back, gagging. "What did you do?"

"I shanked myself, Mandy." Beth glared at her sarcastically and looked around for something to stop the bleeding.

But they were in the woods. People only came out to the clearing behind the school to smoke and drink—or take a break from class. Dressing wounds wasn't something you stole out of a school dance or cut class to do out here. Mac and Ezra were supposed to be right behind them with weed and more beers, but both were highly distractable, and everyone but Amanda knew Mac was trying to get Rosalyn Kesler on the side, so anytime he wasn't in plain view, that was a real possibility.

Amanda looked helplessly in the direction of the school. "Do you want me to get you a tissue?"

The cut was bleeding steadily and stung like venom. "First aid kit? Like a bandage maybe? Check the nurse's office."

Amanda scraped herself off the dirt and ran unsteadily toward the school, a tipsy blur of pink-and-white tulle. Beth stared, transfixed, at the bloody wound on their palm and the bottle fragment that had caused it.

"Fucking downstaters."

"We've been summoned."

Beth looked up, startled. A pair of unfamiliar teens gazed back at them, sizing them up. Both were unconventionally dressed, at least by Ashling standards: one wore a flowing black corset dress with lace gloves and a hat with a veil, and the other sported black jeans, a fuzzy, puffy sweater, and turquoise, cat-eye glasses that appeared to have no lenses. They looked like people you see in fashion magazines, confident and bold and magnetic. People dressed like this on television or at concerts, but not at school.

Beth flushed, embarrassed to have echoed their father's poisonous anti-outsider rhetoric aloud. The idea that newcomers didn't belong in Ashling was hammered into their head daily—it didn't matter if you were born and died in Ashling, if you weren't third generation, you *were* an outsider. Beth considered the guarding of the mountain from outsiders to be silly territorial bullshit. None of them belonged here. This was stolen land. The Whitmans, the Wendells, the Laurences, the Elwoods—they were all outsiders.

"You know," the one in the dress said, sweeping the glass aside with a designer boot and sitting next to Beth. "That was probably left there by a student. I'm Phoebe Crane, by the way. Unapologetic downstater."

"Jack Sawyer." The other one sat on Beth's other side and dug out a Band-Aid from an oversize messenger bag, holding it out like an offering. "Former downstater. I start here in September. Any and all pronouns work for me."

"She/her," Phoebe added cheerfully.

Beth hesitated. People didn't announce their pronouns in Ashling. Beth had decided, after years of parsing through a wilderness of feelings on the subject, that "they" described them best. "She" didn't make them flinch inside the way most gendered words did. It even fit, sometimes. Other times, not so much. But—and this mattered—"they" could get you harassed, injured, or worse if used in the wrong place at the wrong time. Beth had never trusted Ashling to be a safe place, but now that the federal government had *openly* waged war on trans people, some people who had previously kept their hate quiet were emboldened. Beth knew a good number of their classmates were conservative, but it was a slap in the face when Rosalyn, one of Beth's inner circle, had confided her relief that *He* had won the election because *She* was for they/them. Even worse was when Julie had asked Beth what the big deal was? *They* were only one percent of the population. *Deviants,* Randy had said. Amanda had ordered Mac to kick his ass, and he did. But Mac was always up for a fight, so it was hard to get a read on his motivation.

Mom chaired the Ashling women's book club, and when Shira Sanders had suggested a book by a trans woman, Mom had swiftly kicked her out and revised the rules to include books by cis women only. Dad just insisted trans kids didn't exist. It was tempting to argue, to prove him wrong, but not worth the danger of facing people who were more hostile, whose feelings went beyond disbelief to violence. Beth wished they lived in the kind of environment where it felt safe to just *be*. But they trusted their instinct above all else. And that meant being out only to those who they trusted totally and completely. Which did not include strangers in the woods.

"Thanks." Beth accepted the bandage and placed it carefully over the wound, smoothing the adhesive down firmly. "I'm—"

"Beth Whitman." Phoebe smiled. "We know who you are."

That was the first *off* moment. It felt like a clock ticking backward for a second before resuming its forward momentum.

"How?" Beth scanned the path for Amanda's return, for Ezra's appearance, but it was empty; the school's doors remained shut. For an instant, the batshit notion that Jack and Phoebe were ghosts, or maybe vampires, floated through their mind.

"Do you want to hear a story about a dead girl?" Jack asked.

"Everyone knows the story of Veronica Green."

It would take more than that to impress Beth on junior prom night. How could anyone top the countless versions of the Veronica story, each one bloodier, gorier than the last? Telling it was a basic requirement at parties and sleepovers, and you had to put your own spin on it. Sometimes she was a camp counselor, hunted down after wandering off-property. Sometimes she was prom queen, stalked out of the high school gym. She met her end by hunter's knife, rusty machete, screwdriver, crowbar, chainsaw, hatchet, or bare hands, depending on the teller. If you took on the story, you had the obligation to up the stakes, or at least the blood factor. Beth was highly skeptical that two newbies from out of town understood this ritual.

"No one knows the *real story*," Jack hit back.

"Try me," Beth invited.

He did.

"Everyone has their own personal version of hell. For Veronica Green, it was moving to Ashling."

"Weak start."

Phoebe raised a carefully shaped eyebrow. "Wait."

Jack ignored the interruption. "It was dark times for Veronica. Her mother had an affair, and Veronica never forgave her for tearing her away from her other mom, her sister, her friends."

Beth waved impatiently for him to speed it up. The backstory was fluff, filler. It was the blood, the guts that mattered.

Jack went on. "She wasn't what you would call a country girl, but her mother, an artist, was in love with the picturesque mountains. So she bribed Veronica with a dog, Cerberus, and a hive of honeybees, which Veronica tended meticulously. She was an animal lover. This was the way to her heart.

"But Veronica hated Ashling, and she didn't hide it. And Ashling didn't exactly welcome her. There was more to it, of course. In late-90s small-town life, no one bothered to whisper the gay slurs. This was the Matthew Shepard era. Look it up if you don't know."

Beth did know about this homophobic hate crime. It occurred decades ago, in another time and another place. Still, a feeling of deep unease crept over them. Not far from here, not long ago, a Black trans man named Sam Nordquist had been kidnapped, tortured, and murdered. His killers were never charged with a hate crime, supposedly because they knew him and some of them were queer. As if knowing the victim exempted a person from anti-Blackness and anti-transness, as if being queer meant that someone was automatically a safe person.

Of course it didn't.

"Veronica was bullied for being different, for her family

composition," Jack continued. "And once bitten, Veronica was the type to bite back."

"I'm starting to like Veronica Green."

The ghost of a smile crossed Phoebe's lips. "So do we. And if I made the rules, the story would end here. But it doesn't." She glanced at Jack.

"Veronica wasn't very popular," he went on, "but she was very pretty, and she lost her heart to the wrong person. He bet his friends he would sleep with her by prom night, and when she declined, he tried to force the issue. When *that* didn't work, his friends cornered her and locked her up on the roof of the school so she couldn't rat him out. She broke free and went straight to a teacher, who basically told her *boys will be boys, go home and sleep it off*."

"Fuck that guy." Beth's eyes strayed to the school, where the windows were glowing, dark silhouettes of students flitting by like flies. It would be comforting to tell themself that this sort of thing wouldn't happen today. But it would. It did. There never seemed to be any consequences.

"No argument," Jack agreed. "But as I said, Veronica bites back. She figures if the boyfriend didn't listen to *her*, he'd listen to her dog. He was chewed up pretty bad. And this is where the war starts."

"Cerberus bit off his dick and they all lived happily ever after?"

Phoebe grinned at Jack. "See? This is why Beth."

That was the second *off* moment. *Why Beth what?*

"Trust me," Phoebe said quickly, as if sensing their question. "The Phoebe Crane director's cut has a very different ending. But in the theatrical version, a group of the boyfriend's friends retaliated by attacking Veronica's honeybee hive with insect killer."

"That's bullshit." Beth had no love for bees. Ezra was allergic, and Beth had been personally victimized by the movie *My Girl* at a sleepover and had reoccurring nightmares about finding him dead in the woods, his mother's hive having gone rogue. Veronica's story was already vicious, but killing innocent bees was particularly sociopathic.

Jack shrugged a shoulder apologetically. "It's all bullshit, but that didn't stop it from happening. Veronica caught them and had the girls all kicked off the cheerleading team and the boys' gun club shut down."

This last part was more disturbing than all the rest. Because it almost certainly meant Beth's family was involved. Their mother was a cheerleader. Their father was a member of the Ashling High Rifle Club. Beth had once tracked down Veronica's obituary on a dare, and figured out from her death date that their parents must have crossed paths at school, something both were either too traumatized or too superstitious to discuss. And it was starting to become clear, at least in part, *why Beth*. "Tell me what my parents did."

Jack shook his head dismissively. "Veronica took away the one thing that made these guys feel bigger and stronger than her. They got *mad*."

"What did they *do*?"

"They killed her dog."

A lump formed in Beth's throat. As long as they could remember, they had begged for a dog, but their father had been adamantly against it. Now, they wondered. Was this why?

"One of them lured Cerberus off her property and into a coyote trap. No consequences—it was judged an accident. Her word against his."

"Jesus." The lights were beginning to dim inside the school.

Amanda had forgotten all about them. Ezra wasn't coming. No one was coming.

"Well," Phoebe broke in. "His word and the police."

"Bullshit," Jack said, his eyes cold and hard. "Veronica was a warrior. Cerberus was her heart. They knew the only way to take her on was to kill him. Fucking cowards."

This was not the story Beth had been told their entire life. It was worse than the versions with machetes and chainsaws and hockey masks. It was dead bees and dogs. It was deliberate and malicious. It was all the worst you could ever imagine about the people you always feared you had a reason to fear.

And it turned out, you were right to worry.

"I don't want to hear the rest." It had been a mistake to let the outsiders in, because the story was a trap, and Beth could see that now. It wasn't just a story, it had a dark, beating heart, monstrous jaws, and it wanted *Beth*.

"You know the rest," Jack said. "Or mostly do. Veronica knew these guys owned this town, and the only way to get to them was to hurt their pride. So she decided to go after the ringleader and burn down his family's gun shed.

"But they caught her in the act. The whole gang—drunk, riled up, adrenaline pumping. They grabbed the guns. What started as a chase through the woods devolved into a hunt. No one knows who fired the fatal shot. Just that Veronica was found dead with a single gunshot wound in her stomach. She turned to face them in the end."

Beth was crying openly now. *A hunt.* "How can you know any of this?"

Phoebe pulled a battered, leather-covered notebook from her

bag. "For one thing, we have her diary. It doesn't cover the final night, but it tells us a lot."

"And for another..." Jack drew a deep breath. "Veronica was my aunt. My mom was thirteen when Veronica died, and she wanted justice for her sister. My grandmother forbade her from stepping foot in this town. She followed every lead until the case went cold. When my grandma died last summer, I uncovered a trove of Veronica's stuff from her attic, including her diary. My mom's a journalist, and she's pushing to reopen the case, but the Ashling PD was stonewalling her, so she decided to move us up here for a year to harass them in person. They lied to V's mother, but we have a different last name, and my mom thinks if they don't know who she is, they might let their guard down. But she's wrong. It's going to take an unorthodox approach to get to the truth."

"Enter me." Phoebe bowed. "An unsuspecting art student minding my own business. I get a text from a random mutual that some Jack Sawyer needs to talk to me about a matter of life and death." She elbowed Jack in the side. "It turns out, Veronica consulted my grandmother for a summoning spell to contact Cerberus. Gran's a medium. I apparently come from a long line." She shrugged as if embarrassed. "I think Veronica may have established a link to the other side, and we could possibly use it to reach her."

"And you need me because..." It was obvious. Jack was related to Veronica. Phoebe, to the medium who connected Veronica to the spirit world. Beth was connected to one of the people in the chain of events that led to Veronica's death. And there was no way to know who pulled the trigger unless they became involved. The town had closed rank.

Beth *was* trapped, cursed even.

"Because," Phoebe said gently, "of all the villains in the story and their descendants, you're the one we thought we could get through to."

"That was a gamble."

"Was it?" Phoebe showed Beth her phone. On it was an online forum to discuss local issues. "We noticed one participant who consistently criticized this town. A person who sounded a lot like Veronica. Who we were sure would believe us. Only, there is no Liza Grass in Ashling."

"Veronica liked riddles and wordplay too," Jack added. "Liza is short for Elizabeth. Liza Grass sounds like Leaves of Grass, by Walt Whitman. Liza Grass is Elizabeth Whitman. Beth."

Beth nodded a curt concession.

"We're not wrong, are we?" Phoebe pressed. "We need you in order to bring Veronica's killers to justice. They're the law, the government, the media. They own this town. This case didn't go cold. It was put on ice. We can rectify that."

"With no proof?"

Phoebe glanced at Jack, her confidence faltering. "We have a plan, if you'll hear us out."

"Everyone knew what happened." A note of desperation had edged into Jack's voice. "They knew, and they collectively decided to do nothing. There's a seal of silence around the truth about what happened to Veronica, and the only way to break it is from the inside. That's why we need you."

Beth was quiet for a moment. "That's not the only reason, though. Is it? It's to send a message. That they're going to be brought down by one of their own."

Jack and Phoebe exchanged a look, then Phoebe spoke. "Is that something you want?"

Beth set their jaw. "I want them to know the call is coming from inside the fucking house."

Jack grinned, relieved. "They'll get the message."

14

BETH

I am a liar. I was born a liar.

The rest came later, by necessity. And all of this is necessary.

To clarify, I was born smiling. This is fact. My parents have pictures. While Hazel, firstborn, uncomplicated, and sinless from the start, dutifully screamed her lungs out, satisfying the doctors and my parents that she was healthy, I was silent, relaxed, the corners of my lips slightly curled back, and if you want to see it, you can: I was smiling. It's creepy as fuck. Because a newborn baby torn from the only environment that has ever been safe, nurturing, or comfortable is not happy. When you see someone smile and you know they're in hell, you shouldn't be thinking how adorable they are. You should be thinking *my god, that kid needs help*.

If I have ever appeared happy in my fake plastic Country Barbie life, that is a lie. If I seemed like I had my shit together eating lunch with school royalty, dating the son of the most revered person in town, looking and dressing the part of a loyal daughter of the Ashling legacy, that is a lie. It was a lie before I understood how deeply, fundamentally it was a lie.

The truth is this town is poison.

I understand the love my sister has for our home. I believe *home* is a spell, that being born and growing in a place casts a charm over you, binding you to it. The process of sinking down roots, becoming entwined in the earth, inhaling its scent, soaking up the chemicals that leach from the trees and the bodies of ancestors rotting in the graveyards—it makes home part of you, and when you die, you become part of it. That's some dark magic. Because home isn't always somewhere you belong. Take Veronica Green, who came here against her will. Who died and whose murder was covered up. And now, we breathe her, drink her, become her a little every day.

The entire town of Ashling is a lie.

And there will be no peace on this mountaintop until the truth about what was done to Veronica is known.

I will not allow it.

I park the car I stole from Hazel earlier this evening in Phoebe's driveway and glance over at her curiously. She's been texting frantically. "Problem?"

"We've been found out."

My heart begins to pound and my head feels light—like it did when I first met Jack and Phoebe. The night I learned the truth about Veronica Green. As a local legend, she was harmless. But the truth is, Veronica was a real girl my own age. She sat in the same classroom as my parents, ate lunch in the same cafeteria that I do now. Walked her dog along the same trails. Was shot with a real gun, a gun like the ones that hung in my own living room. Bled out and died in the woods where I've walked a thousand times, and was buried behind the church where I've sung hymns about execution, burial, and rising from the dead. The town wanted us to believe she was the fabric of fiction. The only fiction was that what happened to Veronica was somehow removed from the rest of us.

It could happen again. It could happen to any of their kids. Me, for example.

How dare they feel safe.

Phoebe catches me spiraling, places a hand on mine, and squeezes hard to ground me. "Bad choice of words. They're onto *me*. Gran. Hazel got the medium piece of the puzzle."

"Oh." My heart continues to pound, insistent and unrelenting. It's hard to defuse a panic attack once it starts, but at least this one didn't fully take over. Dizziness and palpitations aren't so bad if it stops there. If it progresses to chest pain, numb hands, that fish-out-of-water sensation when I can no longer breathe, I'm going to *believe* I'm dying, and no amount of rationalization will convince me otherwise.

My chest tightens. I kick open the car door, take a few steps into the woods, and inhale sharply. The frozen, pine-scented air is almost medicinal. I don't love much about Ashling, but I love the woods. You can trust the land more than the people living on it. The environment can be brutal—ask the half dozen hikers who die out here each year after underestimating the heat or losing their way in the snow, missing their footing on a steep trail or tracing the edge of the falls. But for me, the trees have always provided a safe haven when the rest of the world became suffocating. I lean against one for support, its rough bark firm and grounding against my skin.

"Are you okay?" Phoebe asks, concern etched into her face. "Come inside and sit for a minute. We can watch *Love Island* and eat Nutella pretzels." She assumes a Cookie Monster voice. "Mmm. Nutella pretzels."

I shake my head. "I should get back. I need to be there when Hazel gets home so she knows I'm okay." The millionth wave of guilt washes over me.

Which, of course, Phoebe clocks immediately. "Hey." She gathers me into a warm, protective hug. "You are not a bad person."

"I somehow don't see Hazel agreeing with you."

She pulls back to arm's length and looks at me intently, her deep violet eyes gorgeously framed by today's selection of impossibly long, delicately curled fake lashes. "We could have done it the other way. But that wasn't going to work, was it?"

That's the part that keeps me up at night. I tell myself I would let Hazel in on the truth if I could. And in the beginning, when we formulated our plan, I believed I made the right call leaving her out of it. Hazel was too close to Mom and Dad. It would have been too big a risk, and too much was at stake. I didn't know I could trust Hazel for sure. I didn't think she would believe two strangers over our parents. So I made the decision to shut her out.

But over the past few days as I've watched her spiral through confusion, anger, and desperation for answers, I've begun to question myself. Was it really that Hazel couldn't be trusted? Or did I not give her the chance because I was afraid if she had to choose sides, Hazel would betray me to protect Mom and Dad? It's not paranoia. She doesn't even like me. And the truth about Veronica's murder has remained buried for decades because people in this town are willing to lie, cheat, and rewrite history in order to protect their loved ones.

I know now, anyway, that Hazel doesn't *hate* me. Although,

anyone would worry when their sibling goes missing. And possession is concerning.

That's the other thing. We designed my performance so it would be equally effective regardless of whether or not anyone actually believed I was possessed. It was an act intended for a specific audience—Veronica's killers, and those who were directly involved in the cover-up. Either Veronica Green had returned from beyond the grave and they should be shitting their pants, *or* someone knew what Veronica knew—and wasn't going to play by the rules.

If the killers *did* buy it, we were going to scare the truth out of them by making them relive the past. Ashling is a superstitious town. In the tradition of *Vertigo*, where a socialite may or may not be possessed by a dead woman, and *The Tell-Tale Heart*, where a guilty man is tortured by the evidence of his crime, we would bring Veronica back into the killers' lives, and torture them until they confessed. The biggest flaw in our plan was that we didn't know who actually pulled the trigger. And when you have no hand to play, you bluff. We were going to unravel a decades-old murder cover-up with a ghost story.

But Hazel caught me way off guard. Hazel not only cared; she believed. After giving every indication over the past year, and let's be honest, most of our lives, that she has nothing but disdain for me. I've always admired my sister. Hazel is my hero, though I might die before admitting it. I love her bravery, the way she seems utterly unable to stop being Hazel. I sometimes feel like I don't know how to *start* being me. Hazel feels her way through life, and I only know how to think my way around it.

Maybe that's also why I haven't told Hazel the truth.

So here's the truth.

The real truth.

When I came home from junior prom, I had already sworn my secrecy to Jack and Phoebe about Veronica and what was to come. But even if I hadn't made that promise, I don't think I *could've* told her. Hazel is innocent. Everyone I choose not to tell the truth about Veronica remains innocent. What we decided to do involved making false statements to law enforcement officers, potentially obstruction of justice, since they would be investigating my disappearance.

It was nightmarish facing her for the first time after deciding I had to keep the truth to myself. Stumbling out of Phoebe's car that night, finding Hazel waiting for me in the darkness, fury radiating off her like a sickness. I already felt numb, emotionally lost. And the night wasn't over. That would have been too easy. Hazel was having *feelings*, and they had to be dealt with.

I'd stared at her, willing her to understand, wishing some unspoken sibling language would communicate that I needed the one thing she never seemed able to give me: time. Hazel never understood my need for space. The need to have secrets and to carve out a little world of my own, one smaller than Bethanhazel even.

Maybe that is selfish.

But it makes me feel safe. The world of Beth is solid, impenetrable. No costumes, no masks—I need to be able to retreat there sometimes. And unlike Hazel, I don't hate her for not understanding. I was just tired and sad.

"Not tonight," I'd said. All the strength left in my body and heart and mind was summoned into those three syllables. *Not tonight.* It was a request, a plea. Give me time, Hazel. Let me build up more strength before I face them. Before I face you. There is nothing left of me right now. I am a ghost. A fucking monster.

I watched my words evaporate in the air between us like smoke.

She moved in front of the door, blocking it. "Yes, tonight."

My heart pounded, a second panic attack building steam as reality set in. "Mom and Dad are asleep," I whispered. But they could wake up. Then I would have to face them. And I couldn't, I could not, I could never.

"You and me tonight," she pushed. "I am sick of you."

Each word slashed like a knife in a horror movie. *I. AM. SICK. OF. YOU.*

I drew a sharp breath, tried to rationalize through that fucked-up feeling that my lungs were no longer absorbing oxygen and I was about to asphyxiate right there on my feet without Hazel noticing anything was wrong. "We can talk about it tomorrow, okay?"

She shoved me. My head was already spinning. It wouldn't have taken much to send me sprawling, but it felt like a long fall, like *Vertigo*, where he spins and spins like a top against a swirling spiral. And then I was lying in the grass, and there was a giant earthworm under my left hand, and it made me think of Veronica, dead in the woods, what happened to her body, and I had to hold in the vomit and a tidal wave of tears. But I'm good at that. I've always been good at holding it in, saving it for Beth world. Because in the real world, the less pain you show, the safer you are. So I choked down the vomit, the tears, the truth, and I said what I had to say to protect Hazel. And it will always haunt me.

"Okay. We won't talk about it tomorrow. You will never talk to Mom and Dad."

She opened her mouth to argue, and I clenched my fists and forced more out.

"Because if you tell them the truth, they will reject you."

She shook her head. "No, they wouldn't."

But they would. I was sure of this, or sure enough not to take that chance. Because now I knew what happened to Veronica Green, a girl who was bullied for having two moms. Veronica chronicled this in her journal. She named names. It's not why she was killed. That came later. But thanks to the diary, I know a lot about our town and my parents I can never unknow. Our mother was one of the cheerleaders involved in the beehive incident. Our father was one of the deadeyes. It's why I had to say yes to Jack and Phoebe. Veronica is a lie my parents told. She is proof that they are not who they pretend to be. They are not safe people.

The worst part is that if Veronica and I swapped places, my parents would have done the same to me. Hazel too. Either of us could have been the body in the woods. Because most of the people of Ashling, including our parents, do not think the life of an outsider is worth incriminating one of their own. And they would see us as outsiders too.

I wanted to tell Hazel, but there was no way to do it without telling her all of it. And everything I knew convinced me that I could not allow Hazel to trust my parents.

So I said the worst thing I have ever said to my sister. *That they would think of her as a loss.*

She told me she hated me and that I was dead to her.

And she called me dead girl.

I asked her not to.

But again. Hazel doesn't listen.

Then I followed her inside, took every gun from the house and buried them in the backyard.

Because I don't know which one of the deadeyes pulled the trigger.

And not loving us isn't the worst thing they could do.

Now, Phoebe squeezes my hand again, hard, to bring me back to the present. "You have done nothing but protect her."

I hope so.

15

HAZEL

The walk back to the house from the woods feels eternal. Black oceans of pavement stretch endlessly between home and the forest where the call happened. Where the wrong daughter, not smart, not a hero, not the *type* to save the day, performed a spell to recall the lost soul. Pretty sure, but not totally sure, that spells are not real. Pretty sure, but not one hundred percent sure, that the lost soul must be that of a teenager and not a demon, god, or monster.

The wrong daughter can't walk much farther. Her arms and legs are sandstone. Her stomach aches, a gnawed-out hollow. A few more steps and she'll be home.

At the end of the road, the house feels strange, somehow off. A walled and carpeted graveyard, soundless and unnerving. The dog's asleep, but he wakes and retreats. The others sleep on. A mother who has fretted herself half dead. A father who doesn't understand where he went wrong. The Other, Beth, asleep on the bed, peaceful and well.

For now.

Only a fool would summon a demon to do her work. A demon has her own agenda. A demon doesn't care how many days you got to spend on earth, or who cut them short, or whether that hurt. A demon hopes that hurt a lot. A monster may be loyal. But take care whose monster you call.

The Other would know better.

But not the one who preceded them both. The legend's daughter of blood and earth.

Here's the th ng.

When Veronica attempted the recall spell, years and years ago, she also hoped she would cause a lot of hurt. She had been wronged, a soul had been taken from her, and she wanted to recall a soul to avenge her loss.

But she was dead before revenge could be taken.

Until now.

16

BETH

When I wake, I can't breathe. Panic starts to set in until the fog of sleep lifts, and I realize *why* I can't breathe. Hazel's face looms inches from my own, her hands planted on either side of my skull, her knees drawn up closely, digging painfully into my chest.

"Get. Off," I gasp.

She stares down at me, blank-faced. "You haven't been honest to me."

"Off." I struggle to push her off with the full force of my arms and legs, but she seems to have gained ten tons overnight. Her face is chalk white, freckles standing out starkly against her ghostly skin, and her dark hair tumbles down chaotically, brushing into my eyes, falling into my mouth when I try to speak.

"Tell me the truth," she says. It's clear she has no intention of budging. Deep, bloodred spots are beginning to cloud my vision, so I nod, choking and swatting at her, until she shifts back and stands.

She sits at the edge of her bed, swaying slightly, like the effort has cost her a lot of energy.

I scoot to sitting and cross my arms over my chest protectively, my lungs bursting. "The hell is wrong with you?"

"Come clean. Just come clean."

My gaze strays to the door.

"They're at a town assembly."

At this hour?

I glance around the room for my phone, but it isn't here. Phoebe has it for safekeeping, to avoid it being confiscated and our plan being discovered. We swore not to break character. The whole plan rests on having the guts to push a bluff as long as necessary. So just this once, the bad guys don't win.

She taps herself on the chest. "Not the enemy. Remember?"

I twist my hands in my lap. The guilt has been crushing. "It's not that simple." I'm already losing the narrative. Shit. I was so on top of this. There is one shot at getting this right.

"Beth. Haven't you let me down enough?"

That is so unfair. I have tried, time after time, not to let her down, not to exclude her, not to shut her out. And I am sick and tired of her telling it wrong. A lot of what has happened between us is my fault, but not all of it. Like when Hazel came out to me, then shut me down when I tried to open up to her. And that is not something I do lightly.

Because while Hazel wears her heart on her sleeve, I keep mine under armor. Three people know I had a girlfriend before Ezra. Julie, my first hand-holding, note-passing girlfriend, Ezra, and Amanda Laurence, the matchmaker of our group. I would have told Hazel if she didn't hate my friends. But she does. Julie and

I broke up, because people change. I met Ezra and was charmed by all his contradictions. He's the son of a rural preacher who has a pride sticker on his skateboard in a town that's not exactly queer-friendly. An athlete with average grades who reads moral philosophy for fun. A gun owner and AOC fanboy, equally devoted to hunting trips with his dad, trans rights, and socialism. Hazel is wrong about Ezra. He has the biggest heart.

Breaking up with Ezra was the hardest thing I've ever had to do, besides lying to Hazel. But he couldn't be trusted with Veronica. His father is a Deadeye. With *everything* else. Ezra was one of the first people I came out to. He's bi himself, though he's low-key about it. His first crush was on a Yankee (as a Sox fan, one of our major disputes) and his first heartbreak was the only out guy at school, who moved away halfway through ninth grade. We started out as breakup buddies and became close friends. Then, later, more. I trusted him with the information closest to my heart: that my gender doesn't fall on either end of a binary. He was a little confused at first, just about the fact that I don't fit certain stereotypes. "You *look* like a girl," he'd said, like this might negate years of confusion, depression, visceral reactions to being called *girl, woman, female*.

"That's gender presentation. Not identity. And that's how it's safe to look in this town."

He apologized. Even allies forget sometimes. There are no out trans people I know of in this very small town, and I don't blame them one bit.

"You don't owe anyone androgyny," he affirmed. And that was that. Ezra gets that I'm okay with the *she* everyone is used to, but I don't love it. So he avoids saying it. He affirms and supports. I don't have a lot of people in my life to do that.

The only other time he's ever questioned me is when he asked, "Still Beth?" The answer is yes. A name is personal, and mine ties me to my sister. It might be the only thing that does. I am half of Bethanhazel. I am Beth Whitman. I am *not* a girl. My pronouns are they *and* she, partly for safety, and partly because *she* doesn't actively hurt me the way *girl* does. I don't know why. I just know how I feel. I prefer *they,* but for now, I accept *she*. That should be enough. For Ezra, it is. For Ezra, I'm always enough.

That's why I trust Ezra Elwood with my heart.

I wish I could say that about Hazel.

Because when I said right back to her, "How gay do you think I am?", her answer said it all—"God Beth, not everything is about you."

That's the problem with Hazel. Anytime I try to share anything personal or difficult, she shuts it down. Then she calls me a liar and blames me for the fact that we're not close. If I am a liar, Hazel made me one—I can shout the truth, scream it at the top of my lungs, and she will only hear what she already believes.

I love my sister. I *miss* her. I've been losing her in pieces as long as I can remember, and not because we have different friends, interests, personalities. It's because we're not real with each other. And any time I try to be, she refuses to engage. Hazel has her version of the world, where she chooses the villains. I don't always want to hear the truth. The Veronica truth is almost unbearable. But the alternative, a growing chasm between us that widens endlessly until we're on opposite sides of the universe, is so indescribably worse.

She looks at me now, waiting, expectant. Her words echo in my ears.

Haven't you let me down enough?

I want to say *no*. I don't think I have let her down. I have tried to be family. She has always pushed me away, closed her ears, rejected the people I have surrounded myself with and the things I loved, my offerings of friendship and truth and shared experience. The only things she has ever wanted to share are fantasy. But that's not what she wants to hear. Nothing will get through the barrier she has built between us. I don't even know who Hazel is anymore. That's the truth. And I still give in, every time, in hopes of winning her back.

"Fine." I close our bedroom door softly and lock it in case Mom and Dad return, then turn around to face her. "I'm not Veronica Green. Veronica Green is dead."

"Yeah," she says dully. She wraps her arms around her stomach and leans forward as if in pain. Her expression is tight, strained, the way I feel when I have bad cramps—the kind that make you genuinely question whether there could be an alien inside you, desperately clawing its way toward the sunlight.

"Do you want me to grab you a Tylenol?"

"Just talk."

"The night I came home late from junior prom."

"When you betrayed me."

"I'm sorry, Hazel. You don't know the whole story. That was the night I met Jack and Phoebe. They aren't who you think they are."

"You don't know that."

I slam my pillow down on the bed, frustrated. "You are making this incredibly difficult."

She shrugs, then gags into the back of her hand, shakes it off, and waves me on. "Go on."

"Phoebe told me what you already know. She's a descendant

of a long line of mediums. One of them knew Veronica Green. Veronica approached her for a spell to summon a spirit after her pet died. Several, actually. A dog and a hive of honeybees."

Hazel nods. "The journal has all of that. She called the dog Cerberus and wrote an elegy for the bees."

"Okay, do you want to tell me what happened next?" I ask, slightly annoyed and slightly impressed at how easily she guessed my laptop password. Hazel stares defiantly, and I continue, "Veronica either lied or was confused about the spell, because she didn't use it to summon her dog. She summoned, or tried to summon, a demon."

"The revenge club. Echo Foxes."

"Right. She was obsessed with Greek mythology, spiritualism, and the occult. She compared herself to Persephone, forced into the underworld against her will, but she named herself Echo, a mountain nymph who had the ability to repeat last words, combined with Fox—three sisters who claimed to communicate with the dead. Veronica performed a summoning, it went wrong, she was killed, and the case went cold."

"That's not the whole story."

"Of course it's not. Someone killed the bees, then the dog. The summoning was her final move in an all-out war."

"And she lost?" Hazel says. It almost comes out as more of a challenge than a question.

"Well... She died, yes. But what if we could get justice for her? Make her killers pay for what they did?"

A spark of interest flickers in her eyes. "How?"

"Force them to confess. Confront them with their guilt. *Tell-Tale Heart* the fuckers."

I wait for an answer, but she's silent. The room is quiet except for the muffled hum of the bathroom fan down the hall. I hadn't noticed it before, and I wonder how long Mom and Dad have been home.

"But who shot the gun, Beth?"

Before I can answer, I hear the bathroom door open and close. The fan switches off, but the humming doesn't stop. It's not so much a humming. It's closer to a buzzing. My stomach tightens and a sour taste gathers on my tongue. *How long has this sound been ringing in my ears, and where is it coming from?* Hazel stares blankly at me, the ghost of a smile resting on the corner of her lips. My eyes drift to the closet door, following the sound as it slowly rises, dread settling over me like a thick, heavy blanket.

My first thought is *please, please not my dog.*

This is what happened to Veronica, isn't it? Before she lost her life, she lost her dog. If you're lucky enough to make it to seventeen without being murdered or having to bury a family member or a friend, that's among the worst things life can throw at you. Because nothing hurts worse outside of the realm of human suffering than the death of a pet.

I approach the closet cautiously, and the dread builds until I can no longer stand it. The buzzing is louder than it should be. It's unnaturally loud, *swarm* loud—and just as my fingertips touch the doorknob, the word materializes in my head: *honeybees.*

I startle and turn to Hazel.

A terrifying smile stretches wide across her face, exposing her teeth the length of her jaw but leaving her eyes dead, untouched.

"Hazel?" My voice comes out a papery rasp.

"The girls were promised springtime," she says. But she slurs the words. They come out melted, fused together, like "the grrls were promst sprngtm."

I stare at her, uncomprehending. I know that line. It's from one of Veronica's poems.

She stands, and I open my mouth to scream, to cry, to ask forgiveness, but none of that happens. Instead, I collapse against the closet, tears streaming down my face, and the pressure nudges the bifold door open a crack, freeing a giant cloud of black, buzzing flies. The stench of death hits then. I stare, unable to look away from the blooming red cloud on Hazel's white T-shirt, an almost heart-shaped mark where she had been clutching her stomach. She approaches, her expression so hard, her movements so rough and jagged that I don't know her. I do not know her. I am terror, and I know nothing else.

The Stranger kneels before me, takes my chin in her hand, examines me curiously, like I am an alien specimen, and says, "All of that's well and good. But that's not how you get revenge."

17

HAZEL

Here's the th ng.
Here's the th ng.
Here's the th ng.
Here's the th ng.
Here's the th ng.
Here's the th ng.
Here's the th ng.
Here's the th ng.
Here's the th ng.
Here's the th ng.
Here's the th ng.
Here's the th ng.
Here's the th ng.
Here's th ng.
the th ng.
th ng.

t h i n g.
t h I n g,
t h I A n g,
t h I A N g,
t h I AM N g,
t h I AM NO g,
t h I AM NOT DEAD g.

18 BETH

It's not my dog.

The rotting corpse in our closet is not Artax.

I discover this when he bounds into the room as the front door slams shut and he dives under my bed, whimpering loudly. I throw myself at him, my face wet, and try to pet him, but he's too anxious to deal with me. He yawns and trembles and shows me his teeth when I attempt to give him a reassuring pat. We huddle for a moment, listening for the Stranger, but all is silent. She's gone.

I jump to my feet, wiping my eyes and nose on my sleeve, somehow strengthened by the anger tearing through me at the idea that someone, some entity, has fucked with my dog. I press my forearm against my nose to suppress the horrible smell and throw open the closet door. The sight alone makes me gag, filling my eyes again.

On the floor, nested in a pile of my old ballet costumes, frilly skirts, gauzy scarves, tights, and leg warmers, is a heap of dead animals, small woodland creatures: squirrels, chipmunks, rodents, maybe a rabbit or two. But they weren't hunted, at least not with a gun or crossbow. They've been torn into and seemingly eaten raw, messily, inefficiently, as if the predator didn't know what it was doing—or was *tasting* the prey, the way they say sharks sometimes make a mistake, bite the wrong species, and move on.

But what predator would stack its rejected meals in my closet?

I approach the bed again carefully, lift the dust ruffle, and examine Artax. He's panting heavily and snarls at me slightly, and I get that terrible *Old Yeller* fear. What if he has rabies? Artax was part of the Veronica plan, but he is my dog, and I would lay down my life for him. We figured if I was going to play the part of Veronica, I needed a Cerberus, and I picked him out from a nearby shelter. But he's not Cerberus, he's Artax. He was never *just* a part in a plan, he is the missing piece in my heart, the dog I begged for since toddlerhood. He chose me as much as I chose him. He has always been wary of my parents, unaccepting of strangers, and merely tolerant of Hazel. Artax and I are a matching set. What scares me is that I don't know what happened to Artax before he became a part of my life. I know nothing about his previous owners. It *is* possible he never had a rabies shot before. And it's possible he was bitten. It's rare, but rabies can have an incubation period of six months to a year. Artax would have been vaxxed at the shelter just shy of six months ago. I watch him, concerned. There's no trace of blood on his fur or muzzle.

What's the alternative? That in an *unbelievable* twist of fate, the plot Jack, Phoebe, and I have been faking has come true, and Hazel has been possessed by Veronica's revenge demon?

Our landline rings, and I leap back, startled. I wait for my parents to answer, but it goes on, uninterrupted. Are they not home yet, and if so, who the hell opened and closed the bathroom door earlier?

I tiptoe out of the bedroom and pick up the phone in the kitchen, peering out the window. Both cars are missing. "Hello?"

All I hear is buzzing on the other end. My heart sinks into my stomach. This time, I know it's not the sound of flies.

"Hello?" I try several times, and then hang up, panic rising in my chest. Why did I ever give up my phone? That's an obvious invitation to the universe to be murdered, even without a potential demon on the loose. I dial Phoebe's number from memory feverishly.

"Hello, darling," she says in a Sally Bowles voice.

"Mayday. Abort. Mission failure. The coconut milk—"

"It's off. What happened?"

"Hazel is possessed," I tell her. "For real. Or thinks she is. I haven't figured it out. But there are mangled woodland creatures in my closet, my dog is not okay, and I don't have a car."

"Okay… I'll come pick you up."

"And honeybees." I close my eyes, aware that I am not getting across the gravity of the situation. We have been playing with fire.

"Be right there." She hums as she hangs up the phone, regular speed.

"Slam the phone down!" I say frantically.

I hang up, then pick up the receiver again and dial a number I haven't used in a long time.

But Ezra doesn't answer, and I have a *My Girl* trauma flashback. The sleepover at Amanda's where her big sister promised we would love this movie her mom made her watch, and *of course* it was the adorable story of a death-obsessed weirdo (*Bethhhhh!*)

and her love interest, the boy next door with the severe bee allergy (*Ezzzzzie!*), until the bee kid is stung to death and the Beth kid has a panic attack at his funeral while all the adults stand around watching impotently like the point of being an adult is to silently witness pain.

I always thought of that kid from the movie as me, standing over Ezra's body, his face covered in little welts, because the marks of death can't always be covered with costumes and makeup. Sometimes you can't look away.

The image in my head of the bee boy morphs, as it inevitably does, into Ezra's. I see his square jaw and delicate lips, soft lashes and round cheekbones, a face that should always be smiling and never still, with his deep, wishing-well eyes that flash summer warm to elfin evil like a mood ring. I blink, and Dead Ezra lies in a casket in his father's church, eyes closed, and not sleep closed, death closed. Lips closed, death closed. In the best of situations, dead people never look asleep; that's another mass delusion. Stung to death by honeybees is not the best of situations.

I slam the phone down and run outside just as Phoebe's car appears at the end of the driveway. She hits the brakes and I sprint out to meet her. Phoebe does not like to mar her perfect antique car on our weather-beaten gravel driveway. I mostly don't blame her. It's uneven, with big rocks and deep mud valleys. Dad is going to have it leveled off one of these days, but it's not at the top of the list of his projects.

I fling open the car door and tumble inside, short of breath.

Phoebe waves calmly, but she doesn't pause singing along to "Stranger Than You Dreamt It" from *Phantom of the Opera*.

I stare at her in disbelief. "Phoeb."

"Elizabeth Whitman, greetings," she sings along to the tune.

"Do you remember the conversation we just had?"

She nods, still looking unconcerned. "You said Hazel was possessed." She glances over her shoulder and backs carefully into the street, heading back toward town.

"I wasn't kidding." I take my phone from her glove compartment, relieved it's been fully charged. I dial Ezra's number again, but once again, it goes to voicemail.

"But that's impossible," she sings with a dramatic expression. "'Cause we made that shit up."

"Okay, can we—" I turn off the music, and she makes a face at me. "You have to take this seriously. We created a road map for revenge, and I think Hazel set loose a demon that's going to execute it." I try Ezra again. Voicemail. Shit.

She sobers up. "Let's hope the fuck not." She chews her lower lip. "So what do we do?"

"I think we retrace the route we mapped out as Veronica's revenge tour: the school, the *Daily Journal*, Ezra's, Julie's, the house of lies. The Deadeyes landmarks. And we make sure our revenge fairy tale is not coming true."

"You do realize how impossible that is? Fairy tales don't come true." But she takes the turn toward Ezra's.

"The school is the first stop on the revenge tour."

"And you've been trying to call Ezra since you got in the car, so we are obviously going to check on him first."

"I love you."

"You should."

I wish impossibility were an effective charm against evil. I'm not sure it is, though. Not sure enough. I try Ezra one more time and then turn my attention to my own voicemail. Fifteen missed calls, a new text from Mom confirming that my parents *are* at an emergency town meeting, and one voicemail since last night, but nothing from Ezra. I listen to the voicemail from Jack.

"Hey Beth. No idea when you'll get this, but call me when you do." He pauses and I hear voices arguing in the background. "I'm worried about Hazel. And I wonder whether we need to think about just ending this. You're right, they're definitely starting to crack. But so is she. I don't think she's as strong as you think she is. She's obsessed. Like Veronica-obsessed. And look what happened to V. Shit. I just lost her. She ran off into the night. Hazel, I mean. In my experience, that rarely bodes well. Call me."

I text him to meet us at Ezra's, then look to Phoebe. "You didn't tell me Jack wanted to give up too."

She avoids my gaze. "I didn't want to influence your decision before you had a chance to think it through. Beth, we have invested a lot in this, but you have *really* gone all-in. You faked a kidnapping. You lied to the police. There are consequences for coming clean."

"We considered all of that before committing to the plan. The consequences are worth it to reopen a cold case and bring a killer to justice."

"Yeah. *If* that's what we accomplish. If we give up halfway through and nothing changes? Are you still willing to take accountability?"

A flare of rage ignites within me. "This whole shitshow is a result of literal generations refusing to take accountability. So yes, Phoebe, I am. I'd never mention your part, or Jack's, so relax."

"If only the *right* person would take responsibility for the *right* crime."

We drive the rest of the way in silence. When we arrive at Ezra's, the driveway is empty, and all the lights are on. The luminaries we set up earlier with Jack have disappeared, which Phoebe also notes with a disappointed frown.

"Deadeyes is gone."

I'm more worried about the front door, which has been left wide open, bright light spilling onto the lawn. Ezra's siblings are staying at his aunt's this weekend while his parents are away. But that open door still gives me chills.

"Where are the children of the corn?" Phoebe asks, her eyes wandering over to the empty swing set with an unsettled look, as if she can read my mind.

"Staying with their aunt." We approach the front door slowly. "The children have nothing to do with any of this."

"Agreed." She touches the door gingerly and pushes it the rest of the way open, then steps inside. She knocks on the open door and waits for a response, but none comes. "Innocent bystanders. Like Veronica's honeybees."

Right. The honeybees. I fill Phoebe in as we search the house for any sign that something happened here, one room, one closet, one hiding place under the bed at a time, starting with the main bedroom. "Hey, right before Hazel went all *I am the keymaster* on me—"

"Gatekeeper," Phoebe corrects, clearing the last bedroom, and we head down the stairs. "The servants of Gozer have highly gender-coded roles."

"Really? Now?"

She shrugs. "If you're going to make a pop culture reference, at *any* time, yes, do it right." She does a quick sweep of the kitchen as I tackle the living room—not much space to hide down here. Or stow a body.

"Okay. Right before Hazel went Zuul on me—"

"—very good."

"—she led me to two highly upsetting discoveries. One, she's been stockpiling dead rodents in my closet. Two—and I want to say this right—she was bleeding Veronica's blood. I think. Her shirt was blood-stained in the abdomen. It was new blood, incredibly freaky." I lead Phoebe back outside and head for the shed, the beehives, and a sense of dread settles over me.

She raises an eyebrow. "Okay, that's serious shit."

"Yeah. Like—try to fake that."

"Why didn't we think of it?"

"Focus. The third thing is that my landline started ringing as she left the house. And when I answered, all I could hear was bees."

Phoebe's eyebrows shoot up to her hairline. She glances toward the hives.

"Also, my dog was acting batshit. I was scared shitless. And before Hazel—or whoever—left the house, she said, *this is no way to get revenge.*"

I open the shed doors. We peer in, phone flashlights aimed into the darkness. A creepy assortment of tools greets us: chainsaws, axes, hoes, shovels that could definitely split a skull in two, an array of electric saws I imagine could dismember a body into bite-size pieces—or at least pieces that would make it very easy to dispose of without being found. And boxes upon boxes upon boxes of ammunition, along with piles of hunting gear. No guns—those are responsibly stowed away from the kids. Blades that could slice through bone, check. Shovels and flashlights, check. Plastic bags and bottles of bleach with thick rubber gloves along with weed killer, insect and rat poison, and potting soil, with stacks of seeds ranging from sunflowers and zinnias to pumpkins and summer squash.

Just your average, unsuspicious toolshed. And I'm not being snarky about that. We all have the tools to be a serial killer. If you think about it too much, you'd never leave your house again.

"No way to get revenge," Phoebe murmurs as we swing the door shut and venture toward several pastel-colored wooden structures where Mrs. Elwood houses her colonies.

"Right." I slow as we approach the hives.

Phoebe halts several yards away. "Why do we have to check the bee colonies?"

"Veronica's bees were attacked. Some kind of supernatural revenge spirit is accidentally summoned and announces that drawing a confession out of the killers isn't sufficient, and I suddenly get a phone call with nothing but the sound of bees buzzing on the other end."

"So the bees called you?" she asks skeptically.

"No, I think I was called by someone being attacked by bees. Someone involved in victimizing Veronica, most likely in the honeybee phase."

"That is twisted," a voice says from the dark, and Phoebe and I scream.

19

BETH

I whip around with my flashlight to illuminate Jack, with Ezra by his side, and Julie Merritt. I should be shocked at the sight of Julie. Furious at Jack for never mentioning her. But the entire world blurs around Ezra.

"You're alive," I say breathlessly, the wind, and intelligent thought, knocked out of me.

Ezra stares at me blankly. "Yeah?"

I deflate. He doesn't know he was in danger. If he did, he wouldn't care that I've been panicking that he might be dead. To Ezra, I'm history. For all I know, he moved on after the party. Maybe that's fair—everyone thinks I'm with Jack. That was the cover story for the time we spent together on the Veronica plot. I tried to stay away from Ezra, but our connection is magnetic, and it always pulls me back. I've been strict with boundaries—no labels, no commitment, everything behind closed doors. But I can't give up the time. Hours spent listening to music and doing homework together. Arguing about the politics of *DuckTales* or the morality of *Batman* over homemade popcorn and root beer. Making out in his room, wondering if this is habit, love, or a mild addiction, feeling guilty that I will always have the upper hand.

I don't have the upper hand now.

Ezra is looking at me like I'm a total stranger. I'm not sure I can handle that. Because before Veronica, he was the one person I could trust with anything. Becoming friends with Jack, who's genderqueer, and Phoebe, who connected me with a group of her amazing friends in the city, was life-changing. But there are things even Phoebe and Jack don't get. A lot of people who don't live in an ultra-conservative, super-isolated micro-town don't understand why you might *choose* to remain in the closet. That it's a matter of safety, and if you haven't lived it, you don't know.

I can't prove it, and I don't want to. Because the way you prove it is when someone is assaulted or dies. You shouldn't have to be murdered to be taken seriously. It's enough that anyone has, ever. It's enough that the majority of my neighbors and some of my friends idolize a president who campaigned on the idea that I should not exist. They loved me when they saw me as their good girl. They'll hate me for being me. I can't do this alone. I can't.

I feel myself start to tear up.

A lot of people don't believe places like this exist in New York. I know it could be worse. At least there are protective laws here. Many states don't have those. But sometimes, especially farther away from cities, law is one thing and reality is another. There are many towns like Ashling in New York, and nearby states. All over the country. Maybe not where law enforcement was complicit in a murder cover-up—but where you could reasonably fear for your safety. Especially if you don't have a solid and vocal group of allies. I wonder if things would be different here if we did. If that would be *all it took* to make a difference?

It's hard to explain to someone who's grown up in a culture of support why you would choose to make a decision they would never make. Like the choice to hide who you are, for now. Just for now. Jack once said to me, "I don't get it. Why let the bad guys win?"

I get his point.

But they're not going to. In a year, every queer senior in town with their head down and mouth shut gets to leave and never look back. Year after year, fewer people stay after graduation, and fewer return. If the bad guys think they're winning, they've never heard of the long game. In the meantime, we find each other and the safe ones among us. When you can't trust your family, you make one. I just wish more people who didn't have to fear for their own safety would speak up for ours. They have to be here. They must be. And maybe that *would* make all the difference.

I look to Ezra, wanting to tell him everything. He's part of the family I made. Now he's a stranger. Because I pushed him away.

"Beth."

I blink, so lost inside my thoughts I didn't notice Jack place his hands on my shoulders.

"I'm awake." It's all I can think to say.

He lets out a long sigh through pursed lips. "Stay with us." He walks slowly toward the bee colonies. "According to Phoebe, you picked up the phone, you heard honeybees buzzing, you thought someone was in trouble."

I nod. "Yes. I realize how it sounds. But you didn't see her. The Stranger."

Jack pauses at the colony and glances back at me curiously.

"That's how I'm thinking of the person that *should* be Hazel. She confronted me like she was Hazel, like she knew everything. She guilted me into confessing—"

"As long as someone gets to know the truth," Ezra interrupts loudly, to no one in particular.

I try not to let it sting. "—and then she informed me that our plan was inadequate and left. While bleeding from Veronica's gunshot wound, but not apparently in pain, and leaving behind a pile of half-eaten rodents in my closet."

"Ew," Julie says.

"So what…Hazel is a vampire now?" Ezra looks at me like I've completely lost the page.

"No," I say, my nerves wearing dangerously thin. "I think she's been possessed by the demon Veronica attempted to summon, and we faked. And now, the Stranger is out there wearing my sister like camouflage. She knows our plan and thinks it could be improved, and she informed me that the only thing she's interested in is revenge. Not justice, *revenge*."

Jack slowly lifts the lid of the bee colony, peers inside, then removes it entirely with a curious expression. "That's odd."

Ezra backs away swiftly. "I can't be close to those. Quick, painful death."

"I doubt it," Jack says. "It's empty."

He ducks his head down to investigate the colony with his flashlight and emerges with a shrug. "Nothing. Ezra, does your mom consolidate in the fall?"

Ezra glances at the small wooden structures. They're so cheerful and pleasant during the day. In the dark, they look like rickety tombstones rising from the frozen earth. "I don't know. She's always feeding them, and eventually she'll seal the hives to protect them from the winter."

Jack edges toward the next one. "It's common to consolidate weak colonies to form stronger ones as winter approaches, but..." He lifts the lid and pans the depths with his flashlight. "Nothing here either."

Ezra doesn't move an inch closer. "She was out here Friday. I saw her. Those bees are her babies."

Jack throws him a contemptuous look, and examines the last hive, the one with *Lillabee* carved into it in messy block letters, coming up empty. "So where did the babies go?"

Phoebe turns to me. "When you got the call with the buzzing, you wanted to come here first. But you didn't want to check the bees. You wanted to check for victims."

"Ezra's allergic. Just triaging. There's a time factor." I avoid Ezra's gaze.

Jack narrows his eyes thoughtfully. "But if the Stranger is doing the whole revenge tour, Ezra shouldn't be on it. He wasn't even alive in Veronica's time."

"The kids have nothing to do with any of it," Phoebe echoes my words back to me. "Innocent bystanders."

"Tell that to Freddy Krueger." Ezra slowly inches closer to the group, satisfied that the bees have flown the colony.

Phoebe looks at him with amusement and an inkling of respect. "Freddy fan?"

"Who isn't? Michael Myers and Jason Voorhees are *Jaws* on land. Mindless, soulless killing machines, basically unstoppable, no real lore beyond *but he was cray and now he's cray dead,* and let's not get started on that lazy shit. Freddy had a score to settle."

"Jason had a score to settle," Phoebe says, her favorite topic engaged.

"No," Ezra says emphatically, "his mom did. Jason is a lump of murder meat."

"This is great," Jack breaks in. "I love the breakthrough bonding going on. But if we can focus for a second on *our* lump of murder meat."

I glare at him.

"Sorry. Our beloved and hopefully stoppable killing machine? She obviously isn't here, nor are the honeybees. Ezra isn't a target because he wasn't among those who targeted Veronica. I think we have a clear objective. Follow the deadeyes map and find the Stranger before she hurts someone. And then, Phoebe, if you could just, you know. Undo it."

Phoebe stares at him. "Undo it?"

"The demon possession?" Jack glances at me for backup. "I think that would be helpful."

"I can't *undo it*. I didn't do it in the first place. Hazel read some ancient text Veronica tracked down, and I wouldn't know the first thing about how to reverse it."

"But it's in your blood. You have the gift." Jack squeezes her hand. "If anyone can do it, you can. You're the Echo Fox."

Phoebe's face goes ashen. She looks to me for help. "I did not ask to be the Echo Fox. The last Echo Fox died. And Hazel..."

"No one's going to make you do anything," I say firmly. "Though your grandmother might know something...right? Could you ask her? Anything is better than what we have now."

She sighs and starts texting as we head back toward the driveway.

Ezra hangs back and clears his throat awkwardly. "I'm done here, right? I'm not dead. You're not dead. You were lying to me the whole time. Everything is out in the open."

"Everything is not out in the open, Ez." I glance impatiently at the others, wishing there was a legitimate reason to stall so I can explain, but there is absolutely no time for that. Phoebe and Jack are climbing into Phoebe's car, and Julie is getting into her truck. Julie, who should definitely not be here. I turn back to Ezra. "Stay with me. I mean, don't be alone tonight."

He gives me a cynical look. "Because of the 'Stranger'?"

"I don't think it would be smart for any of us to be alone right now." I deserve the look he's giving me. Like he has no reason to trust me ever again.

"And is that your opinion as Beth or Veronica?"

"Come on." I swallow the lump in my throat. "I had a good reason not to tell you."

"Did you have a good reason to tear apart my parents' room?"

"Yes."

"I'm all ears."

"There isn't time now. Just come with me, okay? We can give you a ride to your aunt's place."

He sighs and nods, but he does not look happy with me. "Fine. But I'm not riding with you." Before I can respond, he's swung into Julie's truck, leaving me to climb into the back seat of Phoebe's car. I have a bad feeling about this. All of it. But at this point, we don't have much of a choice.

Jack scrolls through his phone and selects the song "Between the Devil and the Deep Blue Sea" by George Harrison.

"Adorable," I deadpan.

"It's on theme," he defends himself.

"So—school first? Deadeye number one?" Phoebe asks. "Should we skip it at this hour?"

"Why would we?" I say. "We're following the revenge map, not the bell schedule. And for all we know, the Stranger could bring her victims along for the ride. Skip nothing."

"Sounds good to me." Jack reclines his seat and begins to sing along with the music. Then he twists his head around and eyes me curiously. "When are we going to tell Ezra and Julie about Deadeyes?"

"When we need to."

But I haven't been completely honest with Phoebe and Jack, either.

Because one of them already knows.

20
BETH

The school looks undisturbed, the way Phoebe and I left it, having put the finishing touches on our deadeyes masterpiece. Nothing like a slash of red paint to liven up a boring pile of brick and cement. The aging old schoolhouse hasn't been updated since Veronica Green walked its pathetic halls alongside our parents decades ago. We did it a favor.

I'm only half joking. Because of all the institutions in Ashling that promise small-town values like community and family, the school is the biggest liar. School is where kids are supposed to be safe. Where adults are supposed to intervene when a girl is isolated and bullied. Are supposed to do something when a student reports that a classmate tried to assault her in his car, *right there* in the parking lot, under the lights, yards from Main Street, in plain-ass view.

Teachers aren't supposed to listen, nod sympathetically, then call the girl's mother and tell her that her daughter was drinking and send her home to sleep it off, with the reassurance that she'll be fine. That nothing happened, after all. Then watch as she puzzles over this, because she told him *exactly what happened*.

You'd think there would be some sort of karmic endgame. That the teacher would be fired in cosmic payback.

But he wasn't fired.

He was made principal.

Amanda Laurence's father wasn't an official member of the Deadeyes club. He was a first-year teacher, fresh off a tour through the Hudson Valley Community College SUNY circuit to collect a degree in education and settle back where he started. He eventually married a student who was a senior during his first teaching year, which is gross even if he wasn't her teacher. And he nepo'd up, like every Laurence in Ashling history ever has and ever will. That's how he earned an honorary place on our Deadeyes list.

"Wait." Ezra interrupts me as we gather on Main Street, just far enough from the school to avoid looking suspicious. "So Laurence was involved with Veronica's death?" He looks uncertain, as if unwilling to accept anything as truth from this point forward.

"Not her *death*," Julie says defensively. "He didn't kill her."

"Where exactly is the line?" Ezra asks, starting to look panicked. "The entire student body treats her like shit. King Dickhead assaults her. Laurence sends her home instead of taking a stand, and then—" He looks to me. "What happened with the bees?"

"The war happened. She had Cerberus attack King Dickhead, so King Dickhead had his friends kill her hive. She got the friends kicked off the cheerleading team, which, by the way, included Laurence's future wife, and his guys retaliated by killing Veronica's dog. She went after him, his guns, his property, and they chased her through the woods with a shotgun."

"Bang, bang," Jack says grimly.

"Fuck," Ezra says.

"I just find it so weird that no one ever heard this version of the story until now," Julie says.

All eyes turn to Julie.

"Yes, they did." Jack examines her carefully. "Everyone who was around when it happened knew this version of the story. They lied about it. What version did you hear?"

She pauses nervously. "The one where Veronica Green is killed by a hitchhiker."

Ezra rolls his eyes. "Even I never believed that."

Jack raises his eyebrows with interest. "Oh yeah? What did you believe?"

I exchange a glance with Phoebe, but she shakes her head slightly, a signal to step back, let it play out.

Ezra ticks off the possibilities on his fingers. "Killed by the boyfriend, the non-custodial parent, or some creeper the mother was dating. That's what statistics say."

Phoebe nods slowly. "Those are actually well-reasoned guesses."

"Not just a hot blond," Ezra says triumphantly to Jack.

Jack shakes his head in disbelief. "Dude, you're not even blond."

Ezra winks at me, and for a second, I feel hopeful. Then he seems to remember he's mad at me and his mask of indifference reappears. Ezra loves to play dumb jock. I think he acts a certain way, sort of clowning, masking his intelligence, because he's always been talked down to and treated like he isn't very capable. Like at some point, he found leaning into that and keeping an invisible wall up was less painful than standing up for himself. We all do that.

Jack is more than the sarcastic snarkbot he plays himself off as. He's incredibly sensitive and angry about what the murder of his aunt as a young girl did to his family. Phoebe is more than confidence and glamour. She carries around massive guilt about her parents' divorce and feeling torn between two sides of a losing battle. The reason she spends so much time in Ashling isn't because she has any love for the wilderness, with all the mud, mosquitos, dead cell zones, and power outages we have to offer. She likes being in a place where she's herself first and an extension of her parents second. We all struggle with that. Ezra is not the Rev. Jack is not Veronica. Phoebe is not her stressful parents. And I could never be mine.

My phone rings, and everyone quiets and looks at me. It's an unrecognized number. I answer cautiously, putting it on speaker, and my heart begins to thump hard and fast when no voice greets us. Instead, I hear a loud, unmistakable buzzing sound, dizzyingly clear.

"Hello?" Phoebe says tentatively. "Can you hear me?"

There's no answer. Just that sharp, relentless, ominous buzz.

Jack grabs the phone and hangs up. "I think we get the point." He looks uncharacteristically shaken. Everyone does. Of course they do. They have to believe me now.

"Okay." Phoebe paces, rapidly typing into her own phone. "We can do a reverse number search."

"That won't work for cell numbers. Virtually all personal numbers are unlisted," Jack points out.

"Shouldn't we...call someone?" Ezra says.

"Like Veronica did?" Jack asks. "Sounds great. You get on that."

"Hey," Ezra says sharply. "What did I do to you?"

Jack, for once, is speechless. He darts his eyes to me, and I shrug him off. *You're on your own, Jack.* I love him to death, but he lets his sadness and anger take over sometimes. He lashes out without realizing what he's doing, or maybe he tells himself it's okay to be an asshole because he's on the right side of things. I don't agree.

"He didn't do anything," Julie says in a conciliatory tone. "This is just really stressful."

"No," Ezra argues. "Jack is always like this." He towers over Jack, but not menacingly. His expression is hurt, frustrated, lost for reason. "You don't act like this toward anyone else. Is it because of Beth? Because I mean, you know that's over. Like, six feet under."

Another punch in the gut.

"No," Jack says, his eyes cast down, his voice soft. He looks like a kid all of a sudden, and I have the urge to hug him, to tell him it's okay, we're going to be okay. But nine times out of ten, Jack isn't a hugger. He's like a cat, sometimes very affectionate and sometimes prickly and standoffish. He needs to approach you. Let you know he's in a people mood. "Beth and I are just friends."

Ezra shoots me another betrayed look. "I think I'm actually starting to lose count of the lies at this point. Okay, well, it's been real. I bid you all goodnight." He turns and starts walking away, into the darkness.

My heart freezes in my chest and I run after him. "Ezra. I know you're mad at me, but please don't do this. Stay with the group tonight. When morning comes, you never have to speak to me again."

"Or we could start the clock now." He doesn't slow his stride or even glance down at me.

"She was sixteen, and she was alone," Jack says, and everyone stops.

Ezra turns to face him.

Jack's frame looks even smaller than usual with the streetlight washing down on him like a spotlight. He shivers in his lightweight knee-length sweater, leggings, and a thin, almost decorative vinyl jacket. "Veronica didn't want to be in Ashling. I can't imagine wanting to be in Ashling." His voice is quiet but intense, and it's soaked through with everything that's ever been unsaid about how hard it is to live in this town if you're someone like Jack, or me, or Hazel. Ashling takes care of its own, but it decides who counts and who doesn't. And then you decide whether it's worth fighting or playing along. Veronica fought. That's what haunts me most of all. She's the *one* person I can think of who fought. And they obliterated her, down to her very memory.

"I wish everyone would stop talking like that," Julie says, and again, Jack glares at her.

"Like what? Like this one generic, random patch of earth is special just because you don't know anywhere else, Jessica?"

"It's Julie," she says tensely.

"Sorry. Long day." He knows her name. I think she knows he knows her name. Things are starting to fall apart. "Ashling is special for exactly two reasons. One, I'm here. You're welcome. And two, it was the site of a highly solvable unsolved murder, subsequent cover-up, and grotesque celebration of that horror by turning her death into a local legend. Please. Your hometown is not special. Your college won't be special either. They're all exploitative academic puppy mills." He sighs an enormous sigh and shakes his head like a dog getting out of the bath. "Glad we cleared the air."

"Maybe she deserved to die," Julie blurts out, then looks horrified.

We all gape at her.

"Not deserved," she backpedals. "That's not what I mean."

Jack raises his eyebrows and blinks. "That's what you said, *Jessica*. How did my aunt deserve to be hunted and left for dead? Like, what's your reasoning exactly?"

"No!" She turns bright red. "No one deserves to be shot. I just mean—you said it yourself, there were two sides to the story."

Jack laughs in disbelief and looks around at the rest of us for backup. "I do not remember saying that."

Julie looks to Ezra desperately. "You know what I mean. She did stuff to them too. No one meant to kill anyone."

"We don't know what anyone meant," Ezra says. "We know no one called 911. That says murder to me."

"I can't believe this," Julie says.

"I can't believe you're defending a murderer," Phoebe says flatly, folding her arms across her chest.

Julie draws a deep breath. "I am saying it's more complicated than just a poor, innocent girl being murdered, and I can't believe no one is admitting it. Because the one thing no one ever wants to admit is when—"

But she doesn't get to tell us the one thing no one ever wants to admit. She's cut off by the sound of five or six gunshots in rapid succession, a bone-chilling scream, and a moment later, a siren wailing in the distance.

Phoebe lunges for her car. "Hold that nugget of wisdom. Fifty bucks says following the siren's call will lure us to the Stranger."

"You're right." I scramble into the car after her and glance over my shoulder. "Catch up with us." I look pointedly at Jack. "Do *not* lose anyone."

He frowns at Julie but nods. "Leave no man behind."

21

BETH

As it turns out, the siren's call leads us to Ed Wendell's house, but we're too late. The scene is total chaos—and total carnage. And it's clear the Stranger was here, or there's something else very wrong in the town of Ashling.

Police are swarming the scene when we arrive, and neighbors have already begun to amass. Jason Diaz is there with his mom and his aunt, and Mel Sanders and her mother—all of them live right up the street, and they look like they've come running out of their houses in pajamas. It's hard to get close, but even from a distance you can see there was a bloodbath here. Whatever went down went down on the front porch, which is eerily lit up by two oil lamps hanging on either side of the large oak door. Bloody handprints cover the blond wood, as if someone were knocking, banging, slamming their fists and palms against it, desperate to get in.

Forgot his keys or couldn't get to them, I hear a deputy say. It's hard to make out much of their conversation. Just snippets. *Dead on arrival.*

That much is obvious. Besides the buckets of blood smeared all over the whitewashed porch and steps, there are *remains*. Scattered in the grass, casually, like this is normal. I react the way I do when I see a dead animal, disemboweled, parts spilling out and scattered by a predator. I try to remind myself that to me, this is cruelty, but to an animal, it's survival.

Then my brain jolts back to reality, and it hits me like a baseball bat to the skull: an animal did *not* do this. I can already hear the theories: *black bear turning over trash cans down the street* and *coyotes reported by tourists in the park*. But this wasn't a black bear or coyotes. Because, like a calling card, the Stranger has left something to remember her by.

On the front door, hanging from the knocker, impossible to miss, is a sprig of bright yellow flowers, prickly and delicate, so distinct in their color and texture that I'm positive what they are, who left them, and who was meant to find them. And it means whoever or whatever the Stranger is, Hazel isn't completely gone. Because the symbol she's chosen as her calling card is witch hazel.

Ezra throws up in the bushes as soon as he arrives, and we relocate to the edge of the woods away from the commotion.

"I did not need to see that," he says.

"None of us wanted to see that." Jack gags into the back of his arm, looking pale.

"This is a nightmare." Julie looks toward the house. "Ed is dead. Oh my god, Mac. Someone should check on him." She looks to me pleadingly, but I still don't feel like speaking to her. Because Julie has been lying to us all along. Before her father was chief of police, he was one of the deadeyes. At the time, his father and brothers made up most of the Ashling police department. Law and order should never be a family business, but that's the Ashling way.

I knew the moment I was dragged into the station as Veronica, Julie was brought in to see if she could get me talking, and when that failed, they treated me like I was in a coma, unaware of the conversations happening right in front of my face. For hours I sat, propped up in a chair like a mannequin. I stared straight ahead, blank-faced, still, while Julie had a *conversation* with her father about how Veronica's death "was more or less an accident," how Chief Merritt understood Julie was mature enough to grasp the difference between murder and accidental discharge of a weapon, how much more harm than good would be done by bringing the past into the light, when it had all been decided years and years ago.

The town has moved on, Jules, you understand? She understood. And then, he'd suggested that she try to spend a little time with me or maybe even the odd one, Hazel, to gauge if we knew enough to amount to a problem.

Yes, Julie. We know more than enough to amount to a problem. But it's all our problem now.

Ezra is already dialing Mac's number. It hits slow, like a storm rolling in. It takes a second to process. The ringtone we all know too well, because it's so obnoxious only Mac *would* have it. The chorus to that old song "What Does the Fox Say" on a maddening loop. And it's coming from the direction of the house. Ezra rises slowly, and I put a hand on his arm to stop him.

"We should stay clear," Phoebe says hesitantly, but Ezra is already shaking off my hand and running. Jack looks at me for help.

"They were best friends since kindergarten," I say helplessly as we chase after him. "He knows Mac is a total douche, but he's still like family."

Ezra gets there first, but we all see it. The ringtone is coming from under the sheet that's been draped over the body. Not Ed's body. Mac's.

He drops to his knees and closes his eyes. "This isn't happening." A cop starts toward him as if to remove him, then sees that it's Ezra and backs off. Julie nods the rest of us over.

Jack hesitantly reaches out and places a hand on Ezra's shoulder. "I'm sorry, man."

I open my mouth, searching, but words are unavailable.

Jason rushes over, but he's not an Elwood, and he struggles frantically to get through the police line, because Mac was his friend too. Julie waves at the cop, and Jason falls by Ezra's side, hands clasped in anguish.

"No fair," Jason says. Then suddenly he rises and walks directly to Mel. "This is your fault."

She looks small and scared. "No, it isn't."

"You told him to die."

"He was being a bully. I didn't mean it literally."

"Yeah? Well, maybe you're a witch."

"Enough." Mel's mother takes her arm and pulls her away, leading her home. The crowd watches hawkishly as Jason's mother and aunt comfort him. But no one challenges his accusation. He's grieving and upset. But witch? Phoebe and I exchange a glance, and a shudder runs through me. And that's when I see them huddled at the edge of the scene, enveloped in shadows, easy to miss amid all the chaos.

The Deadeyes, live and in the flesh.

At least most of them. It's not suspicious. There's reason for all of them to be here. Ed Wendell is bowed over on his knees, his pale knuckles grinding into his eye sockets, heaving silent wails. Chief Merritt stands by his side like a bodyguard, grimly watching his officers work the crime scene. And the Rev crouches by Ed's other side, an arm draped around his shoulders, whispering in his ear. Apparently he lied to Ezra about getting back on the plane.

I stare at them, feeling paralyzed, like my shoes are fused to the pavement. And then, I start running. Merritt spots me first, and the look he gives me is like a smile and a snarl twisted into one. Like the Joker.

"Go home, girl," he says. As if he knows how that particular word cuts. And then, he spits on the ground.

Some people embrace the redneck cliché as an extra *fuck you*, just to let you know they embrace *all* the stereotypes, including the dangerous ones. He's one of them.

"Not." I can't say it fully. But I'm not. And I won't go home.

Ed looks up at me, his eyes bloodshot. "Did you do this? Did you kill my son?"

I stare at him, speechless.

"Ed. It's not her. That's Beth Whitman." The Rev tries to restrain him.

But Ed scrambles to his feet, wild-eyed and sputtering. "How do we know that? Can you prove it?" He looks at me again, and the terror in his eyes makes my blood run cold. "How do we end this?"

"Get a *grip*, Ed." The Rev glances at me, and his gaze is corpse-cold. "You're talking to a lying little brat who knows nothing."

Snap. "I know more than you think." All three of them tense. I have their attention now. "I know what you did to her. I know how you covered it up. And I know why this is happening."

The Rev laughs in disbelief. "You don't even know who she is."

"I was wrong too," Ed drones incoherently. "Not the dog. Not the dog."

Merritt casts him a severe frown and yanks him toward his squad car. "Last warning, girl. As a favor to your parents, I'm looking the other way."

That's the Ashling way.

"Go *home.*"

I look at the Rev again as he begins to slink back into the shadows. Ezra hasn't seen him. None of the others have seen him. A large prayer circle has already formed around Ezra, blocking us from view. "Who was she, then?"

He glances back at me and pauses, and when he speaks, it's like he fades back in time, an immature high school arrogance replacing the comforting, confident reverend. "A freak."

"Is that why you killed her?"

He stills, then takes a slow step toward me. "What would you do if I told you I did?"

A chill ices over my skin.

"Tell the police? Post about it on social media? Or maybe you think you have the guts to kill me."

He stares me down, and I feel defeated. Because I don't have murder in my bones. Not even for a killer. Not even when I'm cornered.

"So you're not sorry," I say.

"For what?" His eyes bore into mine.

"Why did you lie to Ezra?"

He suddenly advances toward me threateningly, and I flinch, aware that we're far enough away from the crowd to be swallowed by the shadows, that the noise of the crime scene would drown me out if I shouted for help, that he is the one who attacked Veronica in the parking lot, that he's probably the one who killed her. And he knows that I know.

He grabs my arms and grips them tightly, and I instinctively go deadweight, like a stubborn toddler; it's my best defense. It throws off his balance, and I kick him off me and grab a fistful of gravel and toss it in his face, my heart pounding.

"You little bitch." He crouches low, rubbing his eyes.

"I'm not a bitch." I back away quickly.

"Stay away from my family," he warns, and then he stumbles into the darkness, down the unlit, winding road.

I am thoroughly shaken. He was always most likely the killer. A part of me wanted to believe that he did it and was tortured by it. Maybe he turned to the church to devote his life to atonement. For this unspeakable wrong that he did, for this life that he stole. But that's clearly not what happened. Chet Elwood is not consumed by guilt. And he sure isn't an innocent man.

And I'm starting to piece together what happened after the murder. The deadeyes: Chet, Chief Merritt, Ed Wendell, and my dad banded together. Mr. Laurence distanced himself from them as much as possible after the girl he didn't believe was killed by the boy he afforded the benefit of the doubt. Mrs. Laurence abandoned the cheerleaders who had been booted from the team, leaving Ashling for college, and eventually returning to marry Mr. Laurence. And Lori Elwood and my mom, the two other cheerleaders involved, never spoke again.

Of course, the Deadeyes would be thoroughly convinced they were the victims. Bad guys always are. I slowly make my way back to the others, my heart filled with dread. If Ezra was mad at me before, he's going to love me when I tell him that his father is a cold-blooded killer.

22

BETH

"This is all wrong," Phoebe murmurs. Her eyes dart between the body, the bloody front door, the witch hazel, the ruined earth. "Mac should have been safe."

"Freddy's rules," Jack reminds her softly. "Punish the children for the sins of the parent."

"That's not Freddy. That's biblical," Ezra says dully. "Oldest trick in the book. Well. Besides creating the universe. That's a neat one to have up your sleeve."

"I was kidding about Freddy," Jack says. "Is that a real thing? Biblical rules, demons? Is the hit list actually the *children* of Veronica's enemies? Because if so..." He looks at me.

"We have *no* time to wait and find out," I say. "Ezra."

He looks at me, distracted.

"Still with me?"

He shakes his head and climbs to his feet dizzily. "No. Uh-uh.

I'm at my limit. I'm going home." He starts to walk, dazed, along the side of the road.

I run to keep stride with him. "But you can't go home. Not tonight. You saw what happened to Mac."

He swallows hard and nods. "Yeah, I've seen enough. I'm not sure why you care. You've done nothing but lie and hide shit from me for an entire year. Well, and poison your parents."

"Stop it." I plant myself in front of him, forcing him to stop. "First of all, I did *not* poison my parents. These rumors are getting out of hand. And second, I am sorry I lied to you, Ez. I'm sorry I didn't let you in, but it wasn't just you, it was everyone. I didn't tell Hazel either."

"That turned out well." He tries to sidestep me, and I block him again.

"I know you're devastated right now, but you're being a real dick."

He pivots and faces me, barely visible in the moonlight. "You have no idea. I thought you were gone. I thought you were worse than dead. But the whole time, in the back of my mind, there was this little voice saying *nah. Beth is lying. Faking it all. Beth would do all of this just to put everyone who cares through hell.* And do you know whose voice that was?"

"Hazel's."

"Hazel's. And my dad's. And *everyone's*, Beth. I was the only person who believed you wouldn't lie to me. And as a result, I was the only person you hurt."

"Hazel believed me in the end."

"And again, look what happened."

Tears sting my eyes. "I didn't do it to put you through hell. I agreed to play the part of a body possessed by Veronica Green to confront the people who killed her. Her case went cold not because no one knew anything. Because *everyone* knew, and they chose to bury it."

His expression softens and he steps in toward me. "But why should that have fallen to you? There are people who do this stuff for a living."

"When there's evidence," I insist. "We're all there is."

He takes my hands, and I have to force myself not to look into his eyes, or I'll tell him all the rest, right now. "You're not telling me something," he says.

"Ezra," I say softly. "You know your dad was part of it. You have to know that."

From his troubled expression, it's clear he does. "That's why you were in his room."

I nod.

"What were you looking for?"

I shrug. "Proof. Evidence. Something tangible."

"But you didn't find anything."

I hesitate, then reach into my pocket. It's not hard evidence, but if I want Ezra's trust again, I need to be completely transparent from now on. "Only this."

He studies the old, creased photo of Veronica standing next to a very familiar hive carved with the word *Lillabee*. But she's not alone. Next to her are a younger version of Lori Elwood, Mrs. Laurence, and my mom. And all three are smiling.

"I don't get it," he says. "*Lillabee* didn't exist until..." He trails off. "Oh no."

I nod. "That was Veronica's hive."

He looks up at me. "Were they friends? I thought Veronica didn't have friends."

I take the photo back, fold it carefully, and put it in my pocket again. I don't like seeing proof my mother was part of it. "Maybe they never were, and this was classic Ashling fake-friendly. But maybe in the beginning they were friends. And then things went wrong."

"My mom *stole* her hive? And built her company off it? After killing the bees? That's..."

"There's a reason our mothers were best friends and don't speak anymore. It must have something to do with Veronica. My mom has forbidden us to talk about her our entire lives. I think it's out of guilt. Maybe your mom sees Lillabee as a tribute. Or maybe it's doubling down."

"But it wasn't our mothers the night of the murder. My dad... How big a part did he play? He wasn't the one who actually...you would tell me that, wouldn't you?"

I hesitate. If I tell Ezra what his father told me, he'll assume the worst, like I did. But he didn't actually confess. "Only Veronica knows who pulled the trigger." That's the truth.

"So my dad was one of the deadeyes." He squeezes my hands hard, as if to steady himself.

"Mine was too. For all I know, he did it." Saying it out loud makes me sick. Though after tonight, I'm pretty damn sure it was Ezra's dad. "They were just a bunch of kids in a rifle club. The name came from the word deadeye, as in *expert marksman*. They had nothing to do with Veronica, until one of them tried to assault her on a date, she struck back, and it all went to hell."

"It was him, wasn't it?" He squints at me, like it's painful to say out loud. "Asking for Chet in the school, the song from the dance, the poems named a king, and he was prom king... My dad was the one who started it all. Wasn't he?"

I nod as the Rev's voice echoes in my mind. *You little bitch.*

Ezra draws a slow, deep breath. "And all this time, you didn't tell me because...what—you thought I wouldn't believe you? Or you thought I would double down on the whole bury-the-town's-dark-history thing? I thought you knew me. Even the bare minimum required to know I wouldn't make myself complicit in the murder of an innocent girl."

"A lot of people would lie to protect their family," I say. "I'm not naive. There's a reason Veronica's death had multiple witnesses and is still unsolved."

"But you know *me*," he says.

I don't answer. You can think you know someone and then find out what they did. The murder has changed the way I look at so many of the people I've grown up knowing and trusting, that I don't know if I will ever feel like I know someone again.

He takes my hand again. "You do know me," he repeats.

I pull away reluctantly. "You should probably know that your dad didn't go back to Miami. He told me to stay away from your family. And kind of grabbed me. I'm okay. But you should—"

"Did he hurt you?" His jaw tightens, fear in his eyes.

"No. But he might have if I hadn't run."

"Fuck that guy. I'm so sorry. I don't think I know my dad." He looks completely lost. I offer him my hand again and he takes it, but he looks like he doesn't remember what to do with it.

"Welcome to the club."

For a moment, the world fades around us. I find myself leaning in, my fingers interlacing with his. But just when I think he might kiss me, he gently pushes me away. “No time,” he reminds me. Only I would try to kiss someone after commiserating over our violent parents. Cool, cool, cool. But what happened was terrifying, and right now I want to feel the opposite of alone.

The longing I feel to reach out and grab Ezra's hand as we walk back to the cars together is overwhelming. So I do it. He casts me a curious look, but he doesn't let go. That's enough for now. This time, he rides with me in Phoebe's car. Julie is on her own at this point. But she follows us to Amanda's. Ezra calls his aunt on the way to check on his siblings, and he tells her to lock the doors because a classmate was just murdered and the killer is at large. Ezra is good at telling the truth without revealing more than necessary. I should get better at that.

Soon the town will probably be in a full-on panic. They should be. Everyone should lock their doors. We have a rough hit list for the Stranger, we think—the kids of every person who tormented Veronica, making *her* revenge list. But there's no guarantee it will stop there. Demons don't make guarantees.

Phoebe brings this up as we arrive at Amanda's house. It's peaceful, with no signs of any disturbance. Her parents' cars are gone, but that's not surprising, even though it's getting late. They wouldn't have missed the town meeting, and since I didn't see them at Mac's house, they probably went out afterward. They're always out with friends, at various clubs and meetings, maintaining their social standing.

But they do have one striking pattern: Mr. Laurence doesn't go hunting or drinking with the deadeyes; Mrs. Laurence avoids the former cheerleaders. I didn't clock this pattern until I read the diary, and then I couldn't not see it. The way Mr. and Mrs. Laurence selectively socialize around the people involved in Veronica's murder seems significant—like the way the grudge between Lori and my mom appears to tie back to Veronica's death. Whether it's out of guilt or self-protection, I don't know. I like to think my mother is motivated by guilt. But maybe it's fear of being exposed. Even in a town that protects its own, there has to be a dread that someday, someone will crack.

Amanda's older sister's car is parked behind Amanda's, in their nicely paved, sunflower-lined driveway. The peace and order of it all is reassuring, and everyone visibly relaxes.

"So—let's review what we know for a sec," Phoebe says. "We know Veronica wanted to get revenge on a specific group of people—we have a list of names. Three cheerleaders and four deadeyes, plus one honorary deadeye. We know the actual spell she used. We don't know for a *fact* that she summoned a demon or tried to. My grandmother is convinced she did. But that's our only real evidence."

"Uh…besides Hazel bleeding a dead girl's blood, chomping down raw rodents, and eviscerating Mac with presumably her bare hands," I argue.

"Oh, anyone could do *that,*" Jack says. "Phoebe has a point, though—we should be careful to sort out what we know and what we think we know. It could be the difference between life and death."

We reach the front door and knock, but no one answers.

Phoebe nods to me. "Try calling again?"

"I am." I try Amanda's cell, but I already dialed her three times in the car and she didn't pick up. Not reassuring, but also not unusual. Amanda doesn't answer the phone. Honestly, who does? But she hasn't answered my texts either.

"I tried her on the way over," Julie volunteers. No one answers her. "Are you guys going to keep up the cold shoulder all night?"

Ezra shoots her a look. "You said Jack's aunt deserved to be murdered. Like, read at least a summary of the room."

"Scan the room's Wikipedia page," Jack adds.

Julie looks to me for help, but I shrug. "CliffsNotes?"

She throws up her hands. "Okay, if you're all going to pile on, fine. I'll go."

A wave of anger runs through me. "You're not here to help. You're only here to find out what we know."

Her mouth drops open. "That is not true."

Jack points to her truck. "No one's stopping you from leaving. Your girlfriend's gone."

I turn to him. "What do you mean?"

He rolls his eyes exaggeratedly. "You definitely have to have a talk with your sister when this is over, because demon or no demon, she deserves better."

I turn back to Julie, white-hot fury filling every cell of my body. "You called her *the odd one.*"

She shifts uncomfortably. "I never said that."

"You said it six feet from my face. When you thought I was in some kind of trauma trance. You're using all of us right now, which is pretty gross. But to pretend to be interested in my sister while she was scared and alone and doesn't have a lot of people to turn to—"

"Don't put your guilt on me," she snaps. "You're the one who did that to her. And you playing the saint now is pretty rich, Beth. Remind us again who actually hurt someone in this scenario."

"I don't know what you're talking about."

"Hazel told all of us what you did. To your parents? The poison?"

I stare at her in shock. This is the second time that rumor has floated back to me. Would Hazel really make up such a horrific lie?

"Well, I didn't," I say defensively. "And I don't know why she would say I did."

"Because you put Hazel through hell. You abandoned her, lied to her, and made her desperate for a friend. All I did was be nice to her."

And this is why I don't trust Julie Merritt. She wears the mask of a honey-sweet, model Christian. She's all *love thy neighbor girl next door*, but in her heart, she cares about Julie first, Julie last, and Julie only. Everything she does, even if it seems kind, is calculated to benefit her. And the second it doesn't, she drops it. She *was* my first girlfriend. But lesson learned. She never cared about me, only being admired. Just because someone is pretty doesn't mean they're a good person. Just because you have important things in common doesn't mean they'll always be on your side.

I don't like that truth, but I value it. And now I'm kicking myself that I didn't pull the plug on this whole thing the second I heard Julie promise to spend time with *the odd one*. Hazel deserves the world, and Julie is the worst, and I hate that she was probably the first girl to show interest in my sister. I can count five girls in Phoebe's friend group off the top of my head who would be a great match for Hazel. And it makes me *livid* that Julie got to her first.

"You weren't nice to her," I hiss. "You used her like you use everyone else. If anyone deserves to be on the hit list, it's you, Julie."

She stares at me in shock, and I register raised eyebrows from the others as I slam my fists against Amanda's front door, then yank on the doorknob. To my surprise, it jerks open. I'm too angry to face the others, and I have the nagging feeling that my last remark went a little too far, but *everything* Julie has done has gone too far. And I have had enough.

"Amanda?" The stillness of the house gives me pause. I turn uncertainly to gauge the others' reactions. Julie is slumped by the door, sulking. Ezra stands close behind me. Jack and Phoebe follow, Phoebe texting, and Jack recording on his phone. "Have you been recording all of this?" I ask.

"Insurance," he explains. "If someone kills us off and tries to bury the evidence, they'll have a harder time."

Smart.

I press forward through the brightly lit kitchen and continue into the den, a cozy room filled with academic certificates and cheerleading awards. That's when the sound reaches us. The sickening, familiar buzzing, low and insistent. A dull drone layered under the ticking of the antique grandfather clock and the crackling of the wood-burning stove. And barely audible under that, there's a soft, intermittent tapping.

"Do you all hear that?" Jack asks, shuddering.

"The tapping or the buzzing?" Phoebe tilts her head toward the ceiling.

"I hear all of it." Ezra steps closer to the wall and places his ear against it. He taps hesitantly and there's a sudden loud and frantic knock in response. He leaps back, startled. "Okay, there's something in there. Someone?"

"Amanda?" I call again. But no one answers. "Well...unless anyone knows how to get into the wall, I think we check out the buzzing first?"

Jack nods uneasily. “Ezra, do you want to wait outside in the car? In case that ominous buzzing isn’t coming from a hive of kittens.”

He looks pained. “I’m not abandoning you guys.”

“Yes, you are,” Phoebe insists, pushing him toward the door. “If you die, you slow us down.”

He relents with a helpless look at me. “Text me 911 if things go south.”

I nod, but the situation is already in Antarctica. If it gets much worse, we’ll be contacting Phoebe’s grandmother from beyond asking her to text Ezra, *sorry took so long to respond.*

We follow the sound down the hallway and around the corner to the bathroom. Here, the buzzing is so loud it’s like it’s being amplified through a speaker. Jack places a hand on the door but I grab it and pull him back sharply.

“Wait. If there’s a huge swarm of bees in there, it could be deadly for anyone, not just Ezra. It would just take more venom.”

Phoebe nods. “She’s right. We can’t barge in without knowing what’s on the other side.”

“There’s a window,” I say. “It’s shuttered when the bathroom is in use, but they keep it open most of the time. I could run around back and try to see in. It might be our best bet.”

“Should we really split up?” Julie asks nervously.

“We already have,” Jack points out. “You and Phoebe can check out the ghost in the wall, and Beth and I can look in the window. Reconvene in the den?”

I nod. “Text at any sign of trouble.”

Phoebe mouths *thanks a lot,* and I lead Jack out the back door and around the back of the house.

"Level with me," he says. "How big a threat is Julie Merritt?"

"A threat? I don't think she is one. She's just not someone to trust."

He tilts his head in a half shake. "I don't know about that. Inserting herself to see what we know? Her dad is a cop. Not any cop, a cop involved in the death of a citizen and responsible for covering it up. I think Julie could be highly dangerous."

It sounds much more disturbing when he puts it like that. "I've known Julie all my life, Jack. I don't like her very much right now, but she's been one of my best friends pretty much forever. You don't go from bratty teen to corrupt undercover cop in the space of high school. It's not a thing in real life."

"None of this is ordinary. At least, it shouldn't be."

We stop at the window and draw a deep breath.

I look at Jack nervously. "Are you ready?"

"No," he admits. "But *ready* isn't an option. Let's do it."

We stand on our tiptoes and press our faces against the unshuttered window of the illuminated bathroom. Then, Jack grabs my hand and squeezes so hard my fingers go numb.

23

BETH

The identity of the girl in the bathroom is unclear, but it is clear that she's dead.

She is sitting upright in the polished clawfoot porcelain tub, her knees drawn up to her chest, head tilted back, mouth wide open in a silent scream, arms wrapped around her legs, fingers digging into her flesh. Her posture indicates pure terror, final seconds dominated by fear and agony.

Every inch of her body is covered with honeybees.

They crawl over the surface of her skin, making her into a living sculpture, a grotesque and fascinating work of art. There is no human part of her visible. There are only crawling and hovering bodies. Flashes of yellow and black churning and revolving, delicate, iridescent wings fluttering like tiny fans, alive. The tile floor is littered with the bodies of the dead who gave their lives in battle, and I remember a bit of trivia, that when a honeybee stings, it loses much of its body with the stinger—the venom sac, bee guts. An awful way to die.

An awful way to die.

With a deep stab of guilt, I realize I'm glad I can't see her face, the welts and wounds. For just this moment, I can exist in the illusion that there *is* no body, there are only the bees, exploring, tunneling. But my stomach turns as I watch them pour in and out of her open mouth, poke out of her nostrils and ears, lay claim to the entire landscape of what I know is a human body. A corpse I used to know.

I start to shiver, slight at first, and then violently. Jack wraps his arms tightly around my shoulders.

"We have to go," he whispers in my ear.

But the poem from Veronica's diary is stuck in my head. I read all her poems over and over, memorized them, locked them up in my heart. Each one was a clue to the mystery of what happened to her and the mystery of Veronica herself. Veronica was a puzzle. The key to her own resolution. And her words were the map. The poems were so few, but so important. I was so sure of that. The honeybee poem was a poem of grief, of mourning. An elegy for winged things.

Spring babies, in winter's land, die
pale, studious daughters
in the valley of the shadow.
The girls were promised springtime
in exchange for sweetness.
That home was not a battlefield
you could be safe in Lillabee, at least, asleep.
In the end, maybe none of them suffered.
But who knew?

Spring babies, in their coffins, do not speak.
Wings lie still
and if you cry, you cry alone.

Her sadness bled through the pages. I believed that, to her, the hive felt like her babies, who were maliciously and cruelly murdered to get back at her for retaliating against Ezra's dad for his attempted assault. It's hard to piece together their reasoning. Veronica had her dog attack him, and the girls hit back by killing her bees. Why did our mothers get involved at all?

I think I understand that one. Ashling *is* a place where you are expected to fight your family's battles. This is the mentality my mother has driven into our heads since we were babies. It's why she forced Hazel and me to be not only friends but allies in the starkest sense of the words. An attack against Chet *would* have been taken as an attack against everyone who loved him. And that would have made Veronica an enemy. Chet almost certainly denied Veronica's accusations, and they almost certainly believed him. He was the one they had known forever.

When Cerberus attacked and Chet was seriously injured, his friends felt honor-bound to respond. And the attack on Lillabee, presumably, was a crime of opportunity. The photograph of the girls with the hive explains the rest. The cheerleaders knew how to get back at Veronica. The bees, her babies, were right out there in the yard, vulnerable, as she said, sleeping. The boys got Cerberus, too, in the end. It was all so sad and needless. Another thought occurs to me, and I share it with Jack as we walk back to the house. "You know what's odd? Maybe not odd. Unfair, I guess."

He throws up his hands. "Oh, all of it."

"Veronica mostly went after them through legitimate channels, and they always fought back below the belt. I mean, she had her dog bite Chet, but that was only after going to Laurence and being told to hush up."

"True. She went through the authorities first. Hence the cheerleaders and Deadeyes getting shut down."

"But they always hit her right where it hurt. Her pets, herself."

He holds the door open for me. "They suck."

I gaze past him into the house, but my shoes feel stuck to the grass. The hallway stretches long and white and spotless, and something about it reminds me of a hospital, in a sad, hopeless way. Hospitals are filled with dying people and corpses on ice. I've spent hundreds of days, entire years of my life, in this house doing homework, watching movies, playing board games, eating family dinners with Amanda, her parents, and her sister Allison. One is dead and the other may soon follow. This house was a playhouse, and now it's a tomb.

I take a deep, shivery breath and step inside. "Do you think there's a link between that and why the Stranger is doing this the way she is? Going after the children? Veronica talked about her bees like they were her children. She called them her babies, her daughters."

Jack sighs. "I mean, who knows? Does it matter?"

"I was thinking about what Phoebe said. We don't know that the Stranger is a demon. We don't know what she is. Why would a demon care about Veronica Green? And if it's not a demon, what is it?"

"Something incredibly loyal to Veronica. Beyond-the-grave loyal."

"Exactly."

We meet Phoebe in the den, and I fill her in on my theory. She then fills us in on *her* situation, which is that Julie got spooked and decided to "guard" Ezra.

"Shock, surprise, horror," Jack says sarcastically. But his annoyance quickly turns into concern. "You should have told us the second she abandoned you. Can we agree from this point forward that we stick together no matter what?"

"Yeah, I should probably catch you up, then," I say guiltily. "I saw the deadeyes at Mac's house. And Chet kind of attacked me. I'm fine. But we need to be careful." Jack offers me a rare hug.

"No more splitting up, and no more secrets." Phoebe looks back and forth between us uneasily. "What did you see out there?"

I hesitate. "More or less what we expected."

Jack gapes at me. "You expected to find a human beehive?"

Phoebe pales. "What does that even mean?"

"Did you ever drop a piece of fruit salad at a picnic and forget about it, and then find it a day later? Like that, except with bees instead of ants, and a human being instead of fruit."

"Imagine the fruit has a mouth and is frozen forever in an endless scream," Jack adds.

"Jesus, okay." Phoebe crosses her arms nervously across her chest as if to ward off attackers. "So it *is* bees. That's helpful."

Jack and I stare at her.

"It could have been termites," she says defensively. "One can dream."

"If you don't mind night terrors," Jack says grimly.

There's another weak knock from the wall, and I knock back with a sick feeling in my stomach. I have no plan. This goes so far beyond what we anticipated when we met that night in the woods, when I learned the truth about Veronica and we formulated the revenge plan. The night that would set this—all of this, bodies and all—in motion.

"Is all of this our fault?" I ask quietly.

"No, I'm sorry." Jack paces anxiously. "I refuse to feel guilty about this. There's no way we could have foreseen actual demonic involvement. That is beyond the standard of care for reasonable scheming."

"You look convincingly like someone who feels no guilt." Phoebe gestures at him, and he suddenly becomes aware that he's been biting his nails and shoves his hands into his pockets.

"You're the one who handed Hazel a summoning spell."

"How was I supposed to know it worked?" she snaps.

"Because of Veronica?" he says incredulously.

"That was a story!"

"Stop!" I whisper-shout. "Unless you want to summon the bees."

Phoebe cringes. "Sorry." She moves along the wall and taps again. "Look, it's stronger here." There's a knock in return, louder. My heart sinks. It's much closer to the bathroom.

"Anyway," Jack whispers, "it was Hazel who summoned the Stranger. Not us."

I glare at him, stung. "Hazel was trying to save me."

"My point is that none of us tried to hurt anyone." He squeezes my hand in apology.

"You didn't actually believe I tried to poison my parents, did you?" I nervously walk toward the bathroom. Phoebe has sealed off the bottom of the door with a damp kitchen towel. Smart.

“Not for a second,” Jack says. “I don’t think Hazel was lying, either, though,” he adds, looking troubled. “She thought she was telling the truth for sure.”

“Hazel’s a victim too,” Phoebe says carefully, leading us further down the hallway. “We need to think about how to draw the Stranger out. I do not think the summoning spell is the way to go. Body-hopping is not going to solve the problem. And we have no idea what’s happening to Hazel while the Stranger is...borrowing her.”

Jack eyes me. “Do you think you could try to reach her? Like use your psychic twin connection to break the spell or whatever?”

I laugh, but it’s a painful laugh. “We don’t even have a close acquaintance connection.”

There’s another knock on the wall, and this one sounds more urgent.

“Phoebe—did you find a way in?”

She nods, stopping in front of a tiny door Amanda and I used to pretend was the opening to a fairy realm. “Through the crawl space. It’s probably how she got in. The problem is that it likely shares venting with the bathroom, putting the person inside at risk of attack.”

“No other way in? Fireplace?” Jack says.

“They have a wood-burning stove, so we can assume the fire-place is decorative *and* we’re not elves.” She eyes him skeptically.

“Have you found a way to communicate besides knocking?” I knock on the wall to keep the line of communication open and receive a knock in return.

“No,” Phoebe replies. “Either it’s Amanda’s sister or Amanda doesn’t have access to her phone. Besides, I don’t think anyone knows Morse code.”

I swallow hard. I hate to wish a horrible death on anyone, but I can't help but hope that Amanda is the one hiding in the wall. "Okay. I think we have two options. One, we open the bathroom window, run for it, and call for help as we make a swift getaway. She should be safe until help arrives."

"Or?" Jack waits.

"Or we tell her to climb back out through the crawl space but risk attracting the bees to the vent and triggering an attack."

Phoebe bites one of her beautifully decorated nails. "The safer bet would be opening the window."

"Not for us!" Jack points out. "I want to live to see us arrested for trespassing at the very least!"

"I don't want a body on my conscience," Phoebe protests, nodding at the wall uncomfortably. "*Another* body," she adds under her breath. "We can't leave her here. She's a sitting duck for the Stranger to circle back and toss in a blender. Or whatever she did to Mac."

Shit. She's right. But before I can say it, my phone buzzes. I glance down at a series of rapid texts from Ezra.

EZRA:
911

EZRA:
911

EZRA:
911

My heart leaps into my throat. "Ezra." I run toward the front door, but Phoebe stops me.

"What's going on?"

"Some of the bees must have gotten to Ezra. He has an EpiPen. As long as it's just one or two and he gets to the hospital, he should be fine. Get Amanda, okay?"

She and Jack run to the back of the house while I sprint to the front door, heart racing. My brain feels useless, my lungs rigid, limbs numb. I count my breaths, try to slow my pulse, but when I throw open the door, my heart seems to stop altogether, a stunning stillness in my chest.

There are no bees.

Ezra and Julie are locked in the car with the lights on, Ezra's face white as a ghost, Julie curled into a ball like a hedgehog warding off predators, her face buried between her knees.

And looming over them is the Stranger.

24

BETH

The Stranger, masked as my sister, stands in front of the car eerily still, head tilted curiously to one side, panting heavily as if she just ran a very long distance.

Her white T-shirt, now soaked deep red, is plastered against her body. Blood covers her arms, her face, her hair. It streaks down her pajama shorts and bare legs in long red ribbons and dyes her once-white sneakers scarlet. A low, guttural humming sound issues from her throat. She slowly raises both hands, bends forward, and presses them against the hood of the car, and then her lips curl back and the sound in her throat rises to an unmistakable snarl.

"Hazel," I whisper, afraid to move closer.

But she isn't Hazel, and she doesn't answer to Hazel. Instead, she crawls forward, and I remember how she trapped me this morning, perched on my chest on all fours. The panic and claustrophobia rushes back, and my lungs constrict again. I gasp for air.

"Hazel," I try again, but my voice is strangled. I am sabotaged by my hummingbird heartbeat and vacuum lungs, and even if it were Hazel, when is the last time she believed a word I said? Ezra catches my eye and motions for me to run. That gets her attention. She whips her head around at me, startled, and suddenly I have the dizzying sense that I'm falling, and then crashing, my head smashing into the ground.

My head spins and everything goes dark. The air is closing in, compressing my body and my lungs. My heart is galloping in my chest and I can't find solid ground, can't bring myself back to reality. And then my eyes focus, and the horrifying truth sinks in: I'm *not* on solid ground. I am surrounded by darkness, suspended in the air, held by the Stranger's unnatural gaze. There is no sound, only Ezra screaming my name silently against the passenger window, the Stranger's accusing gaze, Julie running for her truck as if in slow motion. Slowly, a feeling like pins and needles begins to spread throughout my body, starting in my fingertips and toes, creeping like frostbite to my hands, feet, forearms, calves. I go limp, like little venom stings are putting me to sleep one body part, one organ at a time. Maybe it will be over soon. *Maybe none of them suffered.* Then it stops and I'm falling again, only this time I do hit solid ground, hard.

Sound comes rushing back, the sound of screaming, and I'm lifted, and the pain in my left leg sends sparks throughout my body. Someone carries me into the car and slams the door.

And we're driving *fast*.

"Ezra, what did you do?" Jack asks from the front seat.

I look around, dazed. I'm wedged between Ezra and Amanda, whose face and arms are dotted in little pink welts. She appears to be in shock.

"She'll be okay," Ezra says grimly.

"What did he do?" I ask, my brain dulled by the pain, the panic attack, the fact that I was just suspended ten feet off the ground in some kind of curse state I can only hope has no permanent effect.

"He hit the Stranger with my car," Phoebe says delicately. "But she got right up again," she adds quickly. "She seems in great shape."

I turn to Ezra furiously. "You hit my sister with a car?"

"I was saving your life!"

"You could have killed her!"

"It was a nudge," Jack says. "A break-the-eye-contact thing."

"You couldn't *nudge* her with your hand?" I ask.

"Beth, that entity? Not Hazel," Phoebe says. "She flung you into the air with a glance."

Amanda seems to emerge from her stunned state. "What the actual fuck is going on? The last thing I saw, *not Hazel* creeper tranced into my house and like, summoned these droves of bees without saying a word. Just this spooky smile."

I let the others tell her. My head is spinning. My sister, or some being we don't know how to separate from her, just looked straight into my eyes and tried to kill me. We are losing this battle.

"So our parents murdered Veronica and now some evil, vengeance ghost is hunting *us* down one by one? How is that fair?" Amanda hugs herself. Then, suddenly, "Allison's car was still in the driveway. She left with someone else, right? Julie?"

There's a long silence. Too long.

She grips the shoulder of the front seat. "We have to go back for my sister."

"It's too late," I say. "I'm so sorry, Mandy."

"Prove it." She sets her jaw, but her lower lip trembles. "I won't believe it unless I see it."

"You don't want to," I say gently.

Amanda starts crying. "I need to call Mac."

"He's gone too," Phoebe says, sparing me from delivering more crushing news.

"Who *isn't* dead?" Amanda demands, wiping her eyes on the back of her sleeve.

"Us," Ezra says. "My siblings. We're…statistically looking pretty good so far."

I elbow him. Amanda's lost a sister and her boyfriend in a night. From her point of view, it's a statistical nightmare.

"So what now? What's the plan?" she asks genuinely, like we have an answer. "Stake through the heart? Smash the brain? How do we beat the monster?"

"We don't know," Jack admits.

"How do you not know?" Amanda looks at Ezra accusingly.

"Because this isn't *Twilight* or *Night of the Living Dead*. It's a weird situation. There are nuances," he says.

"We're all going to die," she says, leaning back against the seat, resigned. But it's also a little like an accusation, like we should really have a better possession disaster game.

"Maybe your parents shouldn't have murdered my aunt," Jack suggests.

"Maybe your aunt shouldn't have been a freak demon person," she spits back.

"She wasn't," he argues hotly.

"Excuse me, but yes. She was. Like, she didn't deserve to be murdered. She needed help. And our parents are obviously fucked up. But who summons a demon? Or a god or whatever."

"A god?" Jack looks at her puzzled.

"Yeah like. Real talk. My parents told us the Veronica story. The real one. And the reason no one talks about it is because A. It's fucking sad. And B. It's fucking scary."

Phoebe slows the car like she's going to pull over. "Hang on. I want to hear this."

Amanda points ahead. "Parking lot half a mile up."

I want to hear it too. I'd blown off everything Ed and the Rev said about Veronica earlier as the paranoid ramblings of a grief-stricken father and the cruel words of her killer. But what if that's not the *whole* story?

We pull into the Slashwheel right as I'm starting to feel claustrophobic, so Ezra and Jack help me out of the car to stretch my leg out on the grass. It's definitely broken and extremely painful. Ezra balls up his jacket to prop it up, and then we listen to Amanda, spellbound.

"Okay." Amanda draws a deep, shuddery breath. "So Veronica moved here from the city—"

"We know this part," Jack interrupts.

"Fast forward to junior prom. She goes with Chet Elwood, and, sorry Ez, but he has a reputation. Which he tries to act on, she says no, and he doesn't respect her. So wrong. Luckily, she slams the door in his face and jets, but *unluckily*, when she reports him—"

"To your dad," Jack puts in accusingly.

Amanda nods soberly. "He regrets that he didn't take her seriously, and he's never repeated that mistake. Again, still wrong. But back to Veronica. She decides Chet needs to be taught a lesson."

"We know all this," Ezra says, a little tensely. I guess it can't feel super great to hear what his dad did over and over. "She had her dog attack him."

"No." Amanda looks at him oddly. "*She* attacked him. Only...it wasn't her. It was like she was possessed or something."

I was wrong too, Ed had said. *Not the dog.*

"That's where the 'demon girl' rumor came from," Amanda continues. "Veronica was into the occult. People said she was a witch, that she spoke to monsters and gods. She had this fascination with the underworld. Like Ashling was the gates of Hades. She called it winter's land."

"Right." I nod. "That's straight from her poems."

"So you know I'm not shitting you," Amanda says. "But then our parents really went lowest of the low. They destroyed the bee colony. Ed killed the dog."

"Because he thought that's who shredded Chet, and he was scared he was next," I say.

Amanda nods. "He was always messed up, and not quite in the inner circle. But Chet knew the truth—no dog attacked him. It was Veronica. Or some form of Veronica. And once Chet started talking, I think they convinced themselves she was evil, so their behavior was justified. They were afraid of her."

"She wasn't evil," Jack says tensely.

"Like I said, she probably just needed help or something."

"She tried to get help," I point out. "When no one who was supposed to help did, she turned to a less obvious source."

"A demon?" Ezra says skeptically.

"Amanda said it was like Veronica was possessed," I argue. "And Hazel definitely isn't herself. But I don't think it's a demon. Veronica never mentioned a demon in her diaries. She mentioned one name over and over. Cerberus."

Phoebe whips out her phone and scrolls excitedly. "It's right here in the poems. *I summon a beast. A girl may be beast when you peel back the skin. A hound is a girl's best friend.* She even references three heads. She named her dog after Cerberus, but what if that's also who she was summoning? The girl's best friend."

"Her protector," Jack says. "She referred to herself as Persephone. Reluctant daughter of Demeter, in love with the King of the Underworld."

"So we're dealing with the actual hound of Hades in Hazel's body?" Ezra asks. "Not Veronica's pet Cerberus. *The* Cerberus."

"It would explain a lot," I say.

"How do you defeat Cerberus?" Phoebe asks.

"We don't," Jack says. "We stick to the plan and expose the people who wronged Veronica. Cerberus is Veronica's protector. He's going after the children because he was *summoned* by one of them. We created the generational glitch. When Veronica is no longer threatened, he has no more business here, and balance is restored. That's what my gut says."

"It's a big leap for a gut feeling," Amanda protests.

"Heracles defeated Cerberus by wrestling him into submission without weapons, bringing him back from the underworld," Phoebe reads from her phone. "Does anyone want to try that?"

"We obviously can't physically fight Hazel," I say with a warning look to Ezra.

"I wasn't gonna," he says.

I look at the others, wincing from the pain in my leg. "So we band together, turn in our parents, and hopefully appease Cerberus? Amanda, the fact that your parents confessed to you is crucial. Otherwise, it's Jack's word against all of Ashling."

She nods vigorously. "We end the nightmare."

"You're not doing that."

We look up, startled, to see Julie standing by the side of the road. Julie, who apparently *is* a threat. Because she has been tracking us, stalking us, all this time. And as she raises her shotgun to eye level, it hits me like a gut punch what she's been doing.

She's hunting us.

I almost wish it was the Stranger instead.

25
BETH

Julie," I say, sounding much calmer than I feel. "Put down the gun and we'll hear you out."

"No, you won't." She laughs. "You haven't listened to me once. You won't listen to reason."

"Jules, this isn't you," Amanda says.

"It isn't *you!*" she shouts back. "Since when do you betray your family over a bunch of lies you have no way of verifying? And from a couple of outsiders, who want to move in on our town, our home, and change everything: our history, our values, what's right and wrong. Make it about *them*. They haven't been around for any of it." She turns on Jack and Phoebe. "You don't belong here."

"No argument," Jack says, his hands raised.

"Why don't you just go? Why do you need to drag up old wounds? You don't have this land in your blood."

"None of us have that," Ezra says softly.

"I don't care." Her eyes fill with tears. "It's all we have."

"Please, Julie, put the gun down. We can talk about all of this." I don't move toward her, but I'm getting more and more freaked out. I should have remembered that Julie carries a gun in her truck. Plenty of people do, especially this time of year, when small game season is in full swing, and big game is right around the corner. It just didn't cross my mind that Julie was this kind of a threat.

"No one is trying to take anything away from you," Amanda says. "My sister died tonight. Do you have even an ounce of compassion in your heart? Because if you do, you will put the fucking gun down and treat me like family. *Those* are our values. Not holding your friends at gunpoint like a tragic, spineless incel. My *god*, Jules."

Julie falters. "You promise you won't say a word against my family?"

Amanda stares at her. "No, I don't."

Julie pulls the trigger.

The shot is deafening.

Amanda jolts, then touches her shoulder in disbelief. Blood is already seeping out.

Chaos erupts. Ezra lunges at Julie, tackling her to the ground and wrestling the gun out of her hands. Phoebe cradles Amanda, laying her down gently and getting to work examining the wound and applying pressure. Ezra tears off his sweater to get to his T-shirt and tosses it to Jack, who catches it one-handed and furiously begins tearing it to try to make a tourniquet, but the wound is high. I dial 911.

"How bad is it?" Amanda asks, her voice high and frightened.

"Barely touched you." But there's still a lot of blood. Phoebe presses both of her palms down to stop the bleeding, allowing gravity to assist her.

"Please tell me an ambulance is on the way," Amanda says.

I flash her a tight smile. "They'll be here soon." But I'm on hold. Ambulances can take a long time on the mountaintop. There are only two, and they serve a wide radius.

Julie stares at us, guarded by Ezra, looking like a stranger. "You were going to ruin my life."

"No, she wasn't." I can't even look at her.

"You don't get it," she says derisively. "Your parents are nobodies. My dad, my uncles, my grandfather—they *are* the law. The town collapses if you do this."

"We don't need you," Amanda says weakly, but defiantly. "And you're pretty pathetic if your entire identity is your family."

"Rest," Phoebe orders.

Julie opens her mouth to argue, but nothing comes out. She gapes for a moment, straining, as if there's something stuck in her throat. Ezra takes an uncertain step backward and I inch closer to him. Then, suddenly, Julie is lifted into the air as if being yanked by an invisible puppet string. She hovers ten feet above the ground, staring down at us in frozen terror.

A shriek of horror escapes me.

Across the parking lot, Hazel, the Stranger, Cerberus, is approaching, walking slowly, head tilted in that curious way, eyes staring intensely up at Julie, a blood-soaked nightmare emerging from the darkness. I hand the phone off to Ezra. "Still on hold," I whisper. "I don't think we should move Amanda."

"Please don't leave me here," she says, alarmed.

"We slowed the bleeding a lot," Phoebe reports. "That's the best we can do."

"Okay, but the Stranger could reduce us all to blood borscht in seconds, so risk-benefit," Jack says.

"We have to split up." I look around at the others. "It's our best chance. Phoebe, take your car and get help. I don't know how long we're going to be waiting for an ambulance."

"I'm not leaving you!"

"We have to hedge our bets. I can't go very far. But I can distract her."

"From?" Ezra raises an eyebrow.

"You and Jack moving Amanda to safety. I know you're not supposed to move a trauma victim, but Jack is right. It's too risky to stay put."

"Thank you," Jack says.

"Yes, please," Amanda says. "I have the key to the building. Get me inside. Quickly?"

The Stranger is slowly drawing closer, with those creepy, dreamlike steps. As Ezra and Jack make a kind of stretcher with their arms and lift Amanda, carrying her toward the Slashwheel building, Julie begins to move. There's a low buzzing sound that's beginning to grow louder, and a sick feeling starts in the pit of my stomach. I push myself backward on the grass, away from the horror unfolding in front of me and toward the main building. But movement is slow and painful, and every dip in the ground, every rock and bump is like lightning shooting through my leg.

Julie makes an odd sound, like a painful hum, and tears streak down her cheeks as her lips vibrate, her fingers tremble, her whole body buzzes.

And then I see them.

One by one, honeybees begin crawling out from under her sleeves. From the hems of her pants. From the neck of her jacket. From under her hair. First a trickle, and then an outpouring. And when she finally opens her mouth to scream, they burst forth like a hive cracked open, like her body *is* the hive.

Sheer terror freezes me. It sticks me to the frost-covered grass, numbs my fingers, my face, even my broken leg. Because I understand now the true horror of what happened to Amanda's sister. What almost happened to me. The Stranger doesn't send a swarm of honeybees to chase you down and attack. The Stranger conjures the bees inside you and turns you into a colony to replace the one stolen from Veronica.

I want to look away as Julie is slowly overtaken, claimed as a hive. I want to escape. But the hum is like a curse. Numbing, paralytic. The sight of the bees churning is as mesmerizing and thrilling as it is terrifying. I can't move until it's over. Then, just as suddenly as she rose into the air, Julie's body drops to the ground, still swarming with bees, dead alive.

I flip onto my stomach and crawl desperately for cover, dragging my leg and gritting my teeth with the pain, fairly sure I will not make it. I can hear the Stranger's footsteps behind me, crunching the frost, and I push myself harder. The entrance to the Slashwheel seems impossibly far.

But then the front door flings open and Ezra runs out, lifts me up, and dashes inside, slamming the door behind him, bolting it.

"The ambulance is on its way," he whispers. "Amanda is in the office with Jack on first-aid duty. We're keeping all lights off."

"You know she can probably sense where we are."

"Yeah, well... It's something."

Sneakers squeak across the wooden floor, followed by a metallic thud. Jack snaps on his phone light, illuminating his face in an eerie blue glow. He aims the flashlight at his cargo—a cardboard box filled with a set of heavy, slightly rusted chains and padlocks.

"Security," he pants. "Amanda said these will hold back a tank."

Ezra grabs a set and begins winding it through the bars of the double doors.

I start to untangle another. "Is there another entrance?"

Jack nods, still breathless. "Back entrance, yes." He glances at the door. "But we really barricaded ourselves in here. If she breaks in, we're Pop-Tarts."

Ezra snaps the padlock on the first set of chains, and I hand him a second.

"We didn't stand a chance out there," I argue. "She would have picked us off one by one out in the open. At least indoors we have cover."

"Cover and nowhere to run," Jack says grimly.

"So what, we leave the back entrance unlocked?" Ezra knits his brow. "That feels like a huge gamble."

"Anything we do at this point is a titanic gamble," Jack points out.

They both turn to me.

"What would Hazel do?" Ezra asks.

"How many times do I have to painfully reiterate that Hazel is an unsolved mystery? Besides, that is not Hazel out there. You saw what happened when I tried to speak to her outside Amanda's house. She tried to hive me."

Jack shrugs. "Maybe you said the wrong thing." He looks at the chains. "I have to get back to Amanda. Vote?"

Ezra doesn't hesitate. "Lock it. We can't take any chances. And Beth is right. We wouldn't stand a chance after we got outside. We have to hold down the fort until help gets here."

Jack shakes his head. "I've seen too many zombie movies. The monster always finds a way in. I say we leave an escape route. The windows are too small."

Once again, I'm in the spotlight. "Neither of you felt it toss you into the air and start filling your insides with bees. I want as many walls between me and it as possible."

"Can't argue that." Jack leaves the box with us and retreats to the office. "I really hope I'm wrong on this." He hesitates before rejoining Amanda. "Don't get dead."

"You first," Ezra says.

"Not it," I add.

Jack grins faintly, then slips into the office, closing the door behind him. A metallic click follows.

We're swallowed up in darkness again as his phone disappears with him, and I hear Ezra snapping the last padlock shut in the dark.

"What if we are wrong?" My voice echoes in the empty hall.

"We won't be." He takes my hand.

But we might be. We might be wrong. This could be how we die. In an epic series of spectacularly bad decisions. "It would be my fault. I started it."

Ezra pulls me close against him, as tears begin to sting my eyes. His voice is deep and soothing. "You did *not* start this. Our parents started this."

"But I chose not to tell Hazel. If I did, none of this would have happened. Mac and Allison and Julie would still be alive."

"She or it or whatever wouldn't have listened, Beth. None of us would." He pauses. "I should get the back door. We need to get to cover."

“Right.”

“If we are wrong, though...” Another hesitation. “I should be the one to face the Stranger. It’ll buy you time.”

I stare at him in the darkness. “Are you out of your mind? You saw what she did to Mac.”

“I like to think I’m somewhat smarter than Mac.”

“Not when the test is taking on a godlike monster that has your name at the top of its kill list.”

“That’s kind of the point,” he says quietly. “There’s a reason you’re assuming my name is at the top. My father is the main villain, isn’t he? What if killing me is all it takes to end this?”

“You’re *not* sacrificing yourself. End of conversation. We all get out alive.” But that’s a lie. We’re already down three. And I hate that, now that he’s planted the idea in my head, I wonder if it’s true. What if all it takes to end this is to kill the kid of Veronica’s actual killer—the one who pulled the trigger?

“You’re right. We all get out alive,” he repeats after a moment.

He lifts me again and starts to carry me through the darkness when suddenly there’s a sound behind us. We turn slowly, in dread. It’s not a loud bang, it’s a quiet scratch, like a kitten’s paw.

“Let’s go faster,” I whisper.

“Sure, I’ll throw on my night vision goggles,” he whispers back.

And then the door isn’t there anymore. Pieces of the thick, heavy metal panels are flung into the parking lot, sending strands of bluish white light streaming in. Ezra begins to run, but then the lights flicker on. *All* of the power comes on. The neon lights that make the Slashwheel famous illuminate me, Ezra, and the Stranger, still soaked in blood. The disco ball spins, casting a shimmery glow of hot pink, electric blue, poison purple, and lime green over the scene. The arcade has sprung to life in a dizzying whirl of strobe lights, chimes, game sounds, and random *ka-chings*. Loud music begins to pump through the cavernous roller rink: Gloria Estefan's "Rhythm Is Gonna Get You."

"This is getting surreal," Ezra says. He lifts me over the half wall that separates the skating floor from the rest of the venue and sets me down on the floor, shielded from view.

"What are you doing?" I whisper.

"We're still splitting up, right?"

I nod. It's the last thing I want to do, but it's our best chance. Help is coming. We need to stay alive until it arrives, to get Amanda to safety, and to speak with the authorities—just not the Ashling authorities.

Ezra ducks and makes for the arcade at the opposite side of the building. I glance behind me. The door to laser tag is open. It's a few yards away, and I know every hiding place like the back of my hand. Hazel doesn't. She always barrels through shooting wildly to try to rack up points. The Stranger has the advantage of knowing what Hazel knows, but that seems to mean she also has Hazel's limitations. I crawl over to the laser tag course, but I pause when I hear shouting.

My heart flies into my throat. The EMTs haven't arrived yet, but the police have, which I might have expected. They sent not one but *two* Merritts. Julie's father and her uncle. They both look stricken, but not necessarily *grief* stricken, so my best guess is that they found Julie's body in a similarly unapproachable and unrecognizable state as Jack and I found Allison.

"Don't move."

Both have their guns trained on the Stranger, and for a second,

I stop seeing her as the Stranger, and she's Hazel again. Hazel, who is baring teeth and growling menacingly, yawning her jaws wide—wider than her skeletal structure should permit. And that allows me to glimpse something Hazel also shouldn't have. A row of extremely sharp, definitely not human teeth. Her eyes flash, coal black, a warning, as she arches her back, her posture seeming to alter.

A gun is cocked. I've seen this go wrong before.

"No!" I shout.

I hear the gunshot. I hear it.

But the Stranger is fast. The Stranger is not Hazel. The Stranger is not human. The Stranger seems to blur shapes and forms as she runs. She is a girl, and then she is a beast. She is fact, and then she is fiction. She is present, and then past, truth, and then myth. But this much is certain: heads snatch bodies and lift them, shake them like soft dolls. Teeth tear into flesh. Blood is spilled, *poured* on the shiny wooden floor of the roller rink, and remains are scattered. There is screaming, seemingly endless screaming, but it does end. Then the Stranger is a girl again, standing in a pool of carnage, soaked in blood under a spinning disco ball and neon lights, while the music insists it's the *rhythm* that's going to get you.

I pray to Persephone she does not set her dog on the ambulance workers too.

Then I make the run for the laser tag room.

26

BETH

I slam the door behind me and make my way frantically through the maze in the dark. Jack texts me and I type back while I search for a perfect hiding place.

JACK:

You okay? Please be okay

BETH:

Stranger ate Chief M + 1. Hiding in lasertag. E in arcade

JACK:

Priority #1 keep Stranger away from Amanda until confession yeah?

BETH:

Yes

It takes me a good minute and a half to realize what should have dawned on me right away: the room is quiet as death. Which means no one is following me.

BETH:

She's not here

Jack doesn't answer, and my heart leaps into my throat. If the Stranger kills Amanda, our plan goes to hell.

I reverse course in a panic and force my way back through the maze, my heart beating so fast I can't feel individual beats, just a terrifying vibration, a warning bell, alarms going off that something in me is malfunctioning and dangerous and might imminently explode. A new fear overtakes me. I grasp the wall and gulp air.

Not now, please not now. I can't panic. But my fingertips are tingling, and my foot that can still bear weight is pins and needles as I burst through the door and onto the eerily lit wooden floor. The neon lights are still flashing, but the strobe is on now in addition to the disco ball. The bodies are right where the Stranger dropped them, in pools of blood glossy and slick on the polished floor. A new song blares over the speakers, "Your Woman" by White Town.

For a second, I stand there helplessly, the place seemingly deserted. Then I see her standing motionless outside the office, her head tilted in that creepy, dangerous way. I take a step toward her but before I can open my mouth, Ezra appears from the arcade and runs across the floor. The air is sucked out of my lungs.

Ezra shouts the name *Cerberus,* and the Stranger jerks her head around to peer at him curiously, as if he's an alien specimen, not a threat, but he keeps running straight at her, his face gritted in determination.

My heart is broken glass. My voice is smoke. I try to shout, but the words burn out and die. I try to move, but my legs are numb. I'm walking in someone else's body. Too slow.

Just as Ezra reaches the Stranger, Jack opens the office door, slams it behind him, and places himself between the Stranger and Amanda. The Stranger turns from Ezra long enough for him to barrel into her in what should be a solid tackle. But it doesn't move her an inch. She lowers her head and growls at Jack, and he flies across the room as if hit by an invisible car, slamming against the concession stand and shattering the tempered glass display case.

That breaks me out of my fog. I push forward on pure adrenaline as the Stranger turns back toward Ezra.

He makes eye contact with me just long enough to shout the word "run."

And then she has him. Suspended in the air. Paralyzed. Humming.

"Hazel!" I scream as I limp toward her.

She doesn't turn. Ezra begins to vibrate.

"Veronica!" The smell of blood as I near her makes my stomach curdle. Her muscles are tense, straining, her bloody skin glistening with sweat.

Tears stream down my face as Ezra begins to hum and the shaking begins. I feel myself start to lose him. Like I've lost Hazel. Like I lost my parents, like I have lost everyone. I reach out and grab her arm and try to break her concentration, but she's like a marble statue.

"Cerberus," I try. I slide down to the ground, breaking,

breaking, broken. I cover my face with my hands. I can't look anymore. I can't see or hear or speak anything except *I'm sorry*.

The buzzing stops.

His body hits the ground.

My eyes fly open and they meet Ezra's. He's dazed, but conscious. Not dead. This time he whispers: "Run."

I look up and the Stranger is staring at me.

This time I do.

I run-limp-crawl back to the laser tag room and barricade myself inside, then feel around for shelter. There's an earsplitting crash as she effortlessly breaks through the barricade.

I hear her behind me, her slow methodical footsteps. My phone buzzes in my pocket and I fumble to silence it.

JACK:

Are you okay?

I type carefully, my back against the wall of my favorite hiding spot, a double rock wall.

BETH:

For now. You?

JACK:

Will be. Think Ezra will too.
The hiving was interrupted

The lights snap on. *Great.* The black lights in the laser tag room are fairly dim, but I was counting on darkness. I hold my phone against my pounding heart and strain my ears, but all I hear is the almost inaudible hum of the black light.

A door swings open and slams shut.

Slow footsteps. Heavy breathing. Coming straight toward me.

Shit.

I inch along the edge of the rock wall and duck into another hiding spot, then risk a peek. The Stranger is somehow even more terrifying in the black light, the tiny spots of her white T-shirt that aren't soaked in blood glowing hideously. I wonder if her teeth are normal now, or if they're still unnaturally sharp and jagged. I have to make my way past her toward the door again, but she's blocking the way.

The Stranger stops.

I suddenly get this sharp, sinking feeling, like I'm playing chess against a computer and the algorithm has me cornered. Any move I make, it knows the counteroffensive. Defense is the only option, and it won't work forever. I take out my phone.

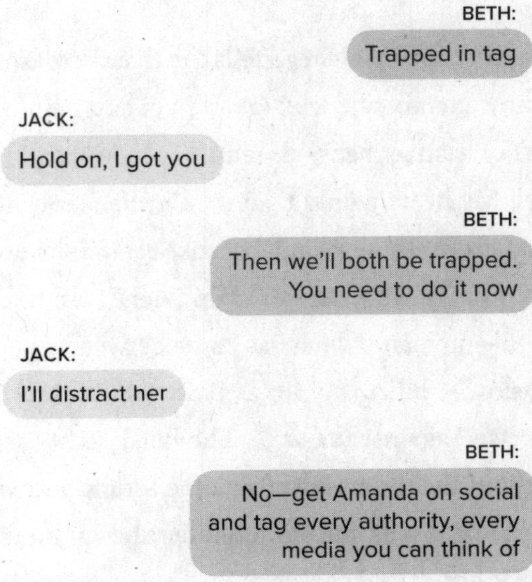

JACK:
We need you too

BETH:
I'll try

The footsteps start again, and I drop my phone into my pocket, my heart pounding. I slip around another corner and assess my options. I could run for the door, but my chances of making it are slim. I could keep hiding, but my time will run out. Or I could text Jack to distract the Stranger and buy a little more time. But I can't keep it up much longer. The pain in my leg is almost unbearable.

With a deadly sense of calm, the truth begins to sink in. I do have one more option. I can pull a Hazel. Instead of thinking my way around the problem, I can face it head on. Make one last epic stand. Go heart instead of head. Trust that some remnant of my sister is left in that shell of a stranger, and fight to tear her back into this world.

Because as much as my head tells me that there is no reaching Hazel, that any attempt will lead to my swift and painful death, my heart doesn't care about sense or reason. My heart still believes in Bethanhazel. My heart would take the Orpheus journey to bring my sister back from winter's land, because even if she doesn't know who or where she is, who else could find her? I am the witch, and she is the wolf—no matter what has come between us.

I stand slowly, biting my lip as pain shoots through my leg, and brace myself against the wall. The black light casts an eerie glow throughout the room. I don't see the Stranger anywhere. But I know she's in here with me. And I know she can hear me better than I can hear her.

"Hazel," I call, and her name is a conjuring. Hazel is a charm. Hazel is a spell. One half of a realm of magic and danger. Of witches and wolves, princesses and poisons, beasts and bloodshed.

Footsteps draw closer.

"I want to talk to my sister."

Another footstep. Deep, uneven breaths. A steady hum, like she's considering whether to growl or swallow it up.

"Tonight, Hazel. You and me, tonight."

Closer now. There's a smashing sound as a wall flattens and I shut my eyes tight and clench my fists. The fear is so palpable, so overwhelming, it's like bugs under my skin. Unbearable and unreal.

"I know I've let you down. I have pushed you away. I have lied to you. I am a liar. I am not Veronica Green."

Another smash, another wall collapses. She emerges from around a corner, in profile. Her back is hunched, mouth gaping, teeth sharp and jaws yawning wide. But she waits. Listens?

"I am Beth Whitman. I am your sibling, your twin. I am not a dead girl. I am not a girl. I want you to know me. I know you are sick of me. I know you are sick."

She tenses. A set of track lights detach from the ceiling and crash down, shattering on the floor, dimming the room even further.

I flinch at the earsplitting crash, at the brilliant explosion of scattered purple glass. "I am here, and I will not leave your side."

The growling starts again, low, then louder. But I am not giving up. I am not giving up on Hazel. I have made up my mind. She turns to me and advances, and all I see is the sharpness of her teeth. I scream in adrenaline and fear and love that is fierce and not all human, "I lied to you about Mom and Dad because I was afraid you would take their side."

She halts, jaws extended, inches away, and in that moment, I am unafraid. And then, slowly, slowly, the Stranger's jaws hinge and close. She draws away from me.

"It was her." Her voice is low and strained.

"Who?"

"She was there for Chet's party." She stares hard at the ground, her black eyes unreadable. "The lights tripped out back, and they went to investigate. They found Veronica by the shed with a can of gasoline. She was going to burn it all. Meat and skins, guns and ammo, all their good things. Chet fired a shot into the air, to scare her off. Veronica ran. Owen loaded a round. And then *she* grabbed the gun. She was never allowed at home."

It suddenly hits me who the Stranger is talking about. Who *she* is. It makes my head spin. "Why?"

The Stranger lifts a shoulder dully. "Fear? Adrenaline? Maybe she was tired of being sidelined. She fired straight into the woods as Veronica was turning to face them. And that was it."

"They won't get away with it," I whisper hoarsely. I feel like I've been sucker-punched. I was so convinced it was Chet. It was his house. He had tried to hurt her before. Mom wasn't even supposed to have been at the scene. But we weren't there. We didn't know anything.

"She already did," the Stranger says harshly.

"It's not over. The Laurences confessed to Amanda. She's live-streaming, telling the whole world what happened right now. I'll tell anyone who will listen."

There's a brief flicker in her liquid black eyes, like a ripple in a midnight lake. "It won't bring her back."

"But it will bring her justice. Everyone who wronged her will be dead or face consequences."

"Owen tried to confess, once. When he realized Beth knew. He tried to convince the others. Elaine wouldn't allow it. She poisoned him. And then she poisoned herself."

That doesn't make sense. And then, it does.

And somehow all the horror until now feels distant, less real.

My stomach is hollow, my whole body broken. Mom tried to poison Dad. Herself too. Me? I try to remember that afternoon. How everything grew so heavy, foggy, and vague. Now, all those odd comments about me trying to poison Mom and Dad make sense. Jack saying he knew I didn't do it, but also believing Hazel didn't make it up. She didn't. Our parents *were* poisoned, and Hazel discovered it and assumed I did it. Of course she did. She had no reason to trust me and no reason to suspect our mother. Our mother, the murderer.

"Hazel. We deserved better parents. But I'm sorry I said they would reject you. I don't know what goes through their minds. I just know I don't trust them—I haven't in a long time. I need you not to hate me. I need to not be dead to you. You're not dead to me. You are alive. I know you're in there." I take a step toward her, and she flinches, but doesn't move. "You are alive, Hazel." Another step. "You are not a dead girl." One more step, and she allows me to put my hand on hers.

She lifts her head and her jaw looks smaller, familiar. I don't see the Stranger's teeth anymore. Her eyes shift to meet mine, and the inky black fades. "Don't leave me."

I catch her as she collapses.

27

HAZEL

TWO MONTHS LATER

The funerals are over, the trials have not yet begun, and for the first time in forever, I'm looking forward to what lies ahead.

I dodged a bullet—no trial for me. I'm not sure how to feel about what happened when I wasn't myself. I know none of it was my fault. But I also know my hands became a killer's hands. My teeth were a killer's teeth. But by the laws of the great state of New York, only a human being with full consciousness can murder. It follows that a person possessed by a mythical beast cannot.

Not that it matters. For me to be responsible, people would have to accept that it happened.

I'm still working on that myself. It's...a process. But we all agree it's time to move forward, and we've decided that the best thing to do is to give Veronica, and ourselves, proper closure.

Which is what brings us to the woods behind Ezra's house with

Veronica's diary, the Ouija board, the ritual supplies, the book with the summoning spell, and a shovel.

It's the dead of night in the dead of winter, which is the worst time to dig a grave. But it's an important day—the anniversary of the day Veronica moved to Ashling. We take turns hacking into the frigid earth, thermoses of hot chocolate providing a sliver of warmth and comfort in the howling wind. There's only a thin layer of snow on the ground, so it could be worse, but cutting through the dirt is like trying to tunnel into concrete.

"Whose genius idea was this?" Jack looks up, red-faced, from the minimal progress he's made.

Beth raises a stubborn hand from the lawn chair where they're watching us comfortably, their cast shielded from the snow by a warm waterproof blanket.

Ezra jumps up from their side and rolls up his sleeves. "That is *not* how you dig a grave."

"My boyfriend, the serial killer," Beth says cheerfully.

"Told you he was trouble." Phoebe looks up from the pile of kindling she's been attempting to ignite for the past hour and flashes a knowing smirk.

They can joke about killers. I can't. Not after we learned the truth about our parents. I know Beth uses humor to deal. But it's still jarring to me. Not only me, I think.

The town of Ashling has been shaken to its core, and nothing will ever be the same. That's not a bad thing. Ashling couldn't stay the same, and small towns are slow to change. It would be a lie to pretend they aren't. But events like these have a way of speeding up that process. Of course, no one knows the real truth. The official story is bears and coyotes and a vicious bee season.

Yeah, right.

Amanda hovers over Ezra's shoulder, offering a stream of advice and criticism, but not a helping hand. No one is going to push it. The past few months have been hard on Amanda. She and Allison had been close, and after her death, Amanda didn't come back to school for a while. When she did, she was different.

Don't get me wrong, Amanda will always be kind of a bossy brat, but now she's my bossy brat. I can admit when I'm wrong—at least, I'm *trying* to. And I was wrong about Amanda. She isn't the person I thought she was. She's clingy and anxious and vulnerable. She doesn't like being alone or going too long without a return text. She doesn't shower as often as I think she probably used to, and she wears the same sweater every day now—the one she was wearing the day her sister and boyfriend both died, before her best friend shot her and then died in front of her.

I like Amanda now. She knows what I did when I wasn't me. A lot of people avoid me because of it, but since Allison's death, we've become strangely close. Maybe because there aren't many people who understand what we all went through. Even though it was different for each of us, we still went through it together. I can't actually imagine my life without Amanda now. That's something I never thought I'd say. She has a good heart. I'm glad I've had a chance to get to know her, even if it was because of all this.

The Laurences didn't deny the truth when Amanda went public. Principal Laurence was willing to testify against the Rev, his wife, Ed, and my parents. The rest are dead. Chief Merritt, and his brothers—there will be corruption charges for the other officers involved in the cover-up. The department now consists of a couple of newbies and transfers from down mountain. I think that's for the best. Fresh start, no baggage.

Before resigning in disgrace, Principal Laurence did a few things to his credit. He publicly apologized to Veronica's family and to the three teachers who left in protest over the book bans. And at Amanda's insistence, he established a generous grant to fund her own lending library to include all books banned in the school and public library. There's no way to control the school board. But thanks to my new friends, I've developed an appreciation for loopholes.

"Hazel, I need you." Beth motions for me to help them up.

"Again?"

They shoot me a pleading look. "I drank a lot of cocoa."

Amanda shrugs at me. "You have pee duty."

This seems highly arbitrary despite being twins. But I help them up, and we start up the path toward the house, shuddering as we pass the shed.

"How are you feeling about all of this? The big burial?"

I shrug. The burial is a gesture. I know Beth likes the idea, but to me, it isn't going to change much. There are plenty of other things that would bring me closure. I'm not sure it could ever be as simple as tossing a few items into the ground and walking away. I've thought a lot about what Beth and I said to each other. Before we really had it out, before we made peace.

I decided I'm not going to write off Ashling, even after all that's happened. I'm looking forward to leaving in a few months for Sarah Lawrence College and getting a little breathing room. But there's a lot of good here, too. For example, Mel.

My girlfriend.

It still feels weird to say those words. Like it might go away at any second. But it's been a month and a half, and so far, no one is going anywhere. In the end, all it took for me to get up the nerve to text her back was a near-death experience. Maybe it was worth it. Because even though it's been hard to open up, it's really nice to have someone who likes me for who I am. A fellow musical theater nerd who doesn't care how judgy and blunt and particular I am. Because she's funny. And silly. And most importantly, honest, unlike an unmentionable dead girl. And when we hang out, just for a little while, I don't stress. The only part that scares me, because it's inarguably too good to be true, is that she is also attending Sarah Lawrence next year. But as a wise person—who I now trust more than anyone in this dark and dangerous world—once said, you can't always assume the worst of people and expect the best. After everything we've been through, I'm ready to hope.

There is a lot of good in Ashling. I'm not like Beth. I see the beauty in this town, including in the people who live here. We are Ashling, too. Beth forgets that there are always people who are isolated and looking for help, like we were. No one is ever alone. Maybe everyone is lonely. But not alone.

I don't want to leave Ashling behind, not for good. I want to make it better. But without people like us, and Mel, Mel's mom—who has taken over the book club—and Amanda who love Ashling and *want* it to grow and change, returning here would be a death sentence. And there are more of us. We just need to unite. I can't help it. I love Ashling. I always have—shitty weather and all.

I don't love the dark things we unburied, or the dark things that lay right there at the surface. But none of us are our parents, and we don't have to accept their way. Our house stands empty now. But it's still ours. A rainbow flag, a trans pride flag, and a nonbinary flag now wave defiantly from the porch. A little light in the darkness. A ray of hope for anyone who needs it. Mel, Ezra, Amanda, Jack, Phoebe, and Uncle Paul's houses sport matching colors. It's one step.

We reach Ezra's house, and I'm struck by how different it feels without his parents. Beth hobbles to the bathroom, and I sit on the bottom step of the spiral staircase, remembering that first time I walked in, awestruck by the impressiveness of it all. Everything bee-related is gone. Ezra's aunt moved in to take care of the kids while his parents are being held until trial. The walls are covered in children's artwork, the floor with blocks and puzzles, slime and art supplies. His aunt is clearly doing her best to make home feel normal. But I can't imagine what it's like to be a little kid and basically have both parents vanish. I wonder what they've been told. I hope not very much. Secrets can be toxic, but they can wait until you're ready.

As for Beth and me, we're temporary Laurences, which is something I never thought I would say. Uncle Paul is officially our guardian for the next several months, but he's allergic to dogs, and Beth refused to be separated from Artax. I refused to be separated from them. All things considered, people have been extremely understanding. I mean, you have to be. Everyone feels sorry for an orphan. And our parents are dead to me.

Beth emerges from the bathroom. "Ready?"

I nod.

They look around mischievously. "We could take our time and defrost."

"That wouldn't be very honest, would it?"

They give me a very persuasive Beth look, and I'm flooded with relief that nothing ever changes *too* much. I still pry open the door, allowing in a gust of icy air, and we head back out into the frigid night.

Beth sighs and flings their full weight against me. "You have to stop punishing me sooner or later."

They say it lightly, but it hits hard, and I cast them a sidelong glance as we make our way back to the others, trying to figure out how seriously they meant it.

I don't think I am still punishing Beth. I don't have hard feelings toward them, specifically.

But grudges?

Oh yeah. I've got those. I've got those in spades.

Everyone keeps saying the anger is going to fade, that time heals, that blood is thicker than bile. And that may be true. But I'm not convinced I will ever speak to my mother or father again. Because how thick does blood have to be to outweigh someone not loving you fully and absolutely for who you are? How much time needs to pass before seventeen years of betrayal starts to feel like less of a knife in the gut—and from the people who are supposed to protect you?

One thing that I think is hard for people to wrap their heads around is this: I'm not refusing to speak to my parents for a mistake they made twenty-six years ago. Even considering that mistake was murdering a girl who was a lot like me. I wonder if they saw it, when I came home with a bloody nose courtesy of Mac Wendell or sat shivering on the porch all night during junior prom. I wonder if that's why Mom pushed so hard to have me accepted in Ashling along with Beth. Because she didn't want me to turn into a Veronica.

Because she knew exactly what could happen to a Veronica. After all, she was the one who dealt the killing blow.

I'm not angry about the murder. I'm haunted by it.

I'm angry about the seventeen years they lived as villains and raised us in their image. I'm angry about every poisonous word they spoke in front of me and my sibling. For the fear they instilled in us to live in hiding in our own homes. The fact is, they rejected me first by making it clear in a thousand ways that I'm not the kind of daughter they want.

After the arrests, I spoke to them one last time. I asked them why they did it. They both refused to answer. I told them that I loved them, but I hated what they did to me and Beth. That I'd never be sure if they were the mom and dad who existed in my childhood memories, or if those were all a constellation of lies and wishful thinking. My mother said she would never forgive me for tearing our family apart. She doesn't understand that I'm not the one who did that. That we were always two halves. She may, someday. But that's out of my control.

My father said I should be ashamed of myself. He didn't clarify why. For turning in my own mother and providing the evidence that she tried to murder him? For killing people, sort of, while I was Cerberus? For simply being Hazel Whitman?

It's my father's words that bothered me. Beth says they shouldn't. Who is he to tell me I should be ashamed?

I don't think my mother feels any guilt over what she did. To her, shooting Veronica was an accident, and because of that, she doesn't think she did anything wrong. Still, in a hit-and-run accident, it isn't the hit that makes the crime. It's the run. The cover-up. And they are *all* guilty of that. My mother may have convinced herself that Veronica was the monster from their glimpses of Cerberus and what he could do. But my father knows what they did was wrong.

It almost cost him his life.

Because Dad was actually going to confess what they did to Veronica Green. Beth's plan would have worked if Mom wasn't willing to kill, even die, rather than take responsibility. I guess attempted murder by his own spouse was enough to scare him back into silence. But still. Dad knows better. So it's a joke that *I* am the one who should be ashamed. He made a nemesis of his own child instead of trying to puzzle out what was wrong. Instead of accepting me, he wished out loud that *something would happen to me*, a statement I now think I understand. My body is a compromise, in my father's eyes. My heart is negotiable. To put it grotesquely, in his mind, some guy ought to set me straight.

So no, I don't see a problem closing that door. Not after everything they've done. Maybe someday they'll admit they messed up and apologize. But after almost thirty years of lying to cover up a "youthful mistake" of murder, they don't have a strong track record of repentance.

That's for another day, though.

Today, we bury the past.

We rejoin the others at the burial place, where once upon a time, our mother fired a gun into the woods and struck down a girl. A girl who happened to be the aunt of Jack Sawyer. A girl who was left for dead by our father, and Ezra's and Mac's. Which was covered up by Julie's and Amanda's mothers. And all of them. And which was avenged, after far too long, by their children.

With the help of a hound.

We gather around the grave with the books, candles, oils, and herbs. The gang scrunches close together. Phoebe curated the entire evening, from readings to a Veronica playlist. Right now she's showing everyone photos of her new Brussels Griffon, Cerberus. I feel like that name choice is tempting fate. But if you can't have a *little* sense of humor about being possessed by the mythical and, as it turns out, eternally loyal hound of Hades, you probably need to lighten up.

Jack is in a texting drama with a guy he met on the train last weekend. I love that the most stressful situation Jack will have to devote himself to for a while is who said what to who, not who killed who when.

Ezra, who has become Jack's unexpected war buddy and close friend after the Veronica nightmare, is propping up Beth. I'm glad they found their way back to each other. I think it's hard to go through something hellish and end up in a good place. But after the smoke cleared on the Veronica shitshow, Ezra was over every day to check on Beth, bringing them books and snacks and movies while their leg healed, goofing off and making them laugh. Now that I know the real Ezra Elwood, I think he's perfect for my sibling. They're perfect for each other.

Phoebe clears her throat, and Jack reluctantly drops his phone into his coat pocket. "I hereby call this ritual of remembrance—"

"No. Nope." Jack shakes his head briskly. "We've already been out in the freezing cold for two hours. Let's bury this and be done."

Amanda's face falls. "That's not closure. I was going to do a reading."

"Compromise," Jack says, anxiously tapping the pocket where his phone is. "Burial now. Ritual later."

"But..." Amanda gazes down at the gaping hole and I get it.

It's not just about Veronica for her.

"I *did* plan an entire ceremony," Phoebe says crossly.

"*One* poem now," I suggest. "Then, the whole ritual later. In a warm, dry place." I raise an eyebrow to Beth.

"Pretty please." Beth reaches out, taking one of Amanda's hands and one of Phoebe's.

Phoebe shrugs. "Indoors, outdoors, we're doing the thing."

Amanda sighs. "Fine." She flips through Veronica's diary. "I'm not going to read 'Elegy.' I'm going to read 'Echo Fox,' which I think is about hope and faith and resistance. And even though Veronica was interrupted, in the end, I think we finished what she started.

Echo fox.
A myth is only a myth
when there is no one left to remember
how it really happened.
A lie is only a lie
when there is no one
willing to believe the truth.
A miracle is made
when faith meets the impossible:
where light comes from darkness
where life comes from nothing
where death is undone.
In the true winter's land, the barren land of bones
and oblivion,
mysteries lie thick and deep, waiting to be excavated.
Three clever foxes told a story and made it true.
And why not?

A universe from nothing, life from the grave,
the miracle is always in the believing.
The sisters knew, and I do too—
If you believe the story, isn't it true?"

She closes the diary and places it carefully in the grave. One by one, we each place an item inside. Jack puts in candles. Phoebe adds the Ouija board. Ezra sprinkles in herbs. After a moment of hesitation, Beth places the oils from the ritual. Which leaves the spell book. I pick it up and feel everyone's eyes on me, and for a moment, I feel self-conscious, like they're watching to see if I'm the real Hazel again, and the only way to tell will be if I can bury the spell book. I drop it into the hole and hold up my hands in a toddler-esque *all gone* gesture.

"Big deal." I shrug.

"Okay then." Ezra shivers. "Can we please do the actual burying tomorrow morning? I'm freezing, and my shoulder kills."

"Poor baby." Beth kisses his shoulder, then looks at Phoebe. "Nutella pretzels?"

"A thousand times yes." Phoebe and Ezra link arms with Beth for the walk back to the house, Jack trailing behind, his face buried in his phone.

Amanda hangs back uncertainly. "You okay? You seem...I don't know."

"Yeah." I hesitate. "Do you think I could have a second alone? One last goodbye?"

"Of course." She hugs me, then hurries to catch up with Jack, reading his text conversation over his shoulder and offering unsolicited advice.

My phone buzzes in my pocket and I half smile at the message from Mel.

MEL:

Ghosts gone yet?

I type back.

HAZEL:

Ghosts are never gone, they just get better at hiding

I send a gif of the librarian ghost from *Ghostbusters,* drop my phone back into my pocket, then turn my gaze back to the others.

I watch them disappear into the trees, then bend down slowly to pick up the spell book, and flip to the page with the summoning spell. The idea is ridiculous. I *am* me again. I don't need the book anymore. Veronica was avenged. It's over. It's all over.

I hold the book over the grave again, but I can't bring myself to drop it. It *is* over.

Of course, some people never *did* truly pay for what they did.

But Beth's plan was good. Cerberus left. He was appeased. Exposing the truth and letting the law take care of things seemed to do the trick. I'm me again. Fully me.

I still can't seem to let go of the damn book.

I glance over my shoulder at the place where the others have vanished into the night. I can faintly hear their bantering voices. They did so well. Really put so much into their little game. It was an impressive feat for a couple of kids who had no idea what they were doing, who they were dealing with. It deserves some credit. And all of that's well and good.

But.

But.

—I open the book—

That's not how you get revenge.

ACKNOWLEDGMENTS

I owe infinite thanks to my editor, Annette Pollert-Morgan, for believing in this book. Thank you for taking it on, for shaping it into its living form, and for your incredible support through numerous revisions as I raced to keep the story consistent with a rapidly changing world.

An enormous thank you to my agent, Ginger Clark, and to everyone at GCL. I feel like I was twelve when I first sent you this manuscript. You never doubted it, even when I did, and without your advocacy, this book would still be in my draft folder. I'm lucky to have you in my corner.

A tidal wave of thanks to the entire team at Sourcebooks Fire, especially to Jenny Lopez. Thanks to Laura Boren, Diane Cunningham, and Thea Voutiritsas. A special thank you to Ash Jon for designing and illustrating a beautiful cover. My thanks to Beth Icard and Shannon Scott.

All the thanks to everyone who read and gave feedback along

the way, especially Maxine Kaplan, Kate Alice Marshall, and Amelinda Berube for your encouragement, critique, and general awesomeness. Thanks to Rebecca Sky, Kim Chance, Tiffany Case, and Jess Pennington for reading the earliest pages and insisting that I keep going. Shoutout to the Spooky Book Club and Allison Varnes.

The biggest thanks to my family: Ben, Ken, Deb, Mike, Chris, Steph, Julia, Frankie, all family near and far. I wish we met more often, but you're always in my heart. Dave, Jan, thank you.

To the special dogs in my life: Ellie, Marshy, Maggie, Leroy, Sammy, and Sansa. You are all loved fiercely; some are missed dearly. My mostly golden girls: Thank you for being a friend.

This book is a fairy tale. A story of revenge and justice and mythical creatures who appear when friends and neighbors and family fail to do the right thing.

Here, in the real world, we have no Cerberus to save us. We have Artaxes for love and snuggles, and thank goodness for that. But the doing, the saving, is up to us.

The world is on fire.

There are friends and neighbors who will come to harm if we do not use our voices. It is a good time to show you care. It's a good time to use your voice. To stand up for every person you see who is not in a good position to stand up for themself. To let them know they are not alone.

Take care of each other. Be a friend.

Thank you for reading.

RESOURCES

ACLU. Legislation tracker.

The Transgender Law Center. Trans-led legal resource.

GLAAD. General resource for the entire LGBTQIA+ community.

The Trevor Project. 24/7 crisis call and chat line. (866) 488-7386.

Trans Lifeline. Peer-to-peer support, trans-run, divested from police. (877) 565-8860.

Transanta. Trans-led mutual aid project that connects anonymous donors with unhoused trans youth.

Erin Reed. A journalist with a Substack that offers coverage of news affecting trans people.

ABOUT THE AUTHOR

Dana Mele is a Pushcart-nominated writer based in upstate New York. Dana's debut, *People Like Us,* was shortlisted for the 2019 ITW Thriller Award for Best Young Adult Novel and is an ALA Rainbow List Selection. Dana's sophomore novel, *Summer's Edge,* was a New York Public Library Best Books for Teens title.